ASTRAY

ARIBOSLIA BOOK I

J. F. ROGERS

NOBLEBRIGHT
— PUBLISHING —

www.noblebrightpublishing.com

Astray - Ariboslia Book I

Cover design by Authorpackages.com
Editing by Brilliant Cut Editing

ISBN: 978-1-9-55169-00-4

Published by Noblebright Publishing
Sanford, ME
www.noblebrightpublishing.com

For my family.

And to those who have not yet found the hope of Christ. I pray the words within these pages lead you to Him—You are loved.

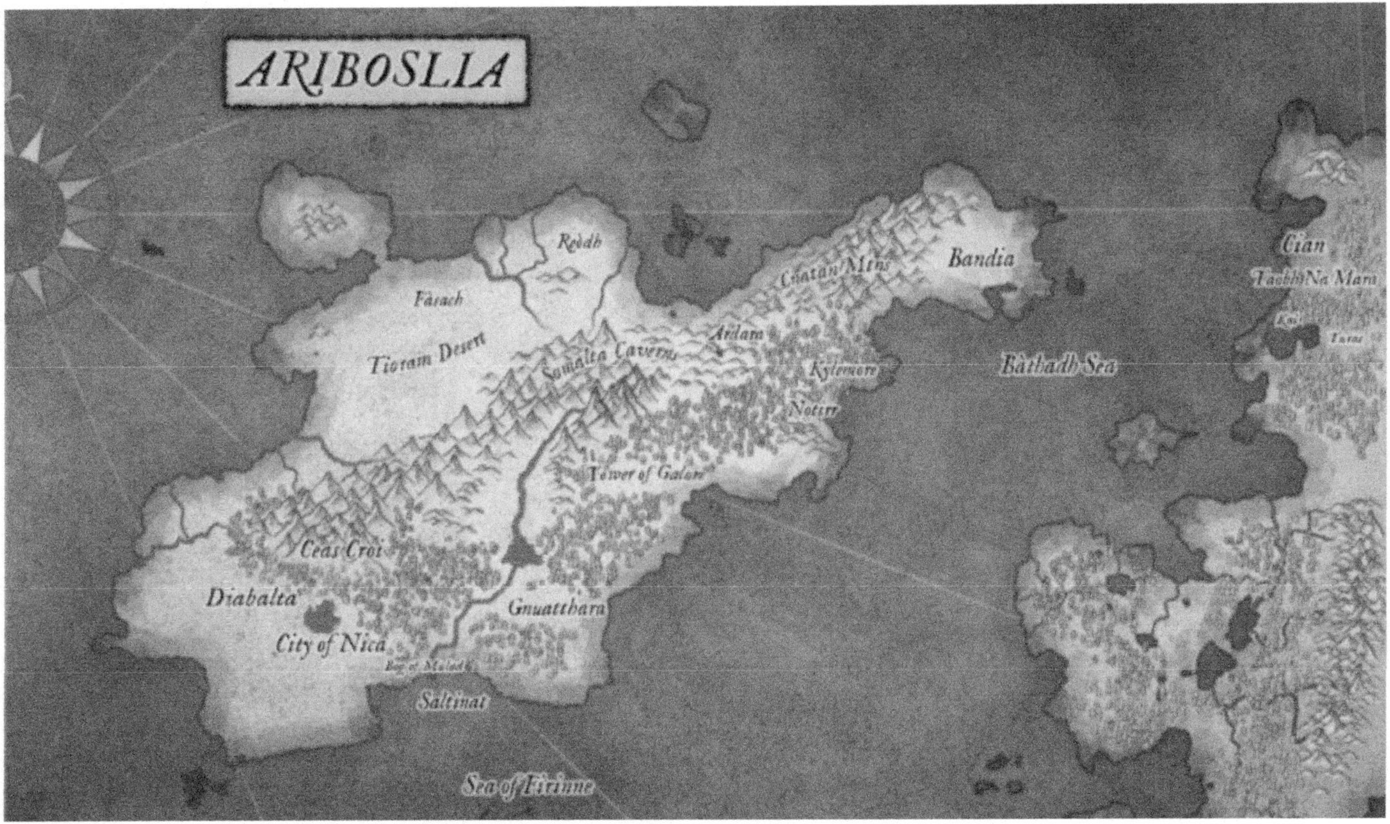
ARIBOSLIA
Rèidh
Fàsach
Tioram Desert
Bandia
Bàthadh Sea
Diabalta
Ceas Croi
City of Nica
Gnuatthara
Saltinat
Sea of Firinne
Cian

PRONUNCIATION GUIDE

PEOPLE

Achaius \ ah-**key**-us \ a Cael from Notirr

Aodan Tuama \ **ay**-den Too-**ah**-ma \ Fallon's uncle

Be'Norr* \ beh-**norr** \ a fasgadair guard

Cahal Fidhne \ kah-**hal** Feen \ a Cael from Notirr

Cataleen \ Cat-ah-lean \ Fallon's mother

Cairbre \ **kar**-bruh \ a legendary hero

Declan Cael \ **deck**-lan Kayl \ a Cael from Notirr

Deirdra \ **deer**-drah \ the love of legendary hero, Cairbre

De'Mere \ deh-**meer**

De'Rahn \ deh-**rahn** \ a fasgadair guard

Eadbhard \ Ay-**dwaar**-er \ Maili's father

Fallon \ **fal**-lawn

Faolan \ **fway**-lawn \ a friend of Fallon's mother

Fiona \ fee-own-ah \ Fallon's paternal grandmother

Le'Corenci \ leh-Core-**en**-chi \ a fasgadair

Maili \ may-lee \ Declan's betrothed

Miloslsv \ mee-**los**-slaf \ a dark pech who forged the zpĕt

Mirna \ Meer-nah \ Fallon's maternal grandmother
Morrigan \ More-ih-gahn \ the original fasgadair
Ryann Mughráin \ ry-an Moo-**ray**-in \ a Cael from Notirr
Tashaundra \ tash-**ahn**-drah \ a Treasach child

CLANS
Ain-Dìleas \ ahn **dill**-ay-ahs \ from Bandia
Arlen \ are-luhn \ from Kylemore
Cael \ kayl \ from Notirr
Treasach \ treh-zack \ from Gnuatthara

RACES
Fasgadair \ faz-geh-deer \ vampires
Gachen \ gah-chen \ shape-shifters
Pech \ peck \ Small, strong people with abilities with stone
Selkie \ sell-key \ gachen who turn into seals

PLACES
Ariboslia \ air-eh-**bows**-lia \ the realm
Bandia \ ban-**dee**-ah \ the Ain-Dìleas kingdom
Bloigh rùm \ bleye room \ a hall in Ceas Croi
Ceas Croi* \ kase kree \ a city in a mountain seized by the fasgadair
Cnatan Mountains \ crah-dan \ mountains surrounding Bandia
Diabalta \ **dee**-ah-**ball**-tah \ a kingdom seized by the fasgadair
Gnuatthara \ new-**tara** \ the Teasach's fortified city
Kylemore \ kyle-more \ the Arlen's tree village
Notirr* \ no-tear \ the Cael's village
Saltinat \ **salt**-in-at \ an underwater selkie city
Tower of Galore \ ga-**lore** \ an enormous tower

THINGS
Bian \ bee-ahn \ when the gachen shape-shift for the first time
Bogle \ boh-gul \ a mythical creature invented to scare children

Cianese \ see-ahn-eese \ a foreign language

Co-Cheangail \ ko-kang-gale \ a committee of United Clans

Drochaid* \ **dro**-hach \ the amulet Pepin created

Gealach Lionadh \ jee-**lahk lee**-on-ad \ the new moon celebration

Glemmestein \ glem-eh-stine \ a mineral that causes in memory loss

Ionraic* \ **on**-eh-rick \ a committee of believers

Sùgh \ sue \ poisonous berries that resemble blueberries

Turnering av Stryke* \ turn-ay-eh-ring ahv streek \ an annual pech
competition of strength

Uilebheist \ oo-deh-bish \ a three-headed monster

Zpět \ sp-**yet** \ the amulet that resurrected Morrigan

*trill the r

PROLOGUE

IN THE FOOTHILLS OF RURAL MAINE

Under the cover of night, hidden in the rickety tree house in the backyard, De'Mere waited, watching. The fort offered all he needed, privacy and the perfect vantage point. He peered into the upper right-hand window of the old farmhouse across the lawn. The alarm clock's glow illuminated Fallon's room in an alien-like green. Only her feet at the edge of the bed lay within view. Their stirring told him she was having a nightmare—again.

He slumped against the rough, far wall and peeked at the sky through wide gaps in the roof. The sun would soon rise. He'd retreat to the wood to rest until it was time to return. Then his real work would begin.

"De'Mere," a thunderous, yet oddly melodic voice called.

De'Mere bristled as chills coursed down his spine. He jumped to his feet, bumped his head on the low ceiling, and dropped to his knees to peer out the windows.

"De'Mere." The voice seemed to float in midair right in front of his face. He fell back, away from the window, and reached out, groping air with his right hand for something solid, perturbed that his otherwise keen eyesight failed him at this crucial time. This must be how a blind man might feel, sneaked up on, spoken to without warning.

"Your time has nearly come." The voice stimulated a fresh course of chills surging throughout his being. It commanded attention, and for a creature such as himself, invoked fear. Its very presence filled the confined space. "Do you remember what to do?"

De'Mere continued his search for clues as to its whereabouts. It seemed to be everywhere. An internal struggle raged between his desperate desire to find the owner of the voice and his equal need to shy away. He craved a glimpse, if only to determine where to draw near or in which direction to run.

"Do you know what to do?"

"Yes," he answered in a hurried, hushed tone, afraid to elicit an unwelcome audience, which didn't appear to concern the disembodied voice. But then, perhaps it wasn't audible to anyone but him. "But how do I make sure she's there?"

"Just do your part. Tonight."

The air no longer squeezed De'Mere like an invisible vise. The unearthly being was gone. He took a deep breath, savoring his solitude. But the hollow cavity within him widened. If only he could fill the void.

He returned his attention to Fallon's bedroom. The sheet lay flat. She must have risen while he'd been distracted. Had she overheard their voices and come outside? He peered down the hole in the floor. The ladder was bare. Careful to avoid the squeaky planks, he crossed to the window closest to the house. He dared stick his head out enough to search the darkness below, hoping it wasn't a mistake. He'd come too far to risk exposure now.

The night was still. As if all living things had been frightened away. The breeze dared not even rustle a leaf. He ducked back inside and searched the path to the house. Still nothing. Crickets chirping in the distance offered the only sign of life.

He glanced back at the house. Light filled the bathroom window. A shadow moved beyond the drawn shade. Releasing the air he'd been holding, he laughed softly at his paranoia. He was much too far away for a mere human to hear.

"Tonight," De'Mere whispered, the word lingering in the air.

After all these years, the time had come. His watching and waiting would soon be over. He'd play his part. The trick would be getting Fallon to play hers.

He descended from the tree house by dropping out the trapdoor. After landing with a soft thud on the unkempt lawn, he ran on all fours for the cover of the tree line.

CHAPTER ONE

The sun's unnatural glow blinded me. Tears coursed down my face as I struggled to take in my surroundings. With each blink, a woman with long, blonde hair dappled in gold sparkles grew clearer. She sat motionless on the sand, watching the ocean waves. I couldn't see her face, but imagined she awaited her long-lost love from beneath the watery depths. A breeze swept across the shore, swirling the white dress around her delicate frame as tresses danced about her face.

The wind carried my name, long and silvery sweet, "Fallon...Faaaaallon."

A shiver ran through me. Was she calling me? Did I know her? A dream. This had to be a dream.

Something about her was familiar. Overcome with an unsettling compulsion to be near her, I walked in her direction. But the woman remained the same distance away. I paused, blinking to ensure I wasn't seeing things, and then quickened my pace. Still, I made no ground. I ran. Again, no progress. Frustrated, I stopped.

The woman slowly turned to face me.

Shadows overtook the landscape as storm clouds choked the sun.

Neither of us moved, yet the woman was closer. The entire scene was now mere feet before me, as if I'd somehow crossed a considerable distance. In one fluid motion, her hair transformed from blonde to black. As the serene face mutated, curiosity morphed into disquiet in the pit of my stomach. I gasped. I recognized deep purple eyes unobscured by thick lenses. The pasty, oblong face minus the acne. Me—only beautiful. With an eerie lack of emotion, the doppelganger's face tilted sideways. My stomach tightened with each passing second that those dead eyes watched me until I nearly doubled over in pain.

Without warning, its mouth widened. Baring sharp, menacing fangs, it lunged at me.

Just before it reached me, my body spasms jerked me awake, as if I'd fallen from the ceiling onto the bed. Entangled in my sheets, I fought to free myself. As reality set in, my thudding heart descended to its natural rhythm. I let out a slow, even breath and glanced at the alarm clock's glowing digits, squinting to make sense of them—3:56 a.m.

Something was off. The air sizzled, as though an unseen electrical current ran through it. I felt a presence. Within reach, yet so far away. The more I grasped for what it might be, the more it evaded me. Something lurked in the shadows. I was certain of it.

I put on my glasses and fumbled with the bedside lamp, knocking it to the floor. I stilled, holding my breath, waiting for whatever remained hidden in the darkness to jump me.

Nothing moved.

Rather than drape my feet over the bed and give any monster lurking there a chance to grab my ankles, I stood and jumped far out of reach. I landed on the creaky oak floorboards and hurried to the bathroom to flip on the light switch before something could sneak up behind me in the dark. I shook my head at myself. If Stacy could see me now, avoiding the boogeyman under my bed, she'd tease me mercilessly.

After splashing cold water on my face, hoping to wash away the dream, I put on my glasses and eyed my reflection. My face, littered with acne no astringent could clear up, scowled back. My purple eyes, magnified in the thick frames, glared. If only I were truly as beautiful as in the dream, for the brief moment before it changed. The fanged creature came to mind. I shuddered, grabbed a towel, and dried off.

I lumbered back to my room and picked up the lamp. The light erased all but a few shadows, which I took time to investigate personally.

I eyed everything with extreme scrutiny, even the flowery, yellowed wallpaper, peeling in places, certain a chameleonlike creature could hide itself there. But nothing bulged. I flung back the once beautiful pink bedding that now looked like something from a hamster cage. Ratty. But the sheet lay flat.

Other than the wear and tear, my room hadn't changed in ten years. Not since Bumpah died. After that, Fiona stopped taking care of...well...everything. She threw money at me every once in a while so Stacy's mom could take me clothes shopping or to doctor appointments. Other than that, she never gave me anything, not even on my birthday.

My birthday. Today. My seventeenth birthday. The first day of summer. I flopped on my bed, grateful school was over until fall, but I couldn't face another birthday without Bumpah. No, I wouldn't allow myself to think about it.

I glanced at the book overhanging my bedside table and snatched it up, eager to escape to the world within its pages. My bookmark fell out, and I grumbled as I found my spot.

Reading about other worlds usually calmed me, but the words refused to sink in. Instead, Bumpah kept popping into my mind. The hollow within me widened. I needed him to pull me out of my funk. I could almost hear him joking, comparing my moods to the New England weather. "If you don't like it, wait a minute," he'd say. Then he'd sing and dance around like a goof. Inevitably, a smile returned to my face.

I needed Bumpah to calm the storm, to make my birthday special.

All I had was Fiona, and she couldn't care less. Instead of loving me as her granddaughter, she treated me like an annoying customer lingering past closing. Or worse.

The whirlwind of darkness engulfed me. Tears slipped down my cheeks. I pulled my knees up and wrapped my arms around myself. My hands ran over the scars, reminding me I could, once more, deal with the pain. But no, I'd promised Stacy, the only one who knew my secret and still cared about me, for whatever reason. Perhaps I should try talking to her God.

"God, if you're really there, I don't know why you'd listen to me, but Stacy keeps asking me to, so here goes. God, I don't know what to do. I'm so angry. All the time. I can't help it. My grandmother hates me. I don't have any family. I'm all al—" My voice cracked and tears poured. "I don't want to be this way." I slammed my fist against the pillow. "Why'd you take my family away? You never even gave me a chance. Are you even there? Do you even care?"

Nothing. No response. I wiped my eyes and returned to my book with renewed focus, determined to escape reality. At least I could tell Stacy I'd tried. If her God was real, He must hate me.

When the sun's rays streamed into the room, overheating me, I found the book open with the pages bent under my face. I folded them back in place, checked for drool, and returned it to my bedside, hoping the librarian wouldn't notice or care. Then I threw on a crumpled pair of jeans and a black T-shirt before heading to the kitchen.

I paused at the top of the stairs and took a deep breath. As I stared at the worn treads, I prepped myself for the off chance that I might come in contact with Fiona. "It's just another day like any other. Don't expect anything from her. It doesn't matter that it's your birthday." No matter what, this year, I would not get my hopes up.

I shuffled downstairs then through the dining room to the

kitchen. Fiona's immense plate collection in the hutch rattled in my wake.

Fiona sat at the kitchen table, eating a late breakfast. She dropped her head, shaggy gray hair falling around her face as she wiped her eyes, and shoved a postcard into the pocket of the drab brown sweater she always wore—even in this summer heat.

I almost turned and left, but I needed coffee. Sighing, I plodded to the coffee maker, eyeing the cracked black-and-white checkered tile as I went. My tangled mass of black hair dangled in my face, shielding me from view.

Fiona slurped her coffee. "Look who decided to grace us with her presence."

I wanted to ask if "us" included her many personalities. I bit my tongue. Instead, I grunted something resembling "morning."

I hoped she'd leave it at that. Nothing good came from conversation with Fiona. The more I allowed the woman to voice her opinion, the greater the chance I'd run away in tears. She was a guilt-trip ninja, striking when I least expected.

"I have something for you."

A warning thumped in my chest. I continued to stir the cream and sugar in my coffee, too much of each. I turned to face her. "What is it?"

"Oh, for Pete's sake, stop gawking and come here, Fallon."

I peered with extreme caution into her outstretched palm.

"Well, take it." She shook the object clasped in her meaty fingers.

Like a game of Operation, I snatched it and removed my hand as fast as possible as if to avoid the buzzing sound. I then backed to a more comfortable distance.

A necklace. I sucked in my breath. The pendent seemed ancient. A heavy circle made from some type of gray stone attached to a leather cord. Seven cone shapes pointed from a circular indent in the center, giving it the shape of a star or a sun. Strange marks, like hieroglyphics, each unique, etched deep between the points.

It had been so long since I'd received a gift I didn't know how to respond. "What is it?"

"Not quite sure. It belonged to your mother."

"My mother?" The amulet fell, the cord caught around my finger. I pulled it to safety and let out a heavy breath. My mother. I couldn't remember the last time she was mentioned in this house.

Fiona's steel-blue eyes lost their sharpness for a nanosecond. "Yes." Then with a quick shake of her head, adding more volume to her frizzy hair, she stood and brought her dishes to the sink. "Well, enough of that."

"No." My mother's ghost had been summoned. I couldn't let it float away.

Fiona stuck out her jaw and glared at me with dead, unblinking eyes. My stomach jumped into my throat. I had ventured into dangerous territory, but I might never have another chance to find out about my mother. I'd searched this house from top to bottom for pictures—any insight into my parents—only to be denied. I tried softening my tone. "I mean...did my mother give this to you?"

Fiona dropped her gaze and returned to the sink. "No. She didn't."

"Well, who then? You've been holding on to it all these years? Why'd you give it to me now?"

Fiona placed her hands on her disproportionately large hips, lowered her head, and sighed. She remained like that, as though worn out from fighting down whatever humanity remained entombed within her otherwise heartless carcass.

After a few eons, she faced me. "Fallon, I really didn't know your mother well. This was given to Nathaniel after her..." She paused as if searching for the appropriate word. "...disappearance. He was instructed to hold onto it until your seventeenth birthday then give it to you. He's not here, so I'm doing it."

"Someone gave it to Bumpah *after* my mother...? Who?"

"I don't know. I wasn't there. He never said."

"But *why*? Why give this to me now? What for?"

Fiona folded her arms across her chest. She leaned toward me. Her pear-shaped frame extended as her face scrunched in a scowl, forcing the peach fuzz to stick out on her upper lip. "I was tempted to throw the stupid thing away. I'm only doing this for Nathaniel. I promised."

Was she for real? I knew she hated me, but this was a whole new level of heartlessness. To want to toss the one thing connecting me to my mother...that was cold. My eyebrow twitched as I tried to think how to respond. I opened my mouth, but words escaped me. Her unblinking eyes bulged in my direction. Words I'd been dying to say for years flew from my mouth. "You're not the only one who lost your family, ya know. I miss Bumpah too. It's not fair. I can't even remember my parents. And I'm...I'm..." I knew what I wanted to say but couldn't bring myself to do it.

"You're *what?*"

Her nasty tone loosed my tongue. "I'm stuck with *you!*"

"Don't try to bait me. Nathaniel would still be here if it weren't for you. He was too old to be chasing after a rambunctious kid. As for my son—let me just say—no parent should outlive her child. *You* miss people you never knew. I lost the only people I ever loved. And where's your mother? I don't know. Her casket is empty next to my son's. Is *that* fair?" She paused as though I might actually reply. "For all I know, she killed him."

Fiona's chest heaved as she gulped for air, her face red. Blotchy. I stood frozen. Though her words stung, they didn't send me crying as they once had. Instead, they fueled my anger. I wanted nothing more than to smack her across the face. I fought to keep my clenched fists by my side. "What about me? I'm your granddaughter, remember? You didn't lose *everyone.*"

Fiona shoved her hands into her pockets. "Oh for Pete's sake, I don't have time for this nonsense. I have more important things to attend to. Not all of us sleep until noon." She trudged out of the kitchen, leaving dirty dishes in the sink.

Blown off again. Fiona didn't have anything to do but send

herself postcards from her dead husband, add to her ridiculous plate collection, and resent being stuck with me.

I dropped my cup into the sink, chipping it, and adding to the pile.

Several fantasies flashed across my mind. Most involved Fiona spinning and falling after a swift blow from a frying pan. Hurtful words I wished I'd said resonated in my mind. I cursed myself for allowing her to suck me in. I should know better by now.

My mind returned to the amulet. My first tangible connection to my mother. I placed it around my neck. It fell heavy against my breastbone. Warmth radiated from the spot, comforting me as if a missing piece of my heart had returned. I held it up to study the markings once more. As my fingers traced the cone shapes, feeling the rough surface, it sparked, like static electricity in the dark. I jumped. The necklace slipped from my fingers and thudded against my chest. My heart skittered. I yanked the stone off and dropped it on the counter.

CHAPTER TWO

I tilted my head and stared at the amulet. No freaky sparks of electricity. No glowing like something from a sci-fi movie. I touched the face as though testing a curling iron. It wasn't hot. Certain it would do something the moment I blinked, I stared at it until my vision doubled and my eyes watered. Still nothing. It must've been my imagination.

Magical or not, I couldn't wait to show this to Stacy. I tucked the necklace under my T-shirt, gave it a quick pat, and rushed from the house. The amulet thumped against my chest as I ran down the path through the woods. When I arrived at the crossroads, I hesitated. Through the graveyard or the long way, as usual? Impatience prodded me forward, chafing against my resistance.

But the graveyard? Not today. As I walked, my mind flitted, thoughts chasing each other: Why had my mother left me the necklace? What would Stacy say? *And* how could I pry more information from Fiona. I envisioned tying her to a chair, shining a bright light in her eyes, and forcing answers out of her.

The path came to an end at the road across from Stacy's house. I crossed the cracked, frost-heaved road to the white cape with navy-blue shutters. Trimmed bushes and Mrs. Pierce's pristine flowerbeds framed their lawn, cut in Mr. Pierce's professional diagonal pattern. I followed the driveway to the brick path up the steps to the breezeway.

Stacy opened the door. "Hey! Happy Birthday!" Her crooked smile lit her freckled face.

I couldn't help but smile in return. It took all my self-control not to show her my amulet. I had to fight the rising laughter, or she'd suspect something. Then I'd be forced to tell her and spoil the fun.

The scent of whatever Mrs. Pierce had baked that morning wafted my way. Cinnamon, apples, and baked dough. My stomach growled. Mrs. Pierce was the best baker in the county. No evidence of her goods remained but the smell. The kitchen was tidy, as usual.

I slipped off my shoes, then followed Stacy through the clean yet comfortably lived in kitchen and living room. My feet transitioned from cold, hard tile to soft wall-to-wall carpeting. Family photos lined the mantle and filled the walls. I could spend hours lounging in this room, soaking up its comfort.

We continued past to the stairs. Stacy flung open her door and flopped on her bed. I shut the door behind us and settled into the purple moon chair.

"So where's the family off to?" I asked.

"Matty had soccer practice." Stacy picked up a magazine and flipped through the pages. "Where's Fiona? Off sending herself another post card?" Only Stacy could ask that question without a trace of sarcasm.

"Probably." Heat flared in my chest at the mention of Fiona's name. I exhaled. "You know, it was sweet of Bumpah to send them when he was alive, but the woman has got to move on. It's been ten years, for Pete's sake." I grimaced. I'd unintentionally used one of Fiona's favorite sayings. "Pathetic."

Stacy frowned, gently laid the magazine down, and walked over to me. She placed the back of her hand on my forehead.

"What?" I asked.

"You sounded concerned about Fiona. I just wanted to make sure you don't have a fever." She giggled. Her nose wrinkled, merging her freckles into a blob. Before I had a chance to reply, her eyes dipped down, zeroing in on the necklace. "What's that?"

"Huh? Oh, this." How could I have forgotten? "Fiona handed it to me on her way out the door. She said it was my mother's..."

"Shut up!" Stacy pushed my shoulder with such force I almost tipped over in the chair. "It was your mother's? And Fiona *actually* gave it to you?" She grabbed the amulet, and I lurched forward before she took my head off. "Why did you wait for me to notice it, loser?"

Before I could say anything, she gasped. "Check it out. Did you see this?" She shoved it in my face, too close to see. "It's glowing."

"What?" I yanked it away and pushed my glasses in place so I could focus. One of the cone shapes pointing from the center was ablaze.

Stacy seized the amulet once more. "It's like a compass or something. It changes when you move it." She held it so I could see. Sure enough, as she turned the amulet, the cone aiming toward the door illuminated. What in the world?

"Let's test it out. What if it wants you to go somewhere?"

"Stacy, that's stupid. It's a stone. How could it *want* me to go anywhere?"

"Are you kidding me? It's glowing." She enunciated the word as though I was mentally challenged. "Aren't you the least bit curious? It belonged to your mother. You know, the one who disappeared mysteriously." She spoke the last part slowly, again, as if giving my feeble mind time to process. "And your rotten grandmother, who never gives you the time of day, suddenly decides to hand it over. Why?"

I didn't know the answer. I shrugged.

"Well, fine then. I'll test it without you."

I moved back, clutching the amulet. "No, you will not!"

"Come on, Fallon. What do you have to lose? Do you have anything better to do today? Seriously." After two seconds of silence, she grabbed my hand and pulled me to my feet. "That's what I thought."

I allowed her to drag me in the arrow's direction and out the bedroom door. Once in the hall, we stopped to consult the compass again. The arrow pointing toward the stairs lit. We sucked in our breath in unison and faced each other. Stacy's eyes bulged, and her mouth hung open in a rare moment of speechlessness.

"See?" Her voice returned, and she danced with excitement. "It *does* want us to go somewhere." She bounced down the stairs like a three-year-old, squealing with delight.

"Normal compasses don't work that way. They point north. They don't care about walls." Stacy disappeared around the corner, oblivious to my insight. How would it know about the wall? How would it know to show the direction, literally, step-by-step, like a GPS?

By the time I caught up to Stacy, she was already out of the house. We continued to follow the blazing arrows.

"Hey, Stace. You mind letting me carry *my* gift."

"Hmmm?" She stopped. "Oh. Sure." She thrust it into my hand.

The amulet guided us toward my house, then at the fork, steered us to the path leading into the graveyard. I hesitated.

It took Stacy several steps to realize I wasn't with her anymore. She stopped, placed her hands on her hips, and tilted her head with dramatic flair. "Oh, c'mon, Fallon, how old are you now?"

"Hey. I actually *considered* coming this way to your house today."

"Wow, you actually considered it. You must've been in a hurry. Or are you getting to be a big girl?" Her head dipped from side-to-side as she spoke the words *big* and *girl* in the most annoying, condescending tone she could summon.

I raised my hand to her face, waved it back and forth as though smacking her, and laughed. I deserved her teasing. But this wasn't the boogeyman under my bed. I didn't think we'd be attacked by some strange creature lurking about graveyards awaiting prey. I wasn't superstitious either. It was the gravestones, marking the final resting place of their inhabitants—Bumpah, my parents—reminding me of death. So inevitable. My short life had been unjustly plagued with it.

The wide path may have been a crude road at one time, though no ruts remained to prove it. Only dirt, roots, rocks, and random patches of weeds. For the most part, the trees were sparse enough to let light filter through.

To avoid further taunting, I followed Stacy at a crawl. She turned. Her body drooped, and her eyes rolled as she waited for me to catch up every few feet. I stalled reaching the creepy part where the path narrowed, but the inevitable occurred. I stopped under the ancient oak trees. Their jagged branches twisted thick and closed in at their peak as if purposefully blocking out the sun to make it eerier. The hairs on my arms stood up like meerkats on the lookout for danger.

To the right was the strange rock formation. I couldn't see it, but I knew its dwelling place. When we were six, we dubbed it the Black Rock. Not imaginative, but we were kids, and it was a dark stone in gloomy woods. I later learned it was a megalith. This one consisted of two perpendicular rocks with another balancing on top, forming a house-like structure—not a natural phenomenon. Stacy and I had so much fun here. The Black Rock had served as anything from a house, a castle, or a jail, to a sacrificial altar. Not anymore. Not since Bumpah died.

"Come on, Fal." Stacy grabbed my shirtsleeve and pulled me into the woods, toward the rocks. The glowing stopped when we reached the megalith. A dead end. I touched the plain stone arrows, turned it over, shook it. Nothing. It was as dull as when Fiona handed it to me —plain stone etchings. "It's dead."

"What?" Stacy asked. "Let me see it."

When I removed the amulet, Stacy took it with a bit more force than necessary, mumbling all the while. This time, she shook it, flipped it over, and shook it again with more vigor before lifting it above her head, waving it back and forth.

"What are you looking for, a signal? This isn't a cell phone, ya loon."

After a few minutes of attempting numerous locations, she gave up.

"Fine." Her arm flopped dramatically as she handed it back to me. "We'll just have to try it out a—Oh, man!" She smacked herself upside the head and headed back the way we'd come.

"What?" I caught up and tried to read her face. "Is something wrong?"

"Mom's gonna kill me. She told me not to leave the house before finishing my chores."

"I take it you didn't finish."

"No. I—" She watched me as I reached up and placed the amulet back over my head. Her eyes widened. "Fal, I thought you were going to stop that!" She pointed to the fresh cut peeking out of my sleeve.

Here we go again. What could I say? Stacy didn't understand. She couldn't possibly. She lived in an intact family in a nice home. Photos of happy moments filled her house and her heart. People cared about her. She would always belong to them no matter what she did. To her, the world held possibility. To me, it promised more of the ugliness I'd already experienced and had no control over.

I avoided her gaze.

She grabbed my shoulders. "Fallon, you're my friend. I love you. What can I do to help?"

Nobody could help someone like me. Cutting was the answer I could find. If I was going to be in pain anyway, I might as well feel something different. And I might as well have some control over it. I dared a quick glance at her face. Her eyes glistened with tears. I hated myself for putting them there. I cast my gaze downward.

"Come to church with us," she pleaded for the millionth time.

I'd placated her by attending a couple of times in the past, but I couldn't handle all the churchgoers. All those eyes, staring...judging. I shook my head.

"I pray for you every day, Fallon."

"I believe it." And I did. Stacy prayed for everything from help removing a splinter to ending world hunger.

She sighed. "Listen, I'm serious. You have to stop. I know I promised you I wouldn't tell my parents. But why should I keep my promise if you can't do the same?"

"I will, okay?" Perhaps it was just wishful thinking. But perhaps someday I would.

"I'll believe it when I see it."

We walked the rest of the way in silence.

Stacy's mother opened the front door. "Stacy Ellen Pierce! I distinctly told you not to leave this house until your room was picked up. Did you do *any* of your chores, young lady?"

Stacy rolled her eyes and ran across the lawn.

Not missing my cue, I waved and walked toward my house, leaving Stacy to her chores and her mom. As much as Stacy complained about her mom, they loved each other. I envied her. It was far better to have parents who pushed you, who *cared* enough to bother, than not.

I looked down at the amulet. It was ablaze.

CHAPTER THREE

M y stomach growled, ready for dinner. It had gotten late. Not that it mattered. Other than food, I had nothing to rush back for. Why had I taken off? If I'd come into the house with Stacy, the Pierces might've invited me to supper. They often did, particularly in the summer when school was out. Then again, Mrs. Pierce was pretty mad. She scared me when she got angry. If only Stacy hadn't been such a slacker.

A wall of gray clouds tumbled in, darkening the sky. It seemed fitting, like the storm within me. How I dreaded going home, eating whatever I could scavenge because Fiona wouldn't bother preparing a meal for me anymore. She'd had enough of that when I turned ten. One of these days, I'm liable to turn into a ramen noodle, I eat so many.

Something landed on my head. I thrust out my hand. More drops plopped on my arm. A rumble sounded in the distance.

"Man!" I picked up my pace. Judging by the oncoming storm's speed, I'd never outrun it. My house was still at least fifteen minutes away.

The clouds let loose, as if God had tightened His fist around them and squeezed.

I ran as fast as I could. The gray sky grew darker still. The fork in the path loomed ahead. Could this possibly get any worse? Dare I go by the graveyard, the fastest way back, my best chance to avoid being hit by lightning? I hesitated for a moment, and then dashed down the path.

My glasses, fogging up and covered with water, rendered visibility almost nonexistent. The windswept rain pummeled me, hindering my progress. My T-shirt and jeans clung to my body, chilling me to the core. The insoles of my waterlogged tennis shoes oozed with each squishy step. I might as well have run through a pond.

The path narrowed, branches rattled, swaying every which way in the crosswinds as if writhing in agony. I neared the creepy part and slowed my pace. My drenched clothing weighed me down. Between my rain-covered glasses and the near-black sky, I practically needed a white cane.

Lightning illuminated the path.

My heart skipped a beat. I recovered and hastened to count. "One one-thousand...two one-thou—"

Rumbling thunder interrupted. Less than two miles away. Too close.

I longed for my house where I could enjoy the storm from my bedroom window, safe. There was something calming about sitting in a dry house while rains pounded and lightning struck. But out in nature? No thanks. If only I could teleport...or fly.

A bolt of lightning shot down. The jagged streak shook the ground. Thunder crashed almost simultaneously. I jumped. My heart leaped into my throat. Smoke filled my nose, and I charged like a spooked horse.

Lightning struck again. A dog stood in my way. My feet stopped before my upper half. Arms wind-milling, I caught myself from falling.

Another flash of light showed the animal— closer. I strained to make it out. Whatever it was, its unmistakable menacing posture sent shivers up my spine. Raised hackles made it appear as large as a pony. White, razor-like teeth shone in the passing light leaving a lingering afterimage.

I fled off the path, heart pounding in my ears. Spindly branches blocked my way. I raised my arms to protect my face. In a small clearing, I dared glance back to find the thing a few feet back. I faced forward and saw the branch too late. My face slammed into it. Before I could register any pain, I was on my back. My head smacked against the unforgiving ground.

Above me, lit by another flash, loomed a featureless pale face with yellow eyes. Then darkness.

CHAPTER FOUR

The bright sun burned my eyes when I tried to open them, making them water. My skull felt like I'd been hit over the head with a blunt object. I groaned. Where was I? What was I doing outside?

My right arm, stuck to the moist earth, itched. I picked it up to scratch the pockmarked skin, wiping away bits of dirt. I touched the back of my head probing a baseball-sized lump and splayed hair as if I'd been dragged along the ground. My muscles ached from sleeping on the earth. Damp clothing compounded my discomfort. My shirt bunched up in the back with leaves clinging to my shoulders. Further evidence of having been dragged. I sat up, peeling my wet backside from the goopy surface. Whoever it was, were they still here?

A chill swept over me as I wiped my eyes with one hand and picked up my glasses off the ground with the other. One lens was broken in the twisted frame. My finger pushed through the hole where the other lens should be.

"Well that's just great." I threw them down, glaring as they skittered away. Though they were farther away, they hadn't grown blurry. My jaw dropped. Could I—Could I see?

I scanned the horizon, which presented itself quite clearly. A field devoid of any ominous creatures—that I could see anyway. I sat in the only dirt patch in the middle of a large field surrounded by forest. Each individual blade of grass in the field glistened from the passing rain. Without glasses, even from afar, I discerned each leaf on every tree surrounding the field. Flowers, scattered about the greenery, popped out in colors I couldn't describe. And the blue sky, littered with wispy white cirrus clouds, looked unreal. Like viewing high definition television when you're used to an old picture tube.

What happened? I've needed glasses since kindergarten.

A cool breeze, carrying unusual chirps and tweets, caressed my exposed skin. The unfamiliar birds twittered in harmony as they flitted from branch to branch.

I didn't wear a watch. And I had no idea which way was east or west to guess the time from the sun's position. It felt like morning. Had I lain out here all night, unconscious? Had someone dragged me here?

Black rock stood to the right of me. I'd recognize the structure anywhere. It was the same megalith as in the woods. But how could it now be here, in the middle of an open field?

Memories of the day before flooded back. The rain. The snarling dog. Hitting my head and passing out. *That* explained my headache.

The face. An odd, pale face shone in the flash of lightning before I passed out. And those eyes—glowing yellow. Had that thing moved me? I shuddered and glanced about once more.

This was all wrong. I shouldn't be able to see anything, never mind these unusual colors and strange birds. And the megalith should be in the woods off the path to the graveyard, not in an open field. This must be a dream. I rubbed my eyes and refocused. Nothing changed. I didn't need to pinch myself—everything hurt.

If this isn't a dream, where am I? How'd I get here?

My legs wobbled as I stood. With each movement, my head pounded. Groaning, I grabbed it in both hands, as if to hold it together, and squeezed my eyes shut. I needed aspirin—and coffee—desperately. I looked down at myself. And a shower.

I couldn't just stand here. No road, no evidence of human life existed. I needed to find someone to explain what was going on... where I was. After scanning the tree line, I found a break in the woods. Perhaps a path. I stepped toward the grassy area, and the blades of grass closest to my feet sunk into the earth. When I stepped back, they shot back up. I rubbed my eyes, blinked, and then moved forward once more. The grass disappeared in a perfect circumference around my foot. I teetered there, with my feet spread apart, and surveyed at the muddy area behind me. Most of it had filled in. What in the world?

Careful not to move too quickly, I walked to the break in the trees. With each step, the grass parted before me then reemerged once I passed. I shook my head. I had to keep moving. Whatever it was, I wasn't going to find answers here.

The soreness in my body subsided as I walked, though my head pounded on, worsening with each step.

At the tree line, the mysterious grass-like substance disappeared. The field showed no evidence that I'd been there. But I was right. It was a path. Or so it seemed. It continued as far as I could see. I had no idea how many miles I shuffled along before it narrowed and disappeared. Too many to go back the way I'd come. So I kept going, hoping the trail would pick back up.

"Croooaaak."

I jerked to a stop. That sounded like a sick frog...or something. It was loud, right next to me. I searched the ground.

"Croooaaak."

No. Higher. Was it in the tree? I peered at a low branch.

"Croooaaak." Part of the tree bulged out—the throat of a big toad. Its body color and rough, warty skin matched the bark. It blended in so well, it might've been invisible until its throat stuck out.

I moved closer.

Its eyes popped open. Wings unfolded, and it took to the sky.

"Whoa." I jumped back. Frogs didn't fly. Or toads. Whatever it was.

What is going on? What is this place? I've been aware of being in dreams before. This felt nothing like it. It had to be real. But how?

My stomach churned. The trees wobbled around me as the direness of my situation set in. I was far from home, in the middle of an unearthly forest—alone. The wavering trees closed in. My chest constricted as though someone stood on it. The tightness restricted my breathing, heightening my anxiety. Those unfamiliar surroundings spun.

I sat and put my head between my legs. Breathe, just breathe.

After what felt like hours of focusing on my breathing, it returned to normal. Aside from branches swaying in the wind, the trees remained rooted to their spots, as they should.

I had no desire to get up and wander. I had no desire to do anything whatsoever. Every muscle in my body felt so tight, every thought consumed with so many possible yet unlikely explanations that I wanted to give up and shut down. Would I wander around here forever? Would I die out here wherever here was? I wanted nothing more than to go home. Would I ever get there again?

Home. What a foreign word. Never in a million years would I have thought I'd refer to Fiona's house as home. Yet that was where I longed to be.

Sitting here, wishing myself home, wouldn't accomplish anything. I had to find something. Food. Shelter. Night would fall. As much as I'd like to pretend this bizarre place with disappearing grass and flying frogs didn't exist, I couldn't be an idiot and wait out in the open, exposed. What might come out at night?

For hours I wandered, hoping the forest would open to reveal something familiar—a road, house, or town—anything. When I came to the same felled tree after walking for miles, I tightened my fists and screamed. Birds scattered from the trees above. I screamed until my throat became dry and sore. Then I sat on the trunk, stifling the tears threatening to burst forward. I lay back on the mossy trunk, closed my eyes, and considered my options. I awoke to water droplets flicking my face.

"Not again!"

The sky had darkened once more. Whether due to the rainclouds or the passage of time, I didn't know. I cursed myself for not finding a dry place to sleep.

Thunder rumbled in the distance. No visible streaks of lightning accompanied it. Thunder clapped a second time. No, it didn't sound right. It didn't sound like it was coming from the sky. It sounded like it was coming from...

I turned and swallowed. The dog I'd seen the night before.

No. Not a dog. A wolf. Only a few feet away. His head lowered as menacing brown eyes peered into mine. Bared lips exposed intimidating, sharp canines. Hackles puffed unnecessarily. His immense frame terrified me without the added bulk.

I kept my eyes fixed on him. With extreme caution, watching for the slightest twitch in his stature, I stood and took a few tentative steps backward. Then I spun and ran with all my aching body had to give.

I fought the temptation to look back. The wolf's panting and heavy footsteps came from close behind. I didn't want to chance his gaining on me by slowing. When I spotted him on my right, I veered left. When he appeared on my left, I angled right. We continued in this way, as though he was shepherding me.

Adrenaline propelled me forward in the dark and rain. Leaping over roots, rocks, and felled trees. Pushing through prickly branches. Instinct took over. I didn't think. I pushed ahead, running for my life.

My foot caught on a root. I landed hard. Pain shot into my knee followed by warmth as blood oozed from the wound. Before checking my knee, I scanned the area, searching for any sign of the wolf. Though it was dark, I could see fairly well. Leaves rustled slightly in the light breeze. Unusual cricket-like chirrups droned on in the distance. Nothing else moved. He had vanished. I had no idea how long he'd been gone. Still, to be safe, I stood and hobbled what felt like another mile while my conscious mind returned to itself and pain set in.

How much more of this could I take?

I headed into mountainous terrain and limped to a rock wall. Determined to find shelter, I searched the wall until I discovered a cavity large enough for me to enter.

The cave embodied three of my biggest fears: things with more than four legs, enclosed spaces, and the unknown. I took a moment to weigh my options. Small enclosure with who-knows-what inside, or becoming one with the wolf's other undigested meals.

Inside, the cave was roomy enough to keep me from panicking—about the size of a two-man tent. I kept my face close to the exit. An occasional breeze swept through, providing temporary relief from the muggy air.

I probed my knee and touched skin sticky with blood. Under my T-shirt, I wore a tank top. To avoid more bruises from the unforgiving rock, I carefully removed my tank top, tore it into strips, and wrapped it around my knee. Not exactly ideal first aid. I needed to wash it when I had a chance. For now, it should work.

How had my life come to this? Now that I wasn't running and had a chance to think, an overwhelming sense of déjà vu came over me. I seemed to recall running through dark, rainy woods from a wolf before. Where did it come from? Why was it chasing me? What did it want?

I feared I hadn't seen the last of the wolf. How odd. It had been near my home *and* in this strange, foreign place. It had to be the same one. Was the wolf the reason for all this? Why hadn't it killed me? I couldn't outrun it. It must have let me go. Was it toying with me?

Cold, alone, and afraid, I did something I used to do as a little girl, something I'd forgotten. I hummed a tune from my childhood. A tune I didn't know the name of or the words to. It was in a foreign language. Yet I could sing it as if it was my native tongue. The repetitive melody sounded in my mind, and I fell asleep.

I woke again, sore and stiff from yesterday's impromptu exercise and the hard ground. This time, thanks to my enclosure, the sun wasn't glaring into my eyes. My clothes had dried a bit. Something else was different too. I was warm. Heat radiated from something beside me. Soft puffs of air escaped in a steady rhythm—it breathed. I held my breath and dared look. The sun shining through the crevice illuminated the cave to reveal a blend of gray, black, and white fur sleeping beside me. The wolf.

CHAPTER FIVE

I froze. How could I escape without waking it? Then again, it could've eaten me, yet it hadn't. I still lay facing the mouth of the cave, the way I fell asleep. The wolf must've stepped over my head to lie beside me. At least it would make my escape easier. Making as little noise as possible, I stole out of the cave.

Once outside, I paused and listened for movement. Satisfied there was none, I released my pent-up breath and hobbled away. I had no idea where I was going. I didn't even know where I was so it didn't make a difference. I needed to put distance between the wolf and me, so I continued away from where I assumed I'd come from the day before. Attempting to circumvent the rocky area, I kept the upward slope to my left.

My mouth felt dry and gritty, my lips chapped. My stomach hurt. I hadn't eaten since—my birthday was Thursday, so today was Saturday? I hadn't eaten since Wednesday? My stomach rumbled as I limped along.

My knee throbbed. I needed to clean the wound.

As if on cue, a faint bubbling emerged from the right. I rushed toward it as fast as my leg would allow. When the brook came into view, I hoped my mind wasn't playing tricks on me, like an oasis mirage in the desert. Sunlight shimmered over the ripples. I eased onto the mossy bank. Steadying myself with one hand, I used the other to scoop water to my parched lips. Most of it ran through my fingers.

A shadow moved across the water on the opposite side. It took a moment to piece together the wavering reflection. The wolf.

I froze. My hand, suspended in midair, dripped water. So I'd be breakfast after all. Moving only my head, I peered up at him.

He held something in his mouth then dropped it. As if sensing my unease, he scooted a couple steps backward, turned, and ran away.

When he was gone, I moved to where the brook narrowed and a few flat rocks above water level allowed me to cross. The water wasn't too deep, but my tennis shoes were beginning to dry. I didn't want to start the process over again.

Once across, I found what the wolf dropped. A rabbit. The wolf offered *me* food? He was helping me? Why? He chased me twice in the last couple of days. *And* he'd snarled. I hadn't mistaken that. There was nothing friendly about it.

Why didn't he catch me? I recalled from my fifth grade report, they could run about forty-five miles per hour. And this one was big. His stride must be longer than an average wolf. I couldn't run fast. So why chase me? What kind of sick game was he playing? He seemed to be alone. Was that why he didn't try to kill me, because wolves attack large prey in packs? No way. My five-foot-five, skinny little frame was no match for him.

I looked at the rabbit again and gagged. Already flies buzzed the carcass. Now what? I was far too squeamish for this. Besides, I didn't have a knife.

"I can't even pick it up," I said aloud as if to excuse myself from the task, not wanting the wolf to think me ungrateful.

I stood there, unsure what to do. My stomach rumbled and gurgled as if to say, "Feed me."

I wanted to oblige. I really did.

First, I needed a fire. I hadn't a clue how to start one. Rubbing two sticks together? Sure, I'd seen it done on television, but it wasn't much help.

I formed a circle with a few big rocks and threw what debris I hoped would pass for kindling into the center. Grabbing a couple dry sticks, I set to work rubbing them together. When my arms grew tired, I switched directions. My hands cramped. Leaning forward hurt my back. Sweat ran into my eyes.

"Ow!" A splinter penetrated my skin. I dropped the sticks, shifted my weight to take the pressure off my back, and wiped the sweat from my brow. After pulling the sliver out of my finger, I sighed. I'd never get a spark like this.

Hunger forced me to persist in my task. I focused my energy on creating the fire and nothing else. I stared at the kindling as though it should burst aflame by the heat of my gaze alone.

It sparked.

"Whoa." I dropped the stick, brought my face close to the smoldering kindling, and breathed life into it. It grew. I had fire. "Ha!"

How did I do that? I hadn't been rubbing the sticks together when it sparked, had I? But I must've been. Fires didn't start by themselves.

Then I remembered the rabbit. How would I prepare it? Particularly with no knife to skin it. I scoured the rocks for one with a sharp edge. One rock had a thin edge, but it was too smooth. I grabbed another and hammered it against the smooth one to rough it up. Small chips flaked away. If I angled it downward, it sharpened the rock. Elated, yet dreading the task ahead, I returned to the rabbit.

I eyed the lifeless carcass until my vision blurred and multiple rabbits lay before me. I yelled to the sky, "I can't do it!"

My shout disturbed what appeared to be blossoms on the tree ahead. Small yellow birds scattered every which way, emitting loud chirps.

Frustrated, I sought something easier to prepare. Or even better, something requiring no preparation at all, like fruit or nuts.

I found success—a half dozen or so bushes with small, round purple berries. I picked one. It resembled a blueberry. Since it wasn't red, I decided it shouldn't be poisonous and tried it. Though it was a bit sour, it was juicy and tasted glorious after going so long without sustenance. Perhaps they weren't quite ripe. Given their deep color, I expected them to be. I didn't care. I attacked the plants, shoving the fruit into my mouth.

The berry supply dried up before my appetite, but it was better than nothing. Feeling more comfortable than I had in some time, I lay down next to the fire.

On the other side of the fire, the wolf gnawed the rabbit. I braced myself, ready to run, and studied him. He glanced at me as if letting me know he saw me and didn't care, then returned to his victim.

It seemed my life wasn't in danger, so I settled back down, keeping an eye on him. I guess he figured the rabbit was free game.

He shook his head. Was he shaking his head at me? He couldn't be. Still, he had a smug expression, if it's possible for a wolf to look smug.

I watched him as long as possible, but my eyes grew heavy. I was half-asleep when he lay next to me. This time, I welcomed his warmth and security.

Sometime after the fire died, I woke. In agony.

My stomach twisted. The pain was sharp as if someone had rammed a knife into it. It lurched. I didn't have enough time to raise myself all the way before puking. When the retching ceased, I pulled away from the vomit and lay back down. Sweat dripped from my forehead and dampened my body.

The wolf stood next to me, staring. He looked confused, like he was ready to act but unsure what action to take.

I puked again then fell on my back as convulsions racked my body. All went black.

CHAPTER SIX

I lay in the cozy bed. Though my body still ached, happiness welled up within me as I snuggled under the blankets. I inhaled a light lavender scent and opened my eyes to—blackness.

The contentment flushed, spiraled downward, and disappeared, dread taking its place. Where was I?

Had I blacked out again? In all my life, I'd never passed out. Now in three days' time, I'd fainted twice?

Something creaked. A door scraped along the ground. Flickering candlelight illuminated the room. A woman with cascading red curls carried the candle in her right hand and a cup in the other. Her dress swished as she neared. I held the covers up, leaving only my eyes exposed, keeping a distrustful watch as she placed the candle on a table. With care, she then lifted the hurricane glass off a lantern and lit the lamp. The small room brightened as she adjusted the wick.

"Good. You're awake. I came to see how you're healing."

Her cheery voice seemed out of place. Did I detect a Scottish accent?

Not sensing a threat, I released my protective covering and wiped my eyes. When I opened them, her round face filled my view. She placed her hand on my forehead for a moment, and then smoothed stray strands of hair away from my face.

"Who are you?" I attempted to back away. The pillow yielded only so much.

"Don't fret, my dear," she said in a cheerful singsong voice. She reached for the covers. "I'm called Kyra. May I take another peek at your wound?" Her words didn't match her lips, like an out-of-sync movie.

How was that possible?

After I nodded, she peeled back the covers. A tan gown had replaced my dingy clothes. Worse, I was clean. My face grew hot. Someone changed my clothes and washed me too? Kill me now.

A fresh cloth surrounded my knee. The woman inspected the wound underneath. "Ah. Much better." She unwrapped the binding. "You had quite a gash on your knee. I stitched it up nice. The scarring shall be minor. Can you sit?"

My muscles ached. I nodded and managed to pull myself up.

She perched on the edge of the bed and reached for the cup she'd brought in with her. "Here, drink this broth." She handed it to me. "This will help you regain your strength."

I nearly dropped the heavy mug, unprepared for its weight. The aromatic steam reminded me how hungry I was. I took a careful sip. It wasn't scalding, so I chugged it.

"Slow, my dear." Kyra removed the cup from my hands and placed it on the table next to the lamp. "You'll make yourself ill again, drinking at such a rate. You were so sick when you got here. Tell me, did something you ate make you so ill?"

"I don't know. The only thing I've eaten in days was some blueberries."

She cocked her head and furrowed her brow.

"Blue berries? Ah. I suspect you ate *sùgh*. They have enough poison to make you very ill. Too many on an empty stomach could've killed you. I'm glad you got to us in time to help you."

"Where am I?"

"Notirr." She trilled the R.

"I'm not here? Huh?"

"Nay." She laughed.

I was glad *she* was enjoying this. An infectious quality infused her melodious laugh. If it weren't for my irritation, I might have laughed with her.

"No-tearrr," she spoke slower.

I watched her mouth. Her lips now matched the word. I repeated her.

She nodded and grabbed the broth. "Our village."

"Where's No-tear?" I accepted the broth from her and sipped it.

"Why, Notirr is in Ariboslia, of course." She frowned. "You really don't know where you are, lass?"

I shook my head.

"Well, how do you like that?"

I wanted to say I didn't like it at all. But it was a bit premature to subject this poor woman to my sarcasm.

"We knew this day would come. It never occurred to me you wouldn't know anything about it. You don't know why you're here then?" The humor was stripped from her voice, the light in her eye dimmed. Worry lines crept across her forehead.

"No." I wished for both our sakes I could reply otherwise. "I don't even know where here is."

"Oh, dear." She clasped her hands together. "You're safe. That is most important. I will have Declan bring you to see Mirna. She can explain everything." She studied my face. "How is it you don't know? How did you get here?"

I shook my head again—clueless.

She smoothed my hair, her eyes large and sympathetic, and then patted my arm. "We'll get it sorted. Not to worry, child. But there is one more thing." She took a deep breath. "When I cleaned your wound, I found some marks on your arms and legs." Her eyes searched mine.

"It's nothing." I averted my gaze and pulled my arm away.

"Would you like to bathe before I call for Declan?"

I nodded.

"Good." Her smile fattened her cheeks. "I'll draw a bath for you." She danced out of the room, dragging the door closed behind her.

I stared after her before returning to my broth. As I drank, I scanned the primitive room. A wooden cabinet with a bowl and a pitcher atop it stood across from the bed. A chair, with a blanket draped over it, sat on the wooden floor in a corner. The small, pizza-shaped room barely fit those items. A rounded wall behind me, the crust of the pizza, sloped to the low ceiling. The lack of windows made the room seem to grow smaller still.

My mind returned to her speech. Her tone was pleasant, soothing even. But her lips. How could their movement fail to match her words? It wasn't the timing that was off like an out-of-sync movie. It was more like a foreign film overdubbed in English. Or was I losing my mind? I must pay closer attention. Sipping my broth, I awaited Kyra's return. And answers.

CHAPTER SEVEN

Never had I longed for a bath more. I submerged my aching body in warm water, leaving only my face exposed. Lavender, mixed with something unidentifiable yet sweet, scented the steam, filling my nostrils, calming my mind. The disquiet in my soul dissolved with the swirling bubbles.

With no clock or windows, only the lukewarm water, absent bubbles, and my wrinkled skin indicated time's passing. After rising and toweling off, I unfolded the clothing Kyra left for me—a dress. I pinched the cloth between two fingers, holding it as far away as I could. I despised dresses.

I emerged from the bathroom to find Kyra and a guy sitting at the rustic, wooden table in the small room I'd passed through earlier. My heart jumped. Wisps of dark hair spilled over the sides of his forehead, almost into his eyes. It flipped up just over his ears and at his neck. And he sat erect. Boys tended to slouch, giving off an air of indifference and slothfulness. Not him. I played with the hair falling into my eyes, trying not to stare.

When they noticed me, they rose. "Ah. Fallon. This is Declan."

Kyra motioned, palm up, in his direction. "He'll take you to see Mirna now."

Sure enough, her mouth didn't match her words except when she spoke names. And she called me by name. I didn't recall telling her. Did I say it in my sleep? No. If I did talk in my sleep, I wouldn't call my own name.

"Of course." With a nod, Declan walked to the door, held it open, and waited. The doorway framed his lean, muscular build like artwork. He studied me with intense, sea green eyes. His gaze heightened my discomfort over wearing a dress.

I wrapped my arms around myself. Kyra nudged me.

Once outside, I understood why all the rooms were so small, oddly shaped, and windowless. They'd built the house into a hillside. Ordinary wood composed its front wall, but the rest was earth and sod. Similar homes lined a twisted dirt path. Each house built into its own small hill.

I had difficulty keeping up with Declan as we wove around homes. He walked so fast, I almost lost him more than once. My knee felt much better, but I still limped slightly. Was he *trying* to lose me?

Around a corner, a dark-haired child wearing a grubby tunic, short pants, and bare feet hollered to a taller boy. The tall boy with a similar tunic under a dark vest squatted and stuck his arms out. The smaller boy threw a piece of wood high into the air. The older boy jumped up and caught it. He held onto the log for less than a second before tossing it to a man on a ladder. The man neatly stacked the log onto a cylindrical pile the size of a woodshed.

The older boy noticed me and stared. The younger child caught a fresh log from the man splitting wood, and then twirled in a circle, preparing to throw the log at the older boy. But the older boy was no longer paying attention. He continued to gaze in my direction.

Once released, the wood sailed, lower in the sky, straight into the taller boy's stomach. The taller boy groaned and fell to his knees as the small boy brought his hands to his mouth, his eyes widened. He turned, presumably to see what had distracted the older boy. I waved. Without blinking, the little boy slowly waved back.

"Fallon! Fallon!" He jumped up and down.

The other men, the two boys, and the girls tending a small garden all waved. We continued greeting each other from afar when I bumped into Declan who had stopped at another hillside home.

"Oh! Sorry." My face flushed as I backed away.

"We're here." He knocked on the door.

An almost inaudible voice from within said, "Come in."

Again, Declan held the door open for me.

Once inside, I paused, waiting for my eyes to adjust. The sun hovered low in the sky, and little natural light spilled through the hill house's single window. Most of the light emanated from candles in wall sconces. An oil table lamp added extra glow to the middle of the room.

A woman walked in from another room carrying two mugs. She tipped her head in Declan's direction. "Thank you, Declan."

He returned the gesture and left.

The woman turned to me. "Have a seat." Her voice might have been smooth and silky years ago. Now it cracked in places. Her long white mane draped over hunched shoulders.

While I sat in the chair she motioned toward, she set the drinks on the table. Once settled into the chair across from me, she looked my way.

I gasped. Purple irises. I was seeing my own eyes in her aged face.

An awkward silence hung in the air.

She cleared her throat. "Do you know who I am?"

"Mirna."

"True. That's what I'm called. Do you know *who* I am?"

"Should I?"

Mirna shook her head and clicked her tongue. She paused for such a lengthy time I feared she'd fallen asleep with her eyes open.

I reached for the drink before me. It tasted like water, but sweeter and more satisfying.

After I placed the heavy mug back, she sighed. "I am your gran."

I almost spat out the drink. Somehow, I managed to choke it down. I coughed. "My gran? As in my grandmother?"

"Aye." She nodded. "The mum of your mum."

"My mother died when I was three," I said, as though my mother's death somehow translated into her death too. How had I never considered my mother might have living parents?

Mirna paused again. Her mouth opened slightly as though she might say something but changed her mind. Her fingers trembled.

I had grandparents, or at least a grandmother, who'd never made herself known to me. Others existed who might have shed light on the mystery of my mother. Someone else might have given me the love I desired. The love Fiona withheld.

Mirna spoke the truth. I'd seen it in her eyes—*my* eyes. My stomach twisted into knots. My throat burned. I was going to be sick.

Any pretense of proper etiquette fell to the wayside. Years of pent-up resentment bubbled inside me. I rose, arms open, slack-jawed. "H–How can it be? If it's true, where've you been all this time? Did you know I was alive? Why didn't you look for me?" My voice came out shrill, growing louder with each question. I wanted to say more, but my mind failed to conjure the words.

Mirna nodded again, as though she expected me to say as much. Hurt dwelled in her eyes.

A pang of guilt tugged at my heart, but anger squelched it. I would not apologize. Instead, I sat back down at the edge of my seat, waiting for her to say something—anything.

She looked up. Did she roll her eyes at my thick-headedness, short temper, or one of my numerous other shortcomings? No. Her gaze didn't return to the ground. It remained fixed on the ceiling. Her lips moved as small children's do when they're learning to read in their head. She took another deep breath and dropped her voice. "I ached to be part of your life. It was not meant to be. The choice was not mine." She clasped her hands together. "This village is the home

41

of your mum and her people. She grew up here. She left to protect you."

I broke free from her stare. Focused on a knothole in the table edge, thoughts bombarded me, weighing me down. "Protect me from what?" It came out in a whisper. Conflicted. I didn't want to know, yet I *needed* to.

"From my son." Her mouth twisted as if her words tasted awful. "There is much you need to know before you will understand. Do you know where you are?"

I shook my head.

"I feared." She straightened and returned her attention skyward. "This will not be easy." She appeared to be addressing Someone above.

I followed her gaze. Finding nothing but ceiling once more, I refocused on Mirna.

Her eyes fixed on mine. "How can I explain? You are in Notirr, a small village in Ariboslia."

"I've never heard of such a place. Where is it? How did I get here?" Bracing my elbows on my knees, I rested my forehead in my hands and closed my eyes. Part of me didn't want to continue, but a larger part hungered for answers.

"That is what is most difficult to explain. Are you familiar with heaven?"

As the questions' absurdity mixed with my discomfort, I laughed. "Heard of it. Never been there."

Mirna chuckled. "I imagine you haven't. I ask you, where is it?"

"Where's what? Heaven?" She nodded, so I shrugged. "I dunno. The sky, I guess."

"But how do you know? Your people explored the sky, am I right? Why is it they have not found heaven? It must be quite large."

"I don't know. Does it even exist? Maybe we just can't see it."

"Ahhhh." Mirna sipped her drink, seeming content with my response. "I think you may be correct. I believe it exists and is invisible to us. That, I know, is what Ariboslia is like. Ariboslia exists right alongside your world."

"My worl—what are you saying?"

"I'm saying you are not in North America or any other continent on your world. This world, Ariboslia, resides on the same planet at the same time as yours—in another realm. Two things cannot exist in both realms at once, with the exception of the megaliths. The same megaliths that exist here, in Ariboslia, also exist in your realm. They are portals between the realms. Do you follow what I say?"

I nearly leapt out of my seat. "Is that how I got here? Through a megalith? Can I go back through the portal and get home? Are there others close by?"

"There are no portals that I know of, nor do I know how to use them. How is it you don't know how you arrived?"

I shrugged, deflating somewhat. "I woke up here. Is there anyone else who could help me?"

"Possibly. But you are here for a reason, Fallon. There are things you must do before you return to your realm. Do you understand?"

Not really. I was far from home, and this woman either couldn't or wouldn't help me. At least, not before doing whatever it is I'm supposed to do. My stomach squeezed in on itself again, threatening to send its contents back where they came from.

"May I see the amulet you are wearing?" She pointed to where it lay beneath my new dress. I glanced down. How did she know I wore it?

"You wonder how I know? It was given to your mum, Cataleen, by a *pech* named Pepin. The amulet allowed Cataleen to enter your realm through the megalith and understand your strange tongue. I know you wear it. If you didn't, you wouldn't be here, and we couldn't speak to one another as we do now. With the amulet, called Drochaid, you understand me, and I understand you though we speak not the same tongue."

I attempted to allow the sheer weight of all she said sink in. It made sense in a twisted, sci-fi way. I was near the megalith when I passed out *and* when I woke up. In fact, only the megalith remained the same—other than the wolf. It explained much of what happened to me in the last few days. I decided to test it. I removed the amulet.

My grandmother spoke, "Mi abair a' firinn."

I watched her mouth as she spoke the words. They matched. I replaced the amulet Drochaid.

She smiled. "I speak the truth."

Once again, as she spoke, her lips didn't align with the words, same as Kyra's. This craziness my grandmother spoke of was the only logical explanation.

So everyone I talked to was going to resemble an out-of-sync movie? I groaned then laughed at myself. That was the least of my worries.

For every question answered, a million emerged. I couldn't sort them to know which to ask first. My mind whirred. It was like inspecting a dirty room, wondering where to start cleaning.

"What about the wolf?" I asked. What happened to him? "Does he have something to do with my being here?"

"Wolf?" She cocked her head. That little tidbit seemed to throw her. "What wolf?"

"At home, a wolf chased me. It chased me here too. At least, I think it's the same one..." There couldn't have been two different wolves.

"Interesting." My grandmother scratched her face. "I wonder...I shall have to discuss this with the elders."

We'd gotten a bit sidetracked. I needed to know about my mother and why I was here. What was I supposed to do?

"As family, it is my duty to explain who you are and why you are here, in due time. It would not do to overwhelm you with much more now."

"But—"

My grandmother raised a hand. "I'll send for Declan. He can tell you more about us as well. I apologize for excusing myself abruptly, but my aging body requires rest. I'll see you at dinner." She smiled a

warm, grandmotherly smile. "My heart rejoices to have you with us."
Then she rose and disappeared through the door where she'd first
emerged.

Right on cue, as though he'd been listening outside the door,
Declan appeared.

CHAPTER EIGHT

My heart sputtered at the mere sight of him. When he opened the door and motioned me to walk through, I ambled past, studying him from the corner of my eye. His gaze remained fixed on something in the dark room as he held the door for me. His other hand trembled.

I took a deep breath, unsure how much more I could take. How could she kick me out without answering my questions? She hadn't helped at all, just filled my mind with more questions, cycling on an endless roller coaster, making my head hurt. With each step into this crazy world, the memory of home further retreated. I feared the world I knew would disappear altogether.

I paused, awaiting instruction from Declan, who'd yet to utter one word to me. His manner irked me. So did his incomprehensible good looks. Not that it took much to further irritate me at the moment. Crossing my arms with a loud sigh, I raised my eyebrows. "Is someone gonna tell me what's going on around here?"

He fixed his penetrating gaze on me. "It was Mirna's charge to tell you."

I shrank back. Great, I was trapped in a foreign land, and *this* guy was my designated tour guide? The brooding type. What was his deal? I didn't care how attractive he was. A creep was a creep. "Look. Will you just tell me how I can get home? That's all I want, really."

"Follow me." He sped away in the opposite direction from where we'd come.

Seriously? He could help me get home? I chased after him, away from the homes in the hills and curious stares of those milling about them. We passed fenced vegetable gardens and horse corrals. Cool, salty air and sporadic seagull calls alerted me to the ocean before it spread into view. The terrain grew rocky, and the surf roared as Declan led me onto a pier. It extended beyond the crashing waves.

I savored the rejuvenating air and gazed at the horizon. Waves splashed against the rocky coast, contrasting with the serene line at the edge of the world. Other than the pristine wooden pier, the coast was bare of buildings or manmade obstructions. My first uncluttered view of the ocean.

Declan sat, allowing his legs to dangle in the water.

"Um, this doesn't look like the way home to me." I tapped my foot.

He continued gazing out to sea.

"What am I supposed to do? Jump into the ocean and hope it takes me home?"

No response.

I dropped my shoulders, lifted my head, and let out an exaggerated sigh. I stared at him, waiting for any kind of response. Nothing. He was an immovable wall.

Not wanting to stand there all day, I slipped off my sneakers, tossed them onto the dock, and plunked next to him. My breath caught as my feet touched the frigid water. I jerked them away before easing back in. The pain gave way to numbness. Closing my eyes, I allowed the salty fresh air to penetrate my mind.

The symphony of crashing waves, accompanied by the cries of gulls, lulled me back to the Maine coast. As a child, I teased the surf, running toward the retreating wave, squealing in delight at its inevitable return. Bumpah snatched me up and held me, allowing the water to encircle my otherwise uncatchable feet.

Oh, Bumpah, if only you were here.

Instead, I was stuck with this jerk who wouldn't even talk to me. "Why do you hate me?" I clutched the dock's splintery edge.

Declan faced me, head cocked to one side, brows pinched together. "Hate you?"

"Yes. You made me chase you down the path. You won't speak or even *look* at me. You must hate me."

He laughed. His dark, expressive eyebrows drew farther apart as his eyes shone, making my blood boil. He closed his mouth, but his shoulders continued to quake in silent laughter.

I pushed myself up to stand, but he gripped my shoulder, pinning me down.

"I don't hate you."

"Then why are you treating me like this? You're not exactly being friendly."

He swirled his feet in the water. "I'm...I guess I'm nervous."

I simmered down a bit. This hot guy nervous? With me? "Why?"

He shook his head, back in brooding mode. "Mirna should've told you. When you were in the bath, Kyra explained how you are unaware of where you are or why you're here. That's not what we expected. Then I listened as Mirna spoke to you. She should've told you. It shouldn't fall on me." He lifted his gaze to the horizon. "She's suffered much loss. I understand this is hard for her."

Unsure what to say, I wiggled my feet in the water.

"If you want to know the truth, I'll tell you what I can. But, *please*," he glanced over his shoulder at me, "don't argue."

I flushed at his intense gaze. What was it about me that made people assume I'd argue? Then I remembered how short I'd been a few moments ago. "Fine." I leaned back on my hands, attempting to disarm my self-defense mechanisms.

"What do you want to know?"

Everything! "Why am I here?"

"That, I cannot tell you. Try again." His eyes softened. Was he on the verge of something resembling a smile?

"Ohhh-kayyyy." I took a deep breath. What *could* I ask? A random thought jumped to my tongue. "Are you human?" Now, why'd I ask that? It was far from the most pressing question in my mind.

"Nay."

My jaw dropped. "Seriously?"

The look he threw me seemed to say, *I thought I told you not to argue.*

"Okay then, if not human, what?"

"We're *gachen*. We're humanlike in this form, but when we reach our *Bian*—that's when we're confirmed into adulthood and learn of our totem—we can transform into our totem form. We're shape-shifters."

This was too much. "So what do you become? Show me."

"Nay, that's not a good idea. Is there anything else you want to know?"

"Why don't you want to show me?"

"Because." He drummed his hands on his legs. "I can't."

"Why not?"

"I have yet to reach my Bian."

"Oh. How does that happen?"

"When it's time, usually around age fifteen, your body just *changes*." He shifted his gaze down. "Or so I'm told."

"How old are you?"

Still downcast, he resumed his drumming. "Seventeen."

"Oh." The way he carried himself and his speech made him appear older.

An awkward silence grew until he chopped it down. "I'm an embarrassment to my clan." His voice deepened, and he seemed to grow. "I'm a Cael. I don't mean I am merely a member of the Cael clan; my *name* is Cael. I'm Declan Broderick Cael IV. I'm the next clansman in line to take a seat on the *co-cheangail*."

I didn't like how he puffed himself up. "What's that?"

"The co-cheangail is the committee of United Clans. There are two representatives for each clan." He returned to normal height.

Not wanting to get into politics, I changed the subject. "So every one of you changes into an animal eventually?"

With hunched shoulders, he nodded, as though it was up for debate.

"I wonder if I will."

"I assumed you would, being the daughter of Cataleen. It didn't occur to me until now that you're half human."

"It never occurred to *me* that I'm half not. Besides, we're both seventeen. So, if I do, my change is delayed too." The idea intrigued me, but it was impossible to envision myself as anything other than me. I changed the subject again, to what should have been my first question. "Any idea how I can get home?"

"If you can find the megalith and figure out how to use the amulet, I would think you can go home anytime."

I slumped. Both would take quite a bit of work. I grasped the amulet. "Mirna said this is what got me through. Funny, I don't remember it."

"What is funny?" He tilted his head. I'd have to be careful about using words he was familiar with in ways that would likely be lost on him. As I formulated an attempt to explain, he continued, "A pech made the amulet. They have the ability to manipulate stone. The pech who made Drochaid must have been powerful. It is a transport stone and enables the user to pass from one realm of existence to the next through the megalith, as long as you know how to use it. This one is also a language translator and a guide—one of a kind."

"How did I get through then? I don't know how to use it."

"Did someone help you?"

"No. I was alo—" I was about to say alone, but the face I saw before passing out came to mind. "Wait. There was someone. I hit a tree branch and blacked out. Just before I passed out, I saw a face."

"What caused you to hit your head?"

"A wolf. I was chased by a wolf." I spoke as though being chased by a wolf was an everyday occurrence in my realm. Where had he gone?

"What did the face look like?"

"It was pale with glowing yellow eyes. That's all I could make out. I couldn't see well."

"Is that unusual in your realm?"

"What? The eyes? On a human, yeah. I've seen eyes look like that on deer in headlights, but human eyes don't reflect light like that."

"Headlights?" His lips matched the sound.

"Uh. Yeah. They're just bright lights." Not only would I have to avoid unfamiliar phrases, I'd have to be careful to choose words he would understand.

He nodded. "Hmm. A wolf. A pale face. Glowing yellow eyes..." Declan crinkled one eye and rubbed his chin.

"What?"

"I wonder if someone from Ariboslia brought you through. Your description sounds like a *fasgadair*. I don't know about your realm, but only they match your description here. Their eyes reflect the light. It could have chased you in wolf form then shifted. Though I must be wrong, for such a creature wouldn't help you."

"What's a fas..." I couldn't remember the word.

"A fasgadair?" In response to my nod he explained, "They're blood-drinkers. I'm uncertain why I mentioned it. I'm sure it wasn't. They wouldn't help you. They would kill you or take you captive."

"A blood-drinker? Like a vampire?"

"What's a vampire?"

"They're mythical creatures who feed on human blood. Once bitten, the victim either dies or becomes undead like them. They have many different abilities, depending on which story you hear."

"Sounds like a fasgadair. They live in your realm too?"

"No. Only in stories."

He studied me with such intensity, I found it hard to hold his gaze. "Are you certain? I mean, how would people in your realm make something like that up? Are there stories about shape-shifters too?"

I nodded. "The most famous are werewolves. They're supposedly cursed by the full moon. That's when they change into wolves and attack. Do you think that's what chased me? A werewolf?"

Declan let out a series of small breaths as he shook his head. "That's foolishness. We can change at will. 'Tis not a curse, but the way we were made. We, the gachen, lived in your realm once. Did you know that?"

"No way. Seriously? When?"

"Long, long ago, until humans revered us as gods. The One True God is a jealous God. Human worship of us made Him angry, so He removed us and put us here, in Ariboslia.

"During the Great Clan War, a couple of daft women made a grave mistake. Their husbands were called to war. The women, worried for their husbands' safety, resurrected Morrigan." His eyes bulged as though willing the severity of this error into my psyche. "Before she was to be beheaded for unmentionable crimes, Morrigan managed to sneak away to your realm where she was worshiped as the Battle-Crow or the goddess of war. It's said the women resurrected her, thinking she would help their husbands win the war. Once Morrigan returned, she wasn't the same. She was no longer dead, yet she wasn't alive either. She was a monster—a demon. She fed on blood. She was, as far as we know, the first fasgadair.

"Once brought back from hell, Morrigan killed the two women. Turning into a crow, she flew to the battlegrounds. They say, once there, in her undead form, she slaughtered almost everyone on all sides of the battle, and then returned to the sky, cawing over the dead bodies. Few escaped the massacre."

"Wait a sec—is this real?" I raised an eyebrow at him.

"It's written in the annals." He nodded, widening his eyes further as if seeking my understanding.

I didn't fully understand, but motioned for him to continue.

"The fasgadair have been strengthening ever since. They kill most of our men. They spare some, either turning them into fasgadair to grow their army or enslaving them to breed more gachen to feed upon. Every once in a while someone will manage to escape, bringing horrifying tales."

"If that's what got me through the megalith, why would it help me? Why didn't it kill me?"

"That's why I say it couldn't have been. Once they turn into their undead state, they're soulless, caring for nothing." His eyebrows pinched together. "When we found you, you were lying outside Mirna's door sick with sùgh poisoning. Your leg was torn up too. How did you get there? How did you know she lived there?"

"I didn't. Maybe the wolf brought me."

"Right, the wolf. The fasgadair," he mulled it over aloud. "Perhaps the wolf is a gachen who protected you from the fasgadair? But why wouldn't he identify himself?" He paused, as if expecting me to answer. "Maybe a gachen pushed you through the megalith after you passed out and came through with you. In any case, we should tell the elders."

"Who are the elders?"

"Seven chosen elders oversee our village."

"What do you think they'd do...to the wolf, I mean. I don't want anyone to hurt him."

"Why would they hurt him? If I'm correct, he's one of us, especially if he's helping you. They might be able to help figure this all out. They may help find him."

That would be nice. For some reason, I missed the wolf. Perhaps because he seemed to have saved my life. Or because he was my only tie to my world, aside from the amulet.

We remained silent a few minutes. The sun lowered in the sky, touching the horizon. The sea began the slow process of swallowing it.

Declan rose, suggesting we go to dinner. Though I stalled, this time he waited and walked by my side. I moved slowly, unsure what awaited me and how much more I could take.

CHAPTER NINE

The ocean behind us, Declan and I trekked back to the village past farmland and stables. We threaded through a maze of dwellings mounded within the earth. The ground leveled, and we approached a large tent surrounded by tables and benches. A sizeable crowd had gathered. Their chatter mingled with the cicadas in the background and random bleats and grunts from farm animals milling about.

Declan's arm grazed mine as we walked. Warmth emanated from the spot and radiated throughout my body. He bent to whisper in my ear, sending a tingle down my neck. "I love this time of year because we eat outside instead of in the dining hall."

Strangers watched as we neared. My grandmother approached. Her cheeks held a tinge of pink, and her eyes sparkled. "My most sincere apologies for dismissing you prematurely, child." She planted a kiss upon my cheek. "I've been ill of late."

The kiss lingered, sticky. I fought the urge to wipe it away. I hadn't been kissed since I was seven—before Bumpah died.

Mirna faced the crowd and cleared her throat. Oh no. Here comes an announcement. Why did I suspect it had something to do with me? If only I could shrink into a water molecule and evaporate into the air.

"Everyone!" Her voice cracked, straining for volume. "Please welcome my long-awaited granddaughter, Fallon!"

The three hundred or so people present cheered. Many rushed to greet me. Some grabbed my arm; others hugged. All tossed their names at me, which I promptly forgot. But their eyes struck me—brilliant greens, blues, or purples, ranging in lightness and depth.

For the first time, I sympathized with celebrities swarmed by adoring fans. Hands with no sense of appropriate boundaries groped at me. The air seemed cut off. My head swam. I searched the faces for Declan.

"Fallon, come, let's eat." Declan spoke louder than normal.

I turned toward his voice. Relief washed over me when he grasped my hand.

My admirers took the hint. Unlike star-crazed fans, the crowd respectfully withdrew.

I took a deep breath.

Once disentangled, we moved to the tables. Declan had become my lifeline, and I held on. He led me to a seat at the table and let go of my hand before sitting next to me. My hand already missed his.

The places were set with gorgeous stoneware—shiny, gray with black specks, hand-painted in intricate blue and green patterns. I touched one smooth surface. "This is amazing."

Mirna sat in the empty seat beside me. "We are known throughout Ariboslia for our pottery." She glanced about as others settled into their seats.

I gaped at the presentation on the table before me: platters of roasted meats, baskets of breads, trays of cheeses, tureens of soups, piles of baked potatoes, and tubs of leafy salads. When Mirna handed me one of the latter, it was so heavy I almost dropped it. I hurried to put some on my plate, pass it, and take the next bowl from her.

Once my plate overflowed, I grabbed a fork, about to dig in. It grew silent. Uncertain, I surveyed the crowd. They clasped their hands together, bowed their heads, and closed their eyes. I didn't know what to do. I bowed too, taking quick peeks at Declan and Mirna, waiting for movement. When they lifted their heads and picked up utensils, I did the same.

Silverware clinked against stoneware, and individual conversations converged into a monotonous hum.

Mirna sliced some soft cheese, spread it on a piece of bread, and handed it to me. "Try this."

The bread crust crackled and flaked in my hand. The inside was still warm and soft. I took a bite. "Oh. This is amazing." The bread didn't have much flavor on its own. Paired with the nutty, salty cheese, it was an entirely new experience. A party of flavors danced in my mouth.

"We are known for our cheeses too." She smiled as I relished the taste.

Declan leaned in to talk over the din. "'Tis unusual to have this much food all at once." The way he gazed at me as he smiled made my skin tingle. "We're celebrating your arrival."

"Why?"

He laughed. "We've waited a long time."

"Waited...for *me*? Why?"

The smile fell. He cast his gaze downward and shifted in his seat. "Well, because you're family."

"That's all?"

He muttered and nodded without meeting my gaze. He was hiding something, but I didn't press him. I probably wouldn't like the answer.

After dinner, men lit a bonfire a few feet from the tent. Musicians played drums and wooden flutes, while others sang and danced. A chaos of people milled about, tons of kids and animals. An occasional sheep, pig, dog, chicken, or duck ambled past. One goat in particular kept following me, rubbing its head against my leg.

Declan laughed. "I've never seen her do that to anyone before."

"There are so many animals. How do you know which ones are

animals and which are those shape-shifter people? What are they called again?"

"Gachen. In this village, we know everyone, including the animals. She's a goat, nothing more."

"So, outside the village you wouldn't know?"

He shook his head. "But most gachen prefer their human form. Except the *selkie*."

"What's that?"

"A shape-shifter like us. But they change into seal form. Or they would say they are seals who change into human form. They prefer to remain in the ocean as seals. But they do have underwater cities where they live in human form."

"Whoa, like Atlantis?"

Declan cocked his head and scrunched his eyebrows at me.

"Oh, right." I waved my hand. "Forgot where I was. Never mind."

The fire grew. Wood popped, sending sparks flying. Shadows bounced with the leaping flames. Haunting melodies from the flutes wafted through the air, intermingling with the tribal beats of the drums, sending shivers up my spine. Cael of all ages danced hand-in-hand in a circle, laughing and singing, sometimes tripping and falling down.

Talk about culture shock—shape-shifters, underwater cities, vampires, amulets...but more: *family*. Family I never knew, and people who seemed truly happy. Which concept most boggled my mind? All ideas were equally bizarre.

Declan ushered me toward a group of people sitting on a grassy hill out of the dancers' way. One girl saw us approach and motioned for her friends to push aside. "Fallon. Declan. Won't you sit with us?" She patted the ground beside her.

I searched Declan for confirmation. He nodded.

Once we'd seated ourselves, the girl who'd spoken placed her hand over her heart. "I'm called Ryann." She pointed to the others, introducing them. I only caught two names: Shonna, the girl with long, red hair, sitting on the other side of Ryann, and Garvey, the boy who'd moved over for us. "So, Fallon, what do you think of our little village?"

What did I think? I couldn't pull together a comprehensive thought, but I had to say something. "It's nice."

"Nice? Well it is that, I suppose." She laughed, brushing away loose strands of golden hair from her face, tossing a chunk of long locks over her shoulder. "Has Declan here been a good host?" Ryann nudged him with her elbow.

The way she teased made me wonder if they were an item. "Yeah," I answered, checking Declan for his response.

"Was there any doubt?" He was hard to read, but he didn't seem to be into her.

"Do you really want us to answer?" Garvey punched him in the shoulder. Declan slugged him back.

Ryann shook her head at them. "So, Fallon, how much do you know about our world?"

"Um. Not much. I know you're gachen. This is Notirr. I have an inhuman grandmother who's still alive. That's about it." Then I remembered Drochaid and the fasgadair. What else had my overwrought mind forgotten?

Ryann's jaw dropped. "That's all? Do you know about the other people in our land?"

"The fasgadair." I tried to recall what else Declan had told me. "Declan mentioned something about pech." What was the other one? "Oh yeah, and selkie."

"How much do you know about selkie?"

"They turn into seals and live underwater." I turned to Declan. "Right?"

He nodded.

Ryann swatted Declan's arm. "You didn't warn her?"

"Warn me about what?"

Declan groaned. "Chances are she'll never see one. Have you?"

"Nay. But our elders raised us with the stories. They knew the importance of being prepared. Don't you think she should be prepared? What if she saw one?" Ryann asked.

"If you think she should know, go ahead, tell her." Declan's hand swept the air as if giving it all to Ryann.

"I'll tell her." Garvey scooted forward to see me past Declan. With his baby face, he appeared a bit younger than the others. "The selkie prefer their aquatic underworld to land. So, as Declan said, you'll probably never see one. They emerge from time to time, in human form. But there's one problem."

"What?" I asked.

"Selkie are like magnets, and we," he leaned forward, his eyes bulging so his wavy blond hair nearly fell into them, "are metal."

"What do you mean?"

"When they come in contact with one of us, we drop everything to be with them." He shook his head. "We remain under their power until the selkie returns to the sea."

"Which they probably will eventually." Shonna moved closer. She, too, appeared younger, but older than Garvey. "Gachen who'd gone missing decades before have returned brokenhearted. We've seen it, haven't we?"

The others nodded.

Garvey cleared his throat. "The selkie don't intend to cause us harm. Their elders try to keep the young with wanderlust at home. But it doesn't always work."

"So I'd never want to go home again if I saw one?" I'd never see Stacy again? What must she think has happened to me? I had to return, if only to calm her fears.

Declan laid a gentle hand on my arm. "Not to worry. It rarely happens."

His touch sent warm shivers up my arm. And his eyes. So full of concern.

"But the power the selkie have over us differs from the fasgadair." Garvey's voice grew louder, stealing my attention from Declan.

Declan pulled his hand away, and I tried to focus on Garvey.

"Did Declan tell you that? The power the fasgadair have?" Garvey asked.

"The power to drain all my blood, you mean?" I half chuckled.

Garvey shook his head at Declan. "You dunderhead. What did you spend all afternoon talking about?" He faced me. "This you definitely need to know. The fasgadair have the power of suggestion. They can make us do their bidding. But it's something those with the aid of the One True God can easily overcome. God can give us strength to overcome the selkie's power, too. The problem is, most gachen won't even ask. Their desire to remain with the selkie runs too deep to reach out for help."

I ran my fingers across the grass tips. "Well that's depressing."

"Aye," Shonna agreed. "But it's important that you know. The selkie are the reason Ariboslia is in peril."

"That's not entirely true, Shonna." Ryann placed her hand on Shonna's shoulder.

Now I was thoroughly confused. "I thought the fasgadair were the problem."

"They are." Declan leaned back on his hands, making his triceps bulge. "But the selkie played a part in why they're here."

"I'll tell her." Garvey hit the crook of Declan's elbow. Declan caught himself from falling. He sat up and swung his fist toward Garvey's jaw. Garvey flinched. Declan stopped short, smiled, and gave Garvey's cheek a gentle pat.

"Boys...boys." Ryann shook her head.

"Anyway." Garvey straightened. "Ariboslia has twelve gachen clans. At one time, we were all united. All twelve clans were part of the co-cheangail, the committee of United Clans. But the northernmost clan, the Ain-Dìleas, turned their back on God. Worshiping false gods, delving into dark arts."

Shonna clicked her tongue. "Not good."

"Nay." Garvey agreed. "The other clans couldn't unite themselves with such evil. They had to sever alliances. Dissent arose among the clans. Some remained loyal to God. Others thought it was more important to remain united, no matter the cost. The co-chean-gail fell apart, and clans waged war against each other."

"That's when the Ain-Dìleas purchased the *zpět*," Shonna added.

"What's the zpět?" All these foreign words were losing me.

"An amulet forged by a dark pech called Miloslsv," Declan said.

"Like Drochaid?" I asked.

"Nay." Garvey threw Declan a look as if to say 'I'm telling the story'. "Drochaid is an amulet forged by a pech. Their beliefs are wrong, but they don't practice dark arts. The zpět contained the darkest of unholy powers—the ability to resurrect the dead."

A breeze swept through, and sparks flew toward us. An owl hooted.

"The clans still in God's favor formed a union called the Ionraic. The Ionraic feared the Ain-Dìleas would invoke the powers of the zpět to resurrect those they'd lost in the clan wars. They sent Cairbre, a gachen warrior, to destroy the zpět. Cairbre was a fearless leader, and cunning. He avoided the seas since the Ain-Dìleas heavily protect the coast. Instead, he planned to sneak up from behind by braving the treacherous Cnatan Mountains. But it is thought that dark powers sabotaged his quest. His men died. All of them. Some fell from steep cliffs. Others starved. Many froze in unseasonably severe weather. Cairbre was the only survivor."

"And here's where the selkie comes in," Shonna added.

"Aye. On his way to the village, he came upon a selkie named Deirdra—"

"Keep in mind," Ryann cut Garvey off, "this was before any of us, the gachen or the selkie, fully understood the power they have over us."

"Yeah...yeah. She fell in love." Garvey groaned.

Was the story over? "What happened?"

"Have you been listening to what we've told you?" Shonna asked. "Nothing. Cairbre stayed with Deirdra. He was so close to the zpět but never bothered going after it. He stayed under her spell."

"How do you know it was a spell?" I asked. "Maybe he was in love with her."

"Maybe he was." Ryann nodded. "We can't know. We do know this—many a poem and song reflect their immeasurable feelings for one another. Her love overshadowed the power of the sea she longed to return to. Perhaps it was meant to be. Perhaps God willed it to be so. His ways are a mystery. Deirdra never returned to the sea, and Cairbre never fulfilled his mission."

"And the Ain-Dìleas resurrected Morrigan." Garvey shook his head.

"That's how we know there's something unnatural between us and the selkie. A curse, perhaps." Declan sounded disgusted. "Who in their right mind would give up such an important mission for a woman?"

"True." Ryann sighed. "Because Cairbre failed to destroy the zpĕt, the first fasgadair entered our world. Many lives have been lost. Many have been enslaved. And many have become one of them. But," her voice brightened, "with the fasgadair as a common enemy, the remaining free clans of Ariboslia have returned to the co-chean-gail. There is hope."

I squirmed. It didn't sound hopeful. To allow such evil into the world because you can't take your eyes off a girl—ridiculous.

"Did Declan tell you about the Bogle?" Garvey grinned.

"Shut your gob, Garvey. Don't you think the girl has had enough for one night?"

"What's a Bogle?" How many more creatures did I need to fear?

Garvey scrunched his face, curved his fingers to appear like claws next to his head. "It's a monster who snatches those who misbehave." He dropped his hands and chuckled. "It's not real—just a story we tell little ones to make them obey."

"Sounds like the bogeyman." If anyone heard me, they didn't respond.

"Speaking of the Bogle and making kids obey," Ryann stood and smoothed out her dress, "it's time to round them up and get them to bed."

Shonna jumped up. "I'll help."

The crowd dispersed. Declan rose and reached out a hand to me. "Come. I'll bring you back to Mirna."

I took his hand. The moment my fingers touched his, a tingle shot up my arm. Heat rose to my face. The faint echo of the sensation remained after I released his hand. I turned and walked back toward the homes, hoping I headed in the right direction.

Behind me, Declan grasped my elbow and directed me to the right. "This way." He chuckled. "I hope those stories didn't overwhelm you."

I viewed him askance. "Is all this true? The selkie. Cairbre. All of it?"

He nodded.

"What about the Bogle?"

He laughed. "Naw. That's just to scare kids."

"Is there anything else I should know?"

"I think the fasgadair are our biggest concern at the moment."

CHAPTER TEN

Hammering woke me. I groaned. The knocking increased, pulling me into reality. "What?"

Mirna opened the door, spilling light into the room. Like a creature of the night, I recoiled from the brightness as she deposited clothes at my feet and picked up the clothing I'd left on the floor. Oops.

"Please get dressed and come out." She lit the lantern by my bed. "I'm going to take you to see Sully." She retreated and began to close the door behind her.

I rubbed my eyes. "Wait. Who's Sully?"

Mirna poked her head back inside. "Sully is a seer."

"A seer? What's that?"

"He has the gift to see things most of us cannot, like the future." Mirna attempted to duck out and close the door again.

"Whoa. Is he, like, a fortune teller?" I propped myself up on an elbow.

"Nay." Her face reappeared, a faint smile playing on her lips. "I'll be outside." She closed the door before I could utter another word.

Reluctant to leave the bed's coziness, but eager to bask in the glow of Declan's gorgeousness, I slid out like a slug and dressed. Perhaps, after the visit with the seer guy, I'd get to see him.

A hand mirror rested on the table. I peered at my reflection. My eyes widened. My usual greasy, lifeless hair shone and bounced. No zits appeared anywhere. My skin, still pale, was smooth. Some might even consider me attractive. Was it a trick of the mirror? The bed, the small table, and everything else was normal. I aimed it back on myself and smiled, enhancing my newfound beauty. What caused this transformation? The dim lighting or the soap I'd used? Or was it this place?

My dream. This is what my face looked like before it morphed and fangs appeared. If this part came true, what about the rest? Would I become one of those monsters I kept hearing about?

A sense of dread seeped into my body and settled in my heart, thick and sticky like black tar. Why did I always have to ruin any moment of happiness?

I FOLLOWED Mirna through the village to see the guy who'd tell my future. What if I didn't want to know? Did I have a choice? Each painfully slow step toward this knowledge seemed to circulate the tarlike dread from my heart to my extremities, further slowing my steps. The thin leather shoes Kyra gave me felt as if they weighed a ton. It became difficult to keep Mirna's agonizingly sluggish pace. Why did I feel as if I was about to meet an executioner, and I'd been found guilty?

I switched my focus to the village. Children helped older siblings or parents tend to their gardens. Some washed clothes in a bucket. Others hung the items to dry. A couple of kids sat next to their mother, each weaving a basket.

The homes thinned and the ground leveled as we approached the farmlands. Cows dotted the meadow. Children carried baskets of eggs and bottles of milk toward the village. Everywhere we went, people paused from their tasks, smiled, and waved.

I returned their greetings, hoping my smile didn't appear as false as it felt. Despite the peace and contentment surrounding me, my mind continued to return to the seer. What would he see in me? Would he confirm that I'd become the monster in my dream?

Mirna led me down a trail in the woods beyond the farmland. The laughter and chatter disappeared. A swarm of flying toads croaked as they flew by, and the ground crunched under our feet. A small cabin came into view. Everyone else lived together in homes built into hills. Why did this man live so differently, so far apart from the others?

A tall man with white hair and matching beard opened the door as we approached. I caught sight of his eyes and gasped. Were they rolled up in his head? No, gray filled the space where irises and pupils belonged. He smiled as though he was happy to see me. As if he could. Could he?

"Come in, Fallon." His cheerful demeanor didn't match his sinister appearance. Something in his voice and smile calmed me slightly. But those eyes. I couldn't stop staring.

"Fallon, this is Sully," Mirna said as Sully pushed the door open and held it while making room for me to enter.

"Well, I'll leave you two alone." Mirna waved and toddled back down the trail.

I climbed the two steps into the cabin, still staring into the gray eyes. They bulged slightly where pigment belonged. I stiffened.

As if sensing my discomfort, Sully closed his eyes. He shut the door and crossed the floor to a small living room without a stick to guide him. He turned back to me, those unnerving eyes aimed right at me, without searching.

"Can you see?" Morbid fascination took control of my tongue. It took a moment to register what I'd just said. My cheeks warmed. Idiot!

Sully chuckled. "Aye, but not in the way you can." He sat in a stuffed chair and motioned for me to sit in a matching chair across from him. "Have a seat, dear one."

I stifled the urge to ask what he meant. How was his vision different? Sensing he had other plans for our visit, I managed to refrain, despite the lack of words filling the air.

He reached for a couple of mugs waiting on the table beside him and handed one to me. Water. Was that a custom? Everyone I visited in Notirr handed me a mug of water. Sully moved about as if he could see perfectly. I envisioned him with his eyes closed and a red Santa hat. Yup. He would make the best Macy's parade Santa ever. Well, the best skinny Santa ever.

After taking a long sip, Sully replaced his mug on the table, folded his hands in his lap, and relaxed his shoulders, as if settling in for a long, pleasant chat. "I've been waiting for this day a *long* time."

I took a sip of the sweet liquid, trying to appear nonchalant and avoid his eyes, in case he knew I was staring. "How long?"

"Oh." His gnarled fingers scratched his liver-spotted head, tousling a patch of what remained of his hair. "About fifty years or so."

"Fifty years!" I set the mug down. It clanged the table, spilling a few drops. "I haven't even been alive that long."

"Nay, your parents weren't born yet either. It makes no difference. There was no need to discuss the matter until it was time for your mother to leave." He reached out for his drink. His hand trembled, probably from old age because he didn't appear afraid otherwise.

"When she left Ariboslia?" I moved to the edge of my chair.

A noise muffled in his throat accompanied his almost imperceptible nod as he sipped from his mug. He swallowed. "Did you know she's a twin?"

"No." My head began to pound. More relatives? Mirna mentioned having a son yesterday. With the information overload, it hadn't occurred to me that I had an uncle. I could only process so much at a time. I rubbed my temples.

"Your gran bore only the two children. Your granda died before their birth. They're..." He tipped his head back and forth sideways a couple times as if trying to loosen the correct word from his brain. "... special. They have certain powers, such as starting fires with their minds."

Sully's words faded to a background murmur. His last sentence echoed in my head... starting fires with their minds. My fire. I hadn't been rubbing the sticks together. Could it be?

"Fallon?"

I blinked. "Huh? Oh. Sorry. What were you saying?"

"I was telling you about your uncle when I lost you. Aodan, your mum's twin brother, let his powers get the better of him. He lusted for more until his hunger consumed the good within him. He joined Morrigan."

I nearly dropped my cup. "Morrigan? The same Morrigan Declan told me about? The first fasgadair?"

Sully nodded. "The one and only."

"So, my uncle is one of those bloodsuckers?"

"Aye. 'Tis true. He's not only one of them. He's their leader."

My jaw dropped. Talk about dysfunctional. What a messed-up family I was born into! "I thought Morrigan was their leader."

"She is. But she prefers to remain in secret. She lets Aodan believe he's in control. Truly he's a puppet." He drew his lips inward and breathed deeply through his nose. "Poor lad was ripe for the picking. Morrigan wanted his unique talents. She used his lust for power to lure him. She enticed him with a kingdom and the abilities unique to the fasgadair: speed, heightened senses, inhuman strength, and power of suggestion. But what snared him was the promise of immortality. His inherited gifts mixed with the fasgadair blood make him a terrifying enemy. Later, with her witchcraft, Morrigan saw what I already knew."

"What?"

"After Aodan's rise to power, his twin sister Cataleen would have a child who would end his tyranny."

"What child?" I glanced about the room as though the person he spoke of might linger. I feared the answer, but nourished a faint glimmer of hope she'd birthed another child.

"You."

As my hope extinguished, my chest tightened making it difficult to breathe.

"When Morrigan told Aodan about you, he tried driving your mum to suicide. One of the special abilities the twins possessed was the mind-link they shared. An ability to communicate, without words, across any distance. When he found out about the prophesied child," Sully tilted both his right hand and his head in my direction, "he opened the link and bombarded her with images to drive her mad. Try as she might, she couldn't block them."

Sully took a slow sip from his mug. "So I shared the prophecy with the village. I already knew Cataleen would be sent to the human realm. Still I had to convince the elders. When Aodan went so far as to convince Cataleen to pick up a knife and aim it at herself, they listened. It was only a matter of time before she ended her life or Aodan sent someone to complete the task."

Something in Sully's deep voice and Scottish sounding accent calmed me. If only his words were more comforting.

"The elders consented to send Cataleen away. Then Faolan, a friend to both Aodan and Cataleen, reappeared. He had left the village with Aodan years before. His return surprised everyone. They marveled over how he had managed to live among the fasgadair without being turned or enslaved. Everyone except me." He chortled. "I am difficult to surprise."

"Did he refuse to become one? Why would they let him live?"

Sully raised his eyebrows. "Good questions. Exactly what the rest of us wanted to know. Just because I know certain things will happen, doesn't mean I know why. Perhaps something within Aodan still couldn't bear killing his friend. Despite all that, Faolan knew as well as I that Cataleen needed to leave. I had already secured Drochaid, your amulet, from Pepin. Cataleen used it to enter the human realm, with Faolan's help."

"And then she met my father and I came along?"

"So it would seem. I'm not capable of seeing into your realm, nor what the One True God does not choose to reveal."

"So why am I here?"

Sully took a deep breath. "When you were three years old, your mum returned to Notirr. She brought your da."

"My da? You mean, my father? Why would she risk it?"

"Something about him needing to know the truth—the why doesn't matter. The moment she returned, Aodan sensed her presence. They tried to leave before he could intercept them, but Aodan's men ambushed them. He had your da killed and your mum abducted."

"How? My father's body was found in the woods near my house."

"The fasgadair followed them through the portal."

"How do you know this? You said you can't see into my world. How do you know my father died there?"

Sully reached to touch my arm, eyes closed. "I have seen your mum. She is enslaved by the fasgadair."

What on earth possessed them to return? If they hadn't, I would've grown up with a family. How could they have—My heart skipped a beat. "My mother is still alive?"

He nodded.

I nearly jumped out of my chair. "Does anyone else know? Do you know where she is? Why haven't you rescued her?"

"Dear child, everything needs to happen according to God's plan. Otherwise, it will result in certain disaster. The fasgadair are faster and stronger. God will protect us, but we must do things His way."

"That doesn't make any sense. Isn't there anyone who could sneak in and save her?"

"Lass, there are so many who need rescuing. We do not have the warriors to free them all. And any attempt to thwart God's plans will only result in harm to oneself or others. His desired outcome will be achieved regardless."

"But what does all this mean? What part do I play in this?"

"You will rescue your mum from her captors and the rest of us from your uncle."

"Me? Are you kidding? I'm a kid. I'm a wimp. I can't rescue anyone." My mouth hung open as I fought to connect the dots. My mother—still alive. Yes, her body never turned up. How often had Fiona complained about her casket laying empty next to my dad's? But how could I save her? I didn't know anything about this place. I wasn't a warrior. I had no skills.

On the other hand, what else did I have to live for? I've never wanted anything more than my parents, and now I had a chance to find one of them. Wasn't it worth risking my life? "How am I supposed to rescue her?"

"How you will accomplish this has not been revealed to me, only that you will. And you will not be alone. You will have the best help possible."

"Well there's a relief." My sarcasm reemerged. "Who's that?"

"God."

"God?" I laughed. I meant no disrespect to the Big Guy, but He'd abandoned me long ago. He wouldn't help me. I'm not even sure I believed He existed. "How is He going to help me?"

"He will give you a gift when you are ready." He dropped his voice. "You think He has failed you, but He hasn't. He has been watching you, caring for you, molding you. All you have been through has made you stronger than you realize. You are growing stronger still."

"Caring for me? Watching me? By taking away my parents and Bumpah, leaving me with an unloving stiff? I doubt it." I crossed my arms.

My insolence failed to agitate him. He remained calm and pleasant. He took a long drink. "When you choose to seek Him, you will find Him. Only then will you begin to understand."

Yeah, right! What a load of bull. "So what is this I'm supposed to do? I don't know how to fight. I can't even cook a rabbit to save my life."

"Follow the amulet."

"Huh?"

"The amulet will guide you. The pech who forged Drochaid is one of the few who worship the One True God. Most pech worship the elements—air, fire, earth, and water—as though they are more than mere sustenance provided by God. The pech have amazing abilities with stone. As God's servant, Pepin has shown what such abilities do in the hands of a true believer. Use it."

"I don't get it. I'm just supposed to wander a world I don't know based on what direction a rock points me?" I pulled it from beneath my collar. "It's not even doing anything. It hasn't for days."

"It will when it's time."

"What if I refuse?"

"Our God is outside of time. He knows all—past, present, and future. I know this to be true, because He revealed you to me many years ago and here you are. All He has shown me has come to be. In my youth, my immaturity, I attempted to thwart His plans. The result was this." He pointed to his eyes. "And the outcome I tried to change occurred regardless. Lesson learned. I no longer attempt to interfere, but to assist." A dreamy quality softened his voice. "I sometimes wonder if part of His plan was to blind me. If the events had not transpired as they had, I would not see as I do today."

"So we don't have free will?"

"To the contrary—we do. As I explained, the outcome will occur according to His will regardless. The question is, will you play the part?"

"It doesn't feel like I have much choice. I'm trapped in a backward world only the Grimm Brothers could've dreamed up, and I have to rescue my mother? How?"

I stared at my shaking hands then placed them under my legs to get them to stop. I wanted to scream and cry. It was hopeless. I would fail. No doubt about it. I. Would. Fail.

Sully placed a hand on my shoulder. "This is much to learn. You have suffered a great deal for one so young. God has chosen you for His reasons. You will learn to trust Him in time. You will not fail."

The dream returned to me. My face. The dead eyes. The fangs. I took a deep breath and dared to ask the one thing I really didn't want to know. "What about the dream? I keep dreaming I become one of those monsters...the fasgadair."

"'Tis but a dream." Sully leaned forward, his gray eyes trained on mine as though he could peer into my soul. "But remember, there is always a choice. Choose wisely."

CHAPTER ELEVEN

Hard wood prodded my back as I rocked in a wooden rocking chair in my grandmother's living room. The chair's rhythmic squeak against the floorboards and a distant hum of cicadas, or some similar sounding creature, filled the air. Afternoon sun streaming through the window dimmed as the shadows in the room lengthened. A slight breeze ruffled the curtains. I stared at the steady flame encased in glass on the table while Mirna knit in silence.

Perhaps I should skip dinner tonight. How could I face them? Now I understood. These people didn't welcome me as a long lost family member. They hailed a savior. Something I wasn't—something I'd never be.

What if I became an epic fail, like Cairbre? What if, like him, my story became a tale of what not to do...shared with generations to come? What if I became the monster I feared? Sully hadn't said it wouldn't happen.

But I couldn't avoid dinner. Scents wafted through the village into the open window, bringing me back to days of Bumpah cooking on the grill in the backyard. My stomach rumbled, reminding me of those first few days in Ariboslia—of true hunger. Phantom pain emerged with the memory.

I followed Mirna along the path between the hill homes to dinner. She remained mercifully silent. We arrived at the tent filling with a large crowd. When spoken to, I plastered a smile on my face, unsure of how to respond. But I was a sham, an imposter, an actress in the wrong play without a script.

Declan pulled me aside. "What's troubling you?"

"Nothin'." Other than the fact that I'd inevitably let everyone here down, and generations to come would tell tales of it. I shook my head, unwilling to dash his hopes.

Others tried to engage me as well. They eyed Declan, questioning him in silence. He shrugged, eyebrows raised and eyes wide in response, showing his complete lack of understanding. I pretended not to notice.

The night passed in a haze. After everything I'd been through, I should be tied up, hugging myself in a love-me jacket and thrown in a padded cell where I could commence drooling. If only I had something sharp to halt my cyclical thoughts and refocus them on tangible pain.

Once in bed, I fought in vain to sleep. The questions, the uncertainty of coming events robbed me of rest. I flitted in and out of nightmares.

The woman with long, blonde hair sat by the shore, watching the ocean waves. The breeze swept across the shore, swirling the white dress around her delicate frame as locks danced about her face. Without turning toward me, she called my name. "Fallon...Faaaaallon."

I'd had this dream before. Was this woman my mother? For the first time, I didn't want to go near her.

The woman slowly faced me.

Darkness rolled in.

"She's here." A deep, masculine voice called from my right.

I jerked my head in its direction. A circle of swirling light pierced the darkness. I moved toward it.

"I can sense her presence. It's almost like...almost like..."

Was the voice coming from the light?

Shadows emerged on the surface of the whirlpool of light. I didn't want to chance getting sucked in, so I craned my neck to peer into it without stepping any closer. A woman with thick, black hair dwarfing her small face narrowed her eyes. Her lips moved, though I couldn't discern a sound.

"Yes. She's here. I'm sure of it," the man's voice came again, a mixture of excitement and malice, laced with a tinge of fear. "Like with Cataleen..."

The woman's eyes bulged. Her face grew larger as she drew closer to the light. She held up her finger. Just as it seemed she'd push through, the swirling light shrunk until it was the size of a pea hovering in the air, then disappeared with a pop. I dared move closer to touch the air where the light had been. Nothing.

I turned back toward the woman by the water. As in my previous dreams, neither of us moved, yet the woman was closer. Her hair transformed from blonde to black. She had become me. Yet again, the doppelganger's eerie face tilted sideways.

Its mouth widened, revealing the sharp, menacing fangs I'd come to expect. I held my arms up to protect my face just before it lunged at me.

I screamed. Mirna was on the bed cradling me in her arms. Never, since the dreams began, had anyone risen from bed to check on me. How I had longed for someone to treat me with such tenderness. Tears sprang to my eyes. She hugged me close, smoothed my hair, and hummed the tune I'd soothed myself with nights before.

I bolted upright and spun to her. "I know that song!"

"You do? Cataleen must have sung it to you. It is a traditional Ariboslian hymn."

So I did remember something about my mother. I lay back down against my grandmother.

"Do you want to talk about it?" she asked. "The nightmare?"

"I've had it for as long as I remember. It starts beautiful with the sun shining. There's a woman in the distance. I try to get to her and —" my voice broke. "I can't do this. I'm not the hero you all expect me to be." Admitting my failings was the nail that cracked the wall around my heart, and it tumbled down. Exposed, I began to sob. My whole body trembled.

My grandmother continued to hold me, rocking, humming the familiar tune.

When my sobs subsided, I worked on breathing. I waited until I could talk without crying again. "What happens if I can't do it?"

"We will love you anyway." Tears flowed once more at the conviction in her voice. How could she love me, a mere stranger, even if I failed them?

SEEMING to understand I needed solitude, my grandmother let me lounge about inside for the day. The dream haunted me. Why had it been so different, as if I had more control over it? I'd never been so aware that I was in the dream, that I'd seen it before and knew what to expect. But most baffling was the swirling light. It was new. What was it?

A frown of worry masked Mirna's face when I refused breakfast and lunch, claiming I wasn't hungry. By dinner, she insisted I eat.

At dinner, Mirna sat me down next to her again. I searched for Declan, but failed to find him. When I finished eating, I waited for Mirna so we could leave. She seemed chattier tonight, perhaps stalling to keep me out longer. As I pecked at the food still on my plate, waiting for her conversation to end, Declan walked over carrying an infant.

"Here." He handed it to me before I could protest. "This is Bedelia. I thought she might help you."

I'd never held a child before, and feared I might drop it. I gazed at the strange, plump little being. Her curious, purple eyes studied me. I returned the stare.

She squinted and pointed a chubby finger at my face. She babbled, stern, as though lecturing me.

I couldn't help but chuckle.

My laughter interrupted her babbling. She scrutinized me further.

I grew serious too. Was she thinking wise thoughts? When she reached to grab my nose, I laughed again. Nope. Just a baby studying my face. I gave her fist a raspberry. She squealed, beginning a game whereby she dared place her fist close to my face and attempted to pull it away before I could get it. Her full-body giggles were contagious.

"See? I told you. She has that effect on everyone." Sitting next to us, Declan put his face close to hers. "No one can resist you, can they?" He planted a kiss on her cheek. My heart swelled that such an attractive, tough-looking guy would be so sweet to a baby.

"Who does she belong to?" I asked.

"She's an orphan."

"Oh." I understood that. "What happened to her parents?"

Declan's eyes flashed, widening for a brief second with increased intensity. "Gnuatthara, a town a few days' journey from here by horse, belongs to the Treasach clan. They wish to create a perfect race of warriors. Any baby born who fails to meet their criteria for the strength to become a fierce warrior or a strong mum is exiled, abandoned."

"That's awful!" I clutched Bedelia closer.

"Aye. We have a small camp near there. They keep an eye on the mountainside where those scheduled for exile are left. We bring them here or to nearby clans willing to take them. Some clans prefer to take the elderly or disabled, so many of the babies remain here."

"They kill the elderly and disabled too?"

"Aye, if the Treasach feel they have outlived their usefulness." His eyes flashed again.

"Ugh! Sick." As a whole, I didn't like people. Yet I could never consider doing something so terrible. "That is despicable! I hate them!"

"'Tis wrong to hate. God created the Treasach and loves them as much as He loves us. Some of them have the goodness of God within them. How else would we rescue so many? Those who disagree with their practices help us."

"Wow. Some of them realize it's wrong?"

Declan scrunched his confused face again.

Was sarcasm completely lost on these people? "If they know it's so wrong, why don't they *do* something about it? Why don't they leave?"

"What good would running away do? All those we help would die."

"I don't know." I glanced around. Most people had finished eating. Kids ran, chasing each other. No wonder there were so many.

"You must understand," Declan added. "They're afraid. They fear the fasgadair. Faith in God is no longer prevalent there. Without Him, they have no reason not to fear. But now, because we have a common enemy, we have a peace between our clans we have not experienced in centuries. Such peace might allow us to make a positive impression on them. Because of this, some are returning to God. We must pray and love them. Perhaps they will recognize their misdeeds."

"I don't get it. How can you love anyone who leaves a child—this child," I turned Bedelia toward him for emphasis, "to *die*." I whispered "die" in the event Bedelia could understand. "How could such a person be worthy of love?"

Declan shrugged. "None of us are worthy. Besides, loving is not something that can be done without help from above. Those of us who depend on His strength are given what we need to do His work. And this is *His* work, *His* desire...that we take care of orphans."

Something changed, as if a dormant switch within me suddenly flipped on. All that had transpired, all that I learned, pressed upon me. This time it didn't crush me. It propelled me forward.

I had to try fulfilling my destiny, or whatever it was. These people, who opened their homes and hearts to me and countless other orphans, must be helped. And the potential reward of finding my mother was far greater than anything I risked.

Declan tilted his head as he seemed to when he was confused. But he didn't scrunch his brows together. His eyes widened. "What are you thinking?" he asked, his voice a higher pitch.

"I can't sit by and do nothing. I have to help. Somehow..."

His intense green eyes fixed on me, twinkling. "You will."

A ripple of warmth coursed through my body. Did the inevitable journey or his gaze cause it? The prophecy of my destiny still scared me, but now I had something more—resolve. There is power in a decision made.

CHAPTER TWELVE

I decided to be sociable and joined Declan and his friends at the fire after dinner. Warm summer air, calming flames, joyous laughter, dancing, haunting tribal music...I drank it all in to the full. I couldn't get enough. I felt stronger, more content than I'd ever felt in my life.

Nothing had changed externally. I was still a foreigner trapped in a strange land. A dangerous mission lay ahead of me. There was no reason to be calm or content and yet, I felt completely at ease. I was exactly where I was supposed to be.

But one thing kept bugging me, invading my peace. The swirling light in my dream.

"So what do you think?" I asked Declan after I'd explained it to him.

"I don't know." He did that thing with his eyebrows when he was deep in thought. His eyes darkened. Adorable. "Have you told Mirna about it?"

"Have you told Mirna about what?" Garvey asked, laughing and out of breath from dancing. He plopped down on the grass in front of us. Shonna and Ryann followed.

"Oh nothing." I pulled at the grass. "Just something I saw in a dream."

"Oooh. A dream?" Shonna leaned closer. Red waves fell from her shoulders toward her face. She tossed them back. "Pray tell."

I took a deep breath and repeated everything I'd just told Declan. "The whole thing is weird, mostly because the dream has always been the same. Always. But now..." I played with a clump of grass in my hand. "I'm completely confused by the swirling lights."

"Did you tell Mirna?" Ryann asked, concern sparking her green eyes.

I shook my head.

"What about Sully?" Garvey asked. "I bet he'd know."

"Maybe." My feet had fallen asleep. With care, to avoid bumping them and sending pins and needles shooting up my leg, I pulled my legs out from underneath me. "Mirna knows about the dream, but I didn't tell her about the light. No one else knows anything except you guys."

Ryann narrowed her eyes. Concerned about the dream? Or perhaps she didn't appreciate being called a guy. "You need to tell someone. I doubt Sully is here, but I'll check." She stood and took off down the hill toward the dancers, disappearing around the fire into the shadows on the other side.

"So you heard a man's voice, but saw a woman's face?" Garvey's face scrunched.

"Yeah. I saw the woman speak, but I couldn't hear her words."

Something moved next to me. "What is that?" I pulled my legs closer. A squat, lizard-looking thing waddled along the ground.

Shonna stood and reached for it. "Aw." She cradled it and petted its back. "It's a fur dragon. Don't you have those in your realm?"

"Uh. No."

"See?" She sat next to me and angled the reptilian thing closer.

It was kind of cute, covered in brown fur rather than scales, but lizard-like angular legs jutted from its elongated body shape.

"You can touch it." Garvey moved closer and reached out to

demonstrate by ruffling a slightly longer tuft of fur on the top of its head, like a circular mohawk.

I gathered it was touchable by the fact that it was sitting in Shonna's lap. The question was, did I want to touch it? It did seem docile. I moved a timid hand toward its head.

The fur dragon's eyes, surrounded by a wide band of black fur, like a panda, followed my hand as it neared. Then it quacked. I jerked my hand away before making contact.

Declan, Shonna, and Garvey all burst out laughing.

"It's okay," Declan said. "They can be vocal. He won't hurt you."

I reached out once more to pet its back. So soft and smooth, like Stacy's velvet throw blanket. The fur dragon closed his eyes. A deep, contented rumble emanated from him.

"He purrs?" I laughed.

"Aw, you found a fur dragon." Ryann's voice startled me. She made her way up the hill with Sully on her heels, walking as if he were a much younger man with perfect vision, but he was hunched as if carrying a great weight.

I pulled away from the fur dragon. Garvey and Shonna scooted away from me to make room for him. The fur dragon's eyes bulged at the disruption. Once Shonna was repositioned, the fur dragon rose. His eyes darted in every direction as if devising the best escape. He quacked, hopped off Shonna's lap, and sauntered off.

Sully smiled, but it wasn't his typical warm smile. He appeared troubled. Extra lines crossed his forehead. His eyes narrowed, and a small groan escaped him. "So. You've experienced the mind-link." He grunted as he lowered himself onto the grass and crossed his legs.

"The what?"

"Do you recall the mind-link I explained that your mum and Aodan shared? You experienced a small dose of it."

"You mean..."

Sully nodded. "You saw through your uncle's eyes. The voice you heard was his."

Shonna gasped.

"Whoa." Garvey's eyes went buggy.

I scanned my friends' shocked faces, certain mine mirrored theirs. How could this be? The last thing I needed was a mental link to a powerful, demonic sociopath. No. It couldn't be. "That was him speaking? Why couldn't I hear the woman? Why was it shadowy...no color?"

"'Tis the beginning. If you don't learn to control it, you'll experience the same thing every time you sleep. It will get stronger. You will hear what Aodan hears. You will see what he sees. The image will sharpen, and colors will emerge. You will even begin to feel what he feels. Then, if you're not careful, it will happen whilst you're awake."

With Sully's back to the fire and little light on his face, his eyes appeared somewhat normal, but dark. "You must learn to control it. If not, Aodan will be able to open the link on his own. If he sensed your presence, he's already working to gain control. He has much experience in this with Cataleen."

No kidding. He nearly drove her to kill herself. His own sister. What would he do to me? I clenched a clump of grass in my fist. "How do I do that...control it?"

"To start, when you're sleeping, if you see the light in your dream, run from it. Don't let him sense your presence. Don't give him a foothold."

"What happens if I'm awake?" My voice was close to becoming shrill. "Will I see the lights like I did in the dream?"

"Nay. You were in your own mind...not reality. Whilst you're awake, it will appear as a vision and take over the true landscape before you. You will see as if Aodan's eyes are yours. His vision will take over." He leaned closer. His gray eyes penetrated mine, and his voice lowered. "If it comes to that, you're in a troublesome spot indeed. You will no longer have control. You won't know where you are or what you're doing. Aodan could walk you off a cliff."

I trembled. That couldn't be possible. Someone else couldn't just take over your body. What was this? *Invasion of the Body Snatchers?*

"I warn you, Fallon. This is serious. This is the reason your mother fled this realm. You cannot let Aodan gain control of your body." Sully's voice had become a growl. I shrank back from his stern expression as if I'd done something wrong. "It can't come to that."

He straightened and softened his tone. "If you sense Aodan's presence in any way, before he gains full control, close your eyes, capture your thoughts. Think about things that bring you joy and peace. But I pray you will not allow it to get that far."

His warning and the dread in his voice left a hollow pit in my stomach. "Is there anything I can do? Can anyone help me?"

Sully nodded, "Aye. God can help. If ye ask Him."

So it had come back to that again. Their God wouldn't help someone like me. My mind wandered back to what had transpired in my dream. The voice. Aodan. He'd mentioned the link, "like with Cataleen," he'd said. Then the woman, whoever she was. She understood. She placed a finger on her lips to make him silent.

My dwindling contentment had reached the bottom. Dread replaced it. The dread of someone who'd been given a death sentence. "They know I'm here."

CHAPTER THIRTEEN

The swirling light appeared in my dream once again. This time, I fought the urge to peer into it and see through my evil uncle's eyes. Sully's warning fresh in my mind, I fled, toward the creepy woman on the shore. When I looked back, the light was gone.

I woke feeling stronger. Perhaps I could do this. Perhaps I could keep Aodan at bay.

At Sully's suggestion, I prepared for the long journey ahead. I started by hiking. Declan joined me. He was good to have around. Otherwise, I'd probably run scared from every strange creature I encountered. I had no way of knowing what was dangerous.

"'Tis good how you were able to walk away from it." Declan leapt over a moss-covered felled tree across the path. "Maybe you already have control over it."

"Maybe." I didn't feel nearly as hopeful as he sounded. "I'm just glad he's not coming after me. Well, not yet."

"Nay. That's not Aodan's style. For one, despite the demon blood surging throughout his body, he still won't allow anyone to touch Notirr. 'Tis his home. A part of him still seems to be nostalgic, which is why we've been safe here."

"But wouldn't he keep fasgadair just outside, waiting to attack the moment I leave?"

"Aodan would expect us to be prepared for that. He knows we'd probably leave during the day when the fasgadair would be in animal form. They're weakest then...easier to kill."

"Why doesn't he send an army?"

Declan laughed a deep, throaty laugh. It took the edge off my fears and filled me with warmth. "You heard Sully. Aodan knows the prophecy. He knows you'll come to him. Why expend the resources? Nay. He'll do as Sully said he'll do, station fasgadair along the way between here and Bandia, waiting for your capture. He'll be too curious about you to kill you right away, from what I hear about him."

I shuddered. "I can't talk about this anymore."

"Shhh!" Declan grasped my shoulder and pulled me to crouch beside him behind some bushes. He peered out over the branches. I followed his gaze and found nothing.

"What are—?"

Declan held a finger to his lips, and then pointed in the direction he'd been watching. "Don't spook them," he whispered.

I checked again and still didn't see anything. Then something pointy moved past some trees. A horse emerged. No, a unicorn.

"Unicorns are real?" I asked a bit too loudly.

Declan's eyes widened as he brought his finger to his lips again, trying not to smile.

I faced the unicorn. It was beautiful, though it struck me as nothing more than a white horse with a perfectly cylindrical, pointy stick protruding from its forehead. It snuffled, swung its brilliant white mane, lowered its head, and shook again. It edged forward and chewed at something on the ground. Its baby followed.

"Oh!" I spun to Declan to be sure he saw. A wide grin stretched across his face, and I watched the baby, a perfect miniature of its parent with a stubby, little horn. So cute! My heart melted. Where was a camera when I needed one?

A sound like a twig snapping rang out from our right, and mama and baby shot off in the opposite direction.

"Awww." I straightened and smoothed my dress. "That stinks. What scared them?"

Declan wrinkled his nose. "I don't smell anything. Hmph. Anyway, unicorns spook easily. I'm surprised we got to see them so close up. Especially with a baby."

"So is it like the legends say? Are they magical?"

"Magical?" Declan's left eyebrow lifted. "What do you mean magical? I've never met an animal that could cast spells, recite incantations, read runes, or mix potions."

"I don't mean like that. Oh, I don't know how...just magical."

"They're just another of God's creation. I assume you don't have unicorns in your realm?"

"Well, we have stories. I never knew unicorns were actually real."

"Of course they are. No human could think up such a being."

I stifled the temptation to point out that it's a horse with a horn sticking out of its head. It didn't exactly require creative genius to come up with. Probably best not to get into a senseless discussion.

Declan asked me more questions about home. Talking about it made it seem closer—like I could hike over the hill and find my dilapidated old farmhouse.

"Stacy sounds like a good friend." Declan wiped perspiration from his brow. "I'd like to meet her someday."

A thrill swept through me. "I would love for you two to meet." My breath came heavy as we crested the hill. The trees parted to reveal the valley and the mountains beyond. "This is beautiful!"

"Aye.'Tis. So, I know you live with your gran, but you never talk about her. Why?" He uncorked his canteen and brought it to his lips. His Adam's apple bobbed up and down as he drank.

I groaned. "There's nothing to talk about."

He laughed and wiped his lips.

"What's so funny?"

"You. You go from happy to angry," he snapped his fingers, "in an instant. I've never seen someone change moods so quickly. And you wear your feelings like a cloak."

I did not! Did I?

"See? Now your face is all red. I embarrassed you. My apologies." He offered me the canteen. "So tell me about your gran."

I grabbed the leather pouch. "Um. I just met her. She lives in another world with a bunch of people who can change into animal form—"

Declan chuckled and shoved my shoulder. "Not Mirna. The one you grew up with."

I found a large rock, plopped onto its mossy surface, and drank. Somehow, the water was still cool. "There's nothing to tell."

Declan sat next to me and placed his arms on his knees. He leaned forward and turned toward me. "What is she like?"

"She's mean. She hates me. End of story." I handed him the canteen.

"That can't be true." He recorked the canteen and draped it over his shoulder. "You thought I hated you too, remember?" He threw me a sideways smile and elbowed me.

I smiled back and sighed internally. His smile could melt the barrier around my heart like nothing else. "No. It's true. She does." I picked up a stick and pushed at the dirt and leaves. "She blames me for my grandfather's death."

"Well," his green eyes twinkled, "did you kill him?"

"No. I didn't *kill* him." I laughed and pushed his shoulder with mine, nearly losing my balance. "He had a heart attack. High cholesterol."

His face grew serious again. "What does that mean?"

"Let's just say it wasn't me."

"Then why does your gran blame you?" He leaned closer. So intent. People didn't listen like Declan. He genuinely seemed to want to know.

"She resents being stuck with me. My father and Bumpah were the only family she had. She never got over Bumpah's death either.

When he was young, he was in the Army. He sent her a postcard every day he was stationed overseas."

"A postcard?"

"It's like a letter, only shorter. He kept sending them, even after he returned home, right up until the day he died. She sends them to herself now and pretends they're from him. It's sad. I guess it's her way of keeping him around."

"Aye. That is sad."

"Yup. I guess she never got over the denial part of the grieving process."

Declan looked at me as if I were an alien again. I was growing accustomed to it. Apparently, he was getting used to not under-standing me. He didn't bother seeking clarification. Instead, he asked, "Does this make you pity her?"

"I suppose so." I shrugged. "I guess I'm usually too mad. I just wish she'd realize I lost them too. But she has no one left."

"She has you."

"She doesn't see it that way." If only she did. A carriage passed on the road a few miles from the village. "What was that?"

"Looks like a transport from Gnuatthara."

"Does that mean—Are Treasach babies in the carriage?"

"'Tis possible."

"Let's go back. I want to see them."

We ran most of the way. I followed Declan down a shortcut to the village. By the time we arrived, I was huffing and puffing. Clearly I needed more running practice.

A couple of men helped a large woman out of the carriage.

"It looks like a couple of elderly women and three babies this time." Declan shook his head and clicked his tongue. "The number seems to be increasing."

"Can we go see?" I asked.

"If you like."

I followed him toward the driver. "Achaius!" Declan called.

The stocky man with unkempt hair turned toward us. A smile

spread across his face, revealing yellowed teeth through his black goatee. "Ah, Declan. How are you, mate?" Achaius walked toward us, extending his right arm.

They wrapped their right arms around each other, gave a couple of quick pats on the back, and parted.

"I'm well, thank you. And you?"

"Ah, God is with us so I'm well also." Achaius smiled at me. "And who is this?"

"This is Fallon. Fallon, this is Achaius."

Achaius opened both arms. I hesitated, and then moved in for an obligatory hug. He wrapped me in a tight squeeze before grasping my upper arms to face me. Looking me in the eyes, he said, "It warms my heart to have you with us."

Heat rose to my face. I smiled awkwardly at the much-too-old-for-me, handsome man. His rugged features looked like they belonged on the cover of a romance novel, except the stained teeth. His eyes sparkled with genuine friendliness. Unsure how to respond to such a welcome, I said, "Thank you. It's nice to meet you too."

Releasing his hold, Achaius returned his attention to Declan. His smile faded. "Things are getting tougher. The Treasach have reason to believe their village will be attacked soon. They're scheduling more executions than ever. And they're tightening security, which makes it more difficult to assist."

"'Tis a good thing you're doing, brother. God will help. How many did you bring this trip?"

"Five." Achaius frowned. "Two elderly women will continue with me to Kylemore. The three babies will remain here." He sighed. "It will take the women a while to adjust." He nodded toward a haggard woman, probably a couple feet taller than me if she straightened, clutching the man helping her down from the carriage. "Keera is losing her sight." He tipped his head at another giant woman holding an infant. She slumped against the carriage's side, causing it to tilt. "Alayna lost her husband. Her children are grown, doing their part to aid the battle. With no one left to care for, she has lost her usefulness. Shame. The Treasach never before would have scheduled an execution for someone like her. They would have found *something* for her to do."

Declan clenched his jaw.

"What about the babies?" I asked.

"Small—as usual. Well, small to the Treasach, normal to us."

Helpless little babies—sentenced to die for not being supersized. It made me sick. I didn't care about the old people. They were part of the problem. Hadn't they allowed this to happen to others? They didn't deserve help after what they'd done. They deserved to die.

CHAPTER FOURTEEN

Before dinner, Declan and I relaxed at our favorite spot on the pier. A flock of ducks bobbed on the waves. No. Not ducks. Their bodies didn't appear to have feathers, but brown skin like a seal, smooth and shiny in the lowering sunlight. One by one they dove underwater. Seconds later they shot back up, then took off, swimming like dolphins, dipping under and over the waves out to deeper seas. In the distance, they looked like grease splattering from a pan in the same direction.

So many crazy things around here. It was as if I'd crossed into a whole different dimension. Oh wait...I had.

My mind returned to the carriage that arrived earlier and the Treasach. My stomach squeezed, wanting to empty its contents at the thought of such sick people, those poor orphans. "I can't stop thinking about those Treasach women. Why should anyone help them? Did they even try to help any of those innocent babies?"

"I understand how you feel, Fallon. But anger won't solve the problem."

"So what will? How are any of you solving the problem? Aren't you helping them?" I glared at him, chest heaving.

"Fallon!" He straightened, met my eyes, brows furrowed. I couldn't tell if I'd hurt or angered him. Probably a mixture of both.

"I'm sorry, Dec."

"Dec?"

"Yeah. Short for Declan. Like Stacey calls me Fal, and I call her Stace. You don't shorten names in Ariboslia?"

He shook his head, one eyebrow raised, his frown twitched as if fighting a smile, probably having difficulty keeping up with my mood swings.

"Anyway, I shouldn't have said that. You're not the problem. I know you're trying to help." I gazed at the sea and kicked the water. "It just makes me so mad."

Declan looked at the water. "I am a Treasach."

"What?" He did not just say what I thought he said. He couldn't have.

"You heard me." He threw me a quick glance out of the corner of his eye, and then returned his gaze to the water. His muscles tensed, and his knuckles whitened as he clenched the pier.

I wanted to reach out to him. Put my arm around him. Something. "How can that be? Aren't you Declan Broderick Cael IV? Next in line for the co-cheangail?" I asked softly.

"Aye. I am." He nodded. "Through adoption." His shoulders hunched as though under a great weight.

He looked normal, not enormous like the Treasach women, not even half as big. So he, probably a normal baby, was scheduled to die? How could he of all people not be as upset about it as I was? "It's not your fault, you know. You're not one of them." I dared place a hand on his arm.

He pulled away. "Remember I told you I have not yet reached my totem?"

I placed my rejected hand on my lap. "Mmm hmm."

"Well, that's my fear—that I'll *never* reach my totem. My parents, my adoptive parents, insist I was scheduled to die because of my size alone. There must be more to it. Something they're afraid to tell me.

What if I fail them? What if their love for me has blinded them to the fact that I am not fit for the co-cheangail?"

I took a deep breath. His confession blew me away. He seemed to have it all together. If someone like Declan felt that way, did everyone have some sort of fear or sense of inadequacy? I wanted to reach out to him, to soothe him, but I held back, unsure. "I'm sorry." So lame, but I couldn't think of anything else to say.

"You're sorry?" He looked at me, his face puckering. "This isn't your fault."

"I know. It's something we humans say, or...full-humans, I mean. When we feel bad for someone and don't know what to say, we say sorry."

"Oh." He gazed out at the sea. "Know what the Cael say?"

"No. What?" My gaze followed his. The sparkling light dancing on the waves calmed my mind.

"We say, 'You are loved.'"

"Oh." I didn't see that one coming.

"Do you know why?" He clutched the edge of the pier and leaned forward, his triceps bulging.

"I have no idea."

"No matter where you are, no matter what has happened, there is a greater purpose for everything." His voice smoothed, sounding dreamy. "Through it all, you are loved by the One True God. He is always with us, guiding, shaping, loving us. This helps us get through trials."

What a strange thing to say. Yet...it made sense. More than saying sorry for something you had nothing to do with. Of course, I wasn't a believer and couldn't bring myself to use the expression. Instead, I blurted, "I cut myself."

His back turned toward me. I didn't look to see his reaction, but focused on my feet splashing the water.

"What?" His tone carried a mixture of confusion and concern.

I took a deep breath. Never before had I brought it up of my own free will. Even Stacy had to pry it out of me. My heart raced, my cheeks warmed, and my voice quavered. "I cut myself." I lifted my dress mid-thigh to reveal the scar nearest my right knee.

"You did this on purpose?" His voice cracked.

I dared peek at him. Tears welled in his eyes. He brought his hand to my leg. His fingers hovered over the scar, and I pushed my dress back into place, overwhelmed with shame.

The seconds ticked by. I wanted to suck the words back in. But it was too late. They floated about in space, and now, in Declan's head.

"Why do you think you do that?"

At the broken silence, I breathed a relieved sigh. Something in the way he asked compelled me to speak without my usual defenses. "I don't know. I'm in so much pain—over *everything*—all the time, with no one to comfort me. I guess, if I'm going to be in pain, at least I want control over it."

To my amazement, Declan nodded. "I can understand. Do you still cut yourself?"

"Not since I've been in Ariboslia."

"Good." He narrowed his eyes at me and smiled. "You better not."

That was it. No psychotherapy. No lecture. *And* it appeared he still liked me. My tight muscles relaxed. I smiled back.

Declan placed a hand on my shoulder and peered into my eyes. "You are loved."

CHAPTER FIFTEEN

W eeks passed. When the swirling light appeared, I followed
Sully's advice and ran away. The last few nights it hadn't
appeared at all. And I stopped checking the amulet to determine if it
was time to move on. I'd gotten comfortable and developed somewhat
of a routine. What began as my daily walk in the cool morning along
the ocean-side, became a run followed by a swim.

Though the scent of the salty air never failed to bring Bumpah to
mind, it no longer saddened me. I liked to swim past the breaking
waves and float, imagining he was floating beside me like he used
to do.

This morning, soothed by his presence, I lay on my back as the
sun warmed my face. Water covered my ears, amplifying my
breathing in my head. My buoyant body rose and fell with each
passing wave. In the vast ocean, I was a tiny being, tossed upon its
enormity. The realization of how small I was minimized my
problems.

At last, hungry for breakfast, I flipped off my back and cut
through the water toward shore. I picked up my towel and dried my
hair.

"Fallon!" Declan's voice made me jump. "I knew I'd find you here."

"Whew, you scared me." I jogged the water from my ears. "What's up?"

He no longer looked up when I greeted him this way—a greeting I couldn't adequately explain. I tried, but hadn't managed to stop using it. He just ignored it entirely.

"Sully called a meeting of the elders."

"Does that mean I'll be leaving soon?" My stomach quivered, as if still rolling on the waves. I gave the ends of my hair one last squeeze before gathering my things to head for the village.

Declan shook his head. "I don't know. My father was speaking with a couple of the elders this morning. They kept their voices low and closed the door when they saw me. It's serious, whatever it is. But we still have to wait for Drochaid."

"When's the meeting? I haven't been to breakfast." On cue, my stomach rumbled. "And I'm supposed to help with the little ones."

"'Tis after lunch."

I loved how everyone gathered for mealtimes. Of everything the Cael did, this seemed most important. Daily events revolved around meals. No one mentioned a specific time, just before or after a meal.

Ryann had convinced me to help with the small children. So I'd taken to eating with them. They jumped around, shouting my name each time they saw me, even if the last time they'd seen me had been moments before.

Their genuine excitement reminded me of Stacy. I wondered, again, what she was doing. I hated to think of her ruining her summer worrying about me. She must have contacted Fiona. What would Fiona say? Was she looking for me? Did she call the police and report me missing? She must have. I'd been gone almost a month. Great, all our family needed was another missing person for the local gossips.

We made our way to the village for breakfast. Children ran or toddled to me yelling, "Fowin" or something resembling it. Their joyous greeting warmed my heart.

"Hi guys." I'm not sure how "guys" translated in Ariboslian, but they responded with giggles and goofy grins.

"Fowin! Fowin!" Colleen tugged on my dress, her blue eyes alight and blond ringlets bouncing. "Sit with me, Fowin."

I squatted to speak face-to-face to my little cling-on. "Of course, sweetie."

She ran into my arms with such force I almost toppled backward. Laughing, I embraced her with one arm and balanced myself with the other.

Once I'd helped serve the kids, I took my food next to Colleen, as promised. She prattled on about the other children as she picked onions out of her eggs. A bit of a mother hen, she liked to correct other kids' behavior then share stories about what they'd done wrong. She sat erect, speaking with the air of an adult as she made faces at wormlike onions dangling from her pinched fingers. I tried not to laugh.

Ryann must have overheard. She got down on one knee beside Colleen, reddish blonde hair falling in waves past her shoulders. "Are you telling stories about the others again?"

Colleen looked down, kicking her dangling feet.

"You have a good sense of right and wrong. And you are helpful with the children. But everyone makes mistakes sometimes, right?" Ryann focused on the little girl, her questions firm and tender.

Colleen nodded, still struck mute.

"When you make a mistake, does it make you feel good or bad?"

Colleen let out an almost inaudible, "Bad."

"And you apologize and try not to do it again, right?"

She offered a weak nod.

"How do you think you make the other kids feel when you talk about them?"

"Not good."

"What do you think you should do?"

"Stop telling what other kids do wrong."

"A good choice." Ryann smiled, opening her arms.

Colleen flew into them with as much eagerness as she had with me, but now, she had tears in her eyes.

Ryann stroked Colleen's curls. "You are loved, dear child."

Colleen returned to her meal. Her eager chatter resumed, but the content changed to a detailed explanation of precisely why she hated cooked onions.

What a transformation. Never had I witnessed anything like that back home. All I'd seen there were passive dads, yelling moms, and bratty kids. With the exception of Stacy's mom, of course. But even she didn't have the gentle finesse Ryann displayed.

The kids all helped with the cleanup from breakfast while the men and older boys returned to other chores. I delivered Colleen and a few others her age to their teachers, then headed to the field for my daily defense lesson, another one of Sully's suggestions.

Sloane, the defense instructor, was not what I expected from a trained fighter. He was well muscled, but only in proportion to his slim body. He was short for a full-grown man, too. I could look him in the eye.

"All right, let's try it again." Sloane reached around my neck and put me in a chokehold. Following his instruction, I planted my feet, tucked my chin, grasped his arm, and pushed back as I slid my body out sideways.

"Good. Again."

"If someone really wants to choke me, I doubt I could get out so easy."

"That may be true." He wrapped his arm around my neck once more. "Assume you are unable to free yourself. Where are your arms?"

"Down here." I flapped them by my side.

"Right. Remember, as long as your arms, legs, or head are free you have a weapon. What could you do? Can you move your head?"

"No. It's stuck."

"So head-butting isn't a choice. What about your legs?"

The more I moved my legs the tighter the resistance on my neck. I coughed. "Not comfortably."

"What about your arms?"

My arms flapped awkwardly at my side. He held me so tight, my arms didn't have enough range of movement to gather strength to hit him hard enough to release me. But I could scratch his arms or his face, though the thought of doing so sickened me. "I could scratch you." I lifted my hands to his arm and gently pressed to demonstrate.

"Exactly. When you are locked in battle, you must free yourself by any means. There is another option. Can you think what it is?"

"Not a clue." Speaking wasn't easy in this position.

"If you are ever stuck like this, struggling to breathe, turn your head and tuck your chin. Even if it's too tight to get out, you will be able to breathe if your throat is not constricted. Go ahead, tuck your chin."

I obliged.

"Now what can you do?"

I knew what I could do. Bile lodged in my throat. "I could...bite your arm." His arm muffled my voice.

"Right." He released me. "Remember, the best fight is no fight. But if you have to, use everything you have to get away: hit, kick, scratch, bite. Use what God gave you. Make it fast and make it count so you have time to get away. The fasgadair are strong, but they are not invincible. They feel pain too." He turned and waved back at me. "Follow me."

We headed toward the classrooms. Sloane stepped up into one of the buildings, and I followed. Ancient looking weapons lined the rustic cabin walls and countertops. He retrieved something from the cabinet against the far wall, turned, and handed me a stick.

The smooth wood slid comfortably into my hand. I tipped the surprisingly sharp point to the light, even as I fit my fingers to the grooves carved for them to slip into. It fit perfectly...like it had been made for my hand. I arched a brow. "A stake?"

"Aye. I carved it for you. Keep it on you at all times. Do you remember how to use it? I know we've moved to more defensive maneuvers, but you'll need the stake to kill the fasgadair." His back straightened as he waited for my response.

Most of what he'd taught me was a blur. I'd never be able to stick the thing into anyone's ...*anyone's*...A full body shudder rocked me.

"We'll practice more tomorrow. I still have to patch up the straw dummy. You made quite a few holes in some interesting places." He laughed, rubbed his hand along the five o'clock shadow growing on his scalp, and faced the cabinet. "There's one more thing." He reached in and removed something wrapped in cloth. He delicately peeled the dark blue material away to reveal a dagger. Sloane held the blade carefully so the material fell away from the braided steel grip and furled around the intricate tree with roots etched into the pommel.

I didn't want to touch it. "What do I need that for?"

"There are other things out there besides fasgadair. You may need to defend yourself."

"How am I supposed to carry two weapons?" I tucked the stake into my belt.

"I'll give you a sheath for the dagger. You should keep the stake just as you have it now."

"But how will I know which weapon I'll need?"

"Keep them both on you. You'll know which one to use when."

"You have too much faith in me."

He waved the grip at me as if I'd forgotten he wanted me to take it. I hadn't forgotten. It had been so long since I'd held something sharp with the exception of at the dinner table. But this was different. This was a sharp instrument meant for doing damage. What if, somewhere along the way in this journey, I resorted to my old habits? I didn't want to go back there. I couldn't go back there.

"Remember," he began in his lecture tone, "defense is more important than offense. Stay away from a fight if you can. But if you need to, use this. You shouldn't go out there completely unarmed."

I grasped the handle delicately and balanced the heavy weight, staring at the long blade. It bulged evenly beyond the grip and merged to a sharp point. I couldn't picture myself using it. The idea of plunging it into anything squishy...I shuddered.

"Tomorrow, I'll show you how to use the dagger. Good job today, Fallon."

"Yeah, right." The compliment grated. "We both know I'm dead if a fasgadair attacks me."

He chuckled, and the otherwise imperceptible lines around the corners of his eyes and mouth popped out, betraying his age. "You'll be fine. I have no doubt."

I threw him a disbelieving glance.

He smiled. "Look at you. You're stronger than when you started. Your stamina has improved. But the best fight is no fight at all. Focus on getting away as quick as you can. We need you alive."

No problem. Running away was my greatest skill.

CHAPTER SIXTEEN

W hen I arrived for lunch, I was too nervous about meeting
with the elders to eat or give the kids attention. I formed my
mashed potatoes into a volcano, a pool of butter melting in its center.
I cut strategic ridges out of the tip with care to allow butter to drip
down the sides. When I rose to help the kids pick up, I'd found I'd
entertained them without meaning to. I laughed at the sad little
replicas of my masterpiece on their plates.

Once the area was clean and the children shuffled away, I found
Declan.

"Where are we meeting?" I asked.

"Right here." He stopped at a table, sat, and patted the next chair.
"Sit."

When I drummed my fingers on the table, Declan reached over
and flattened my hand. An electrical surge at the point of contact ran
up my arm. Had he noticed? I glanced sideways at him. His twinkling eyes and upturned lip made my heart flutter. I smiled back, took
a deep breath, and slipped my hands under my legs.

All the tables filled, except the one furthest from the entrance.
Nervous chatter grew to an indiscernible buzz. Sully, Mirna,

Declan's father, and others I didn't recognize, moved to the empty table and sat facing the crowd.

Declan III stood and raised his arms. When the murmurings subsided, he began, "Sully, the elders have gathered today at your request. What news do you bring?"

Sully cleared his throat. "Morrigan and Aodan know of Fallon's presence."

Gasps filled the air followed by anxious whispers. Many eyes trained on me as if searching for a reaction. But this wasn't news to me.

"Are they on their way?" someone shouted from behind.

"We must flee to the Cnatan mountains!" another yelled from the other side of the room.

Sully attempted to speak, but the deafening shouts overpowered him. Declan's father pounded on the table. When the voices simmered down, he spoke, "Please, let's hear what Sully has to say and discuss the matter, one at a time."

Sully's gray eyes roamed the crowd. "Aodan won't attack his home village. He knows the prophecy and her mission. He is confident she will come to him and plans to set up traps along the way to Diabalta for her capture. He doesn't want her dead...yet."

Well, that was comforting.

"Are you going to send her straight into the traps?" I couldn't see the speaker.

"How will she fulfill the prophecy?" came another shout.

Watching everyone talk about me as if I weren't there unnerved me, like an out-of-body experience watching doctors perform surgery on me.

"Of course we won't send her into a trap. Where is your faith? She is in God's hands. He will lead her as He has thus far. He will use Drochaid, which will soon point Fallon on her way. The time has come to determine who will accompany her, so they may prepare to leave."

"Agreed." Declan's father gave a sharp nod. "Have you insight on this?"

"I do. God has shown me. Cahal Fidhne, Ryann Mughráin, and your son, Declan Cael IV, are to accompany her. On foot."

A renewed clamorous buzz erupted throughout the Cael. Declan and I looked at each other, eyes wide and mouths open. This I had not expected. I clamped my mouth shut and faced the elders, attempting to listen while they debated my future, but my mind kept returning to my traveling companions.

Declan would go with me! But who was Cahal? And Ryann? An inch or two taller than me, thin, a few years older at most. Sure, she was nice and great with the kids. But no way would she have that kind of effect on *vampires*. And I didn't know what to make of her. She tended to focus on her work rather than chat, making her difficult to get to know. So serious. All the time. Why would she accompany me on this quest? What could she offer?

Then again, what could *I* offer?

I returned my attention to their arguments. Mirna, Declan's father, and many of the others agreed with Sully. But, despite Sully's venerable history of accurate predictions, many debated with him.

Declan nudged me. "Your grandmother and my father know better than to argue with Sully. They've been elders the longest and have no doubt where Sully gets his knowledge. See the younger man on the end? The one without much gray?"

I nodded. "The one who insists we should be allowed horses for transportation?"

"Aye. He hasn't quite learned yet. Neither have they." Declan pointed to two slightly older men who agreed more warriors should accompany us. "They lack faith."

I guess I did too. Though I hadn't learned to ride, I'd much prefer a horse to carry me. And warriors to accompany me. No, I wanted an army to protect me. My enemy knew I was here. He was waiting for me. He was so sure he'd overtake me that he wasn't concerned about keeping me alive. For a little while anyway. And for what purpose? I swallowed hard.

"At least we have Cahal." Declan leaned over, halting my downward spiraling thoughts.

"Who's Cahal?"

He turned in his seat and pointed behind us. "Three tables back. The big one."

He was easy to spot, he towered head and shoulders above the rest. He would have stuck out of the crowd even if he'd been much shorter. Hardly any Cael had dark hair or eyes. He had both. Black hair fell into piercing black eyes. And he didn't have much of a neck —it was more like a tree stump, thick. Taught skin clung to the veiny muscles his sleeveless tunic exposed. His gaze dropped from the elders to me, catching my stare. I elbowed Declan in my haste to turn around.

"Sorry!"

Declan waved it off. "All is well."

"The guy's a giant." I hoped he wasn't as mean as he looked. Or perhaps he'd just been intently listening. Either way, it was a good thing he was on our side. I almost told Declan how thankful I was to have at least one warrior type accompany us. But given what he'd shared about his past, I didn't dare. The last thing I wanted to do was make him feel inadequate. And despite Cahal's stature, he was only one man. How many bloodsuckers waited to pounce me? Three companions. Only three.

Declan's father stood and raised his arms again. "It has been decided. Cahal Fidhne, Ryann Mughráin, and Declan Cael IV will accompany Fallon Webb on her quest to fulfill the prophecy of our forefathers. They will follow Drochaid on foot. God be with them."

God, I hope You're there. We're going to need You.

As the sun went down, I lay on the soft grass near the ocean, listening to the surf. Declan by my side, I stared at the stars, trying to forget evil forces wanted me dead. I breathed deeply to steady my racing heart, attempting to stuff down the rising fear and focus on the millions of pinpricks of light splattering the night sky. "I wonder if those stars are the same as the ones back home." Declan didn't respond to my rhetorical question. "Have you ever wondered how big those teeny stars really are?"

"Aye." A piece of grass dangled from his mouth.

"Did you know our sun is only a medium-sized star?"

"Nay."

"That means some of those stars are large." I sighed. "They must be incredibly far away to seem so small."

"I never thought of that."

"Makes you feel small, doesn't it?"

"Aye, and all the more amazed by God."

"I can't even conceive of a being Who could've created such an immense universe." I tried to comprehend the notion and found my puny brain incapable. "Have you ever heard of the Big-Bang Theory?" I doubted he had, yet some similar theory could exist here.

"Nay. What's that?"

"Well, I don't fully understand it, but I guess it's the thought that random particles collided in space and created all this. The idea is that, over billions of years, life will spontaneously occur and evolve. According to the Theory of Evolution anyway."

"What's that?"

"When small changes in a species lead to new species, or something. They say we evolved from apes."

"What do you mean? Humans can shape-shift too?"

"No. In my realm, apes are apes and people are people. We don't change into anything else. The theory is that apes populated the world first. Over time, their bodies straightened and grew taller, their faces changed, and they became less hairy and more brainy."

"Do they think we came from apes too? We originated in your realm."

"I don't know. I hadn't thought about it. I guess you would have."

"Who thinks these things?" He huffed. He turned on his side and rested his head on his hand.

"Scientists."

"Are these 'scientists' thought to be intelligent?" The term must not have translated into gachen or Ariboslian or whatever they spoke. He stumbled over it.

"Yes, they're educated."

"That doesn't speak well of your means of instruction."

"Huh?"

"Look at this sky. You say some of these stars are larger than our sun. Look at our world and people, what complex and amazing creatures we are, and you say we," Declan hesitated, "evolved," he over enunciated the word, looking at me questioningly as if to see if he had it right, "from apes?"

"I didn't say it." I put up my hands. The way they presented these concepts in school seemed reasonable. Yet, when I tried to explain them to him, they sounded absurd.

"The created can't turn themselves into something they weren't created to be. Particles can't collide and create order. How can educated people think such things? These are foolish ideas."

"Yeah, like suggesting a computer could program itself."

"A what?"

"Never mind." I didn't want to go there. It would lead to never-ending questions and inadequate responses.

"Only God could have breathed life into us and provided us with this perfect home."

I didn't respond, but I couldn't help but agree that sounded more logical. Whether it was random particles or a Creator who created life, it seemed any theory required some element of faith. And randomness required much more. And now, I needed more than a little faith in this Creator who could possibly save me and my three companions from walking straight to our deaths.

Or perhaps we needed what any army immediately sought when facing an attack, or walking into a trap. Intelligence. We needed intelligence.

I had access to that, didn't I?

Perhaps Sully was wrong. Perhaps my greatest weapon against Aodan was the mind-link. What if I looked...just to see where he was, what he was doing, what he was planning against me? Just to gain intelligence. Wouldn't that be the best way to avoid any traps?

Tonight, if the swirling light appeared, maybe I'd take a look.

CHAPTER SEVENTEEN

That night, as I dreamt, I walked toward the woman with my eyes trained on the air to my right where the swirling light usually appeared. Sizzles, like water droplets hitting a hot pan, sounded in the air. Specks of light burst like fireworks, but they didn't fall, or leave trails of light behind. They grew in number, swirling until they formed a complete circle. Shadows flickered, and the creepy voice broke through in a disjointed fashion, as if over a bad cell phone connection.

The picture cleared, and the sound improved. Two pale-faced men in hoods stood before Aodan. The lips of the one on the right moved.

"She hasn't left Notirr. But when she does, we'll be ready. Go. You know what to do."

Man! Seconds too late. What had he just told them?

"Fallon."

Startled, I spun toward the sharp whisper. The woman on the shore was still far away. No one else was around.

"I know you're there, spying on me." He clicked his tongue in a "tsk-tsk-tsk" manner. "I expected more from the prophesied child."

My body jerked. Every nerve tingled. I squeezed my eyes shut. Please go away. Please go away. I opened my eyes. The light was gone. I breathed deep and relaxed as I turned toward the woman and prepared for her attack to wake me.

The afternoon following the elders' meeting, I helped Ryann prepare the next batch of stoneware to be shipped for trade. She painted intricate designs while I glazed.

I wanted to talk to someone about the mind-link. About a way to find out what Aodan was up to without raising his awareness. But Ryann was probably the last person I should approach. Perhaps I could feel her out. I dipped the pot into the glaze, filled it, swirled it around, and dumped it out to coat the interior. "What do you think about going on the quest?"

"There is not much to think about. God has called me, and I will do what He asks."

"Aren't you nervous?"

"Why should I be nervous?"

"Oh, I don't know. We're only marching to our deaths. What's there to be nervous about?" My snarky attitude resurfaced. I couldn't help it. Her couldn't-care-less attitude grated my frazzled nerves. But she unintentionally answered my question. I definitely could not talk to her about the mind-link. Her thinking was about as black and white as they come.

She placed her bowl on the counter. "I'm being inconsiderate. Please forgive me. You're not a believer so you don't understand. But I promise you, all will turn out well." She placed her arm around me, squeezed, and returned to her task.

She meant well, and the matter-of-factness in her voice didn't come across as condescending despite her words. Still...something rubbed me the wrong way.

"I must tell you." She reached for another pot to paint, her tone indicating a serious subject encroaching. "I have seen you and Declan together."

Seen us? Like we were doing something wrong? This conversation had taken a turn I never would have suspected. I could feel mother hen striking again. This time, I was the target. It was one thing for her to talk to the kids like that, but I was only a couple of years younger. I bristled, preparing for attack. "Yeah? What about it?"

"You seem quite comfortable with one another."

What was her issue? "We're friends."

"Has he told you about Maili?"

"No. What's maili?"

"You mean *who*. She is the daughter of an elder in Kylemore. Declan is the son of an elder in Notirr." Her fingers still, she looked at me like I should be getting some sort of hint.

I raised my eyebrows to illustrate my cluelessness.

"Declan and Maili are betrothed."

"So?" I steeled myself to remain indifferent, but my body betrayed me. My face grew hot. I struggled to keep a steady hand.

Ryann's eyebrows flickered, as if registering my response. She turned back to her work. "I wonder why he has not told you about her." Ryann focused on the bowl, her skilled hands swirled about its surface, leaving expert designs behind.

I shrugged. "Why should he? It's not like we're going out or anything."

"Going where?" She placed the completed masterpiece on a tray, pushed stray hair away from her face with the back of her wrist, and wiped her hands.

"No, I mean, seeing each other..." Yeah, that helped. In response to her tilted head and bewildered expression, I attempted to come up with another saying with the same meaning, something more out of date. "Courting."

She nodded and returned to her work. "Still, he should have told you. I see how he looks at you, so be warned, Declan is not available."

An uncomfortable laugh escaped me. "You don't beat around the bush, do you?"

Ryann turned her attention to me. "What's around the bush that I should beat?"

"Ah...Nothin'. Just a saying." I put all my energy into spreading an even coat of glaze over my bowl, relaxing a bit when she picked up the next piece and resumed painting.

Man! What was her deal? What was I supposed to do, stop being friends with him? Tell him to go away? Make him stop looking at me? Then her words broke through my irritation, *I see how he looks at you.* I fought a smile and peeked at Ryann to make sure she didn't notice. Not much got by her.

A warm sensation spread over my chest—more than an excited-about-a-boy feeling. It was external, as though I'd spilled coffee. Finding nothing on my dress, I checked under the neckline. An arrow on the amulet was aglow. I dropped my bowl. Ceramic shards skittered across the floor. Ignoring them, I pulled it out to show Ryann.

She nodded. "'Tis time."

AN HOUR LATER, we stood on the road on the outskirts of the village, the stone wall surrounding the perimeter at our backs. Drochaid pointed down the dirt road which disappeared into the thick woods— the unknown. Archers surrounded us, their eyes trained on the forest on all sides. My stomach churned. If protection wasn't necessary out there, in the forest with whatever evils waiting to pounce on us, why have it here? Where was the complete faith in their God to protect me now?

Sully waved his hand at them. "Bah, such unnecessary fanfare."

"If there is anything out there, won't they just follow us and wait until we're alone to attack?"

"You give Aodan too much credit. He is arrogant. Much too confident in his own understanding and abilities."

"So he doesn't have minions camped out, watching me, prepared to follow me? You said—"

Sully rested his hand on my shoulder. "Child. Have faith. You must be cautious and follow Drochaid." He handed me a heavy pouch full of green dust. "Sprinkle this behind you as you walk. It will mask your scent, making it difficult for the fasgadair to track you."

I nodded. My fears remained, but I was thankful for such an invaluable, albeit unusual, gift.

"Use it sparingly. A little goes a long way, and you have a long way to go, especially since you're taking the indirect route." He winked and gave a little knowing smile.

I surprised myself by rushing to hug him. He must have expected it though, being a seer.

Sloane patted my back. "Remember, the best fight is no fight."

Mirna kissed me goodbye and hugged me close when I hesitated to leave. "God will provide. Not to worry, child."

The whole village seemed to have converged on the road. Everyone cheered. Tears pooled in many eyes. I attempted to blink them away, and wipe inconspicuously at the one that escaped. In my head, Munchkins sang, "Follow the glowing Drochaid," and we marched away following the arrow on the amulet. Unease rose in my gut. I'd grown comfortable in Notirr, but this new venture reminded me I was a stranger in a dangerous land. I gulped and pressed forward despite my fears, in hopes, by some miracle, I could help these people. Whether I succeeded or not, I prayed the end of the road would lead home. I needed Stacy. I needed things to be familiar, predictable. Safe.

We'd only walked a couple of miles, but I already grew tired and sweaty from the heat of the midsummer day. How I despised the heat. As I brushed the sweat from my brow, a gray and white dog crossed the path ahead.

"Wolf!" I called out, unaware until that moment how much I missed him. He had saved my life before. Perhaps he would do it again. When he sauntered over to me, I dropped to my knees and hugged him, laughing. "Maybe we'll survive this suicide mission after all."

"This must be the wolf." Declan spoke up.

"Yes." I beamed, hoping he'd stay with me this time. An intimidating wolf traveling with us would be a great comfort. I was thankful for Cahal as well. Seven feet of rippling muscles. Biceps the diameter of my head. The battle-axe across his back probably weighed as much as me. Surely, his presence invoked fear in all who crossed him.

I scanned my companion's faces. None appeared impressed. They stood arms crossed, scowling.

"Sully didn't say we'd be accompanied by a wolf." Ryann eyed him with distrust. "This isn't part of the plan."

"Sully told us who we'd leave with, not who we'd meet or pick up along the way." No matter what, Wolf was coming with me.

Declan planted his feet and peered down at him. "If you are one of us, reveal your identity so we might discuss the terms of this journey." He took the satchel off his shoulder. "I have clothes you can change into." He eyeballed Cahal. "I'm sure Cahal has some too, if you need something larger."

Cahal rolled his eyes.

Wolf yawned as though he had no intention of revealing himself, if he was, indeed, one of them.

I didn't care who or what he was. I trusted him. "He's coming."

Declan stepped toward me and touched my arm. "Fallon, you don't know who or what it is."

When Wolf grumbled, Declan glanced his way before continuing, "You don't know what its intentions are."

"Look. He's already saved my life once. He's coming."

One by one, we set off. We didn't argue further, nor did anyone attempt to conceal the distrustful eye they glued on him. Wolf didn't appear to care.

So we walked on. Cahal marched in front, scanning the wooded hills like a Secret Service agent. Declan sandwiched me between himself and Wolf. I watched the amulet, trying not to weave into their paths. Ryann trailed us, sprinkling Sully's dust.

When the sun disappeared over the horizon, we made camp.

"Rest." Cahal unsheathed his battle-axe and wielded it as if prepared for attack. "I'll take first watch."

CHAPTER EIGHTEEN

The popping lights began forming a circle when a growl rang out from my left. I turned to find nothing there. The growling grew louder as if right in my ear.

Wolf growled. Lying beside me, his rumbling vibrated against my back. He nudged me with his nose and got to his feet. Head low, he peered in the direction from where we'd come.

"Is it fasgadair?" I whispered, as though he'd answer.

Yet he did. He looked me in the eye and nodded.

My body went numb.

Wolf growled again, low and threatening. Whether in warning to us or to our potential attackers, he succeeded in waking Declan and Ryann.

"Get your weapons," Declan whispered. Eyes wide, he lifted his sword.

Cahal, ready and waiting, searched for what Wolf already saw, smelled, or otherwise sensed.

I couldn't move. Declan pulled me to my feet and tried to put the stake in my hand, but my fingers didn't want to grasp it. The smooth wood felt foreign. What had Sloane told me to do?

I looked at the minuscule weapon, and my stomach rolled. What if I needed to use it? I couldn't puncture someone's skin, let alone plunge it into squishy muscle to pierce a heart. Would I even have the strength if I could manage to aim at the right place? A fasgadair was a bit tougher than a straw dummy.

As I clutched the weapon, fear prickled my body. Wolf raced toward something in the woods. Cahal followed at incredible speed, considering his girth. Declan and Ryann sprinted off after them.

They left me. I didn't want to follow. But I couldn't stay. Alone. Unprotected. Didn't Sloane say to run? Run where? What if I lost everyone? An owl hooted, making me jump, giving me the nudge I needed. I bolted after them.

In the dark woods, I'd already lost them. My throat closed. I searched for clues to their whereabouts and clutched my hands over my mouth, fighting the urge to shout for them. Ahead branches rustled and twigs snapped. I followed. As I neared, shuffling feet, snarls, and grunts as well as the thud and whisper of slashing blades disrupted the night. I stopped.

The noise faded in the distance, replaced by my rapid breath and pounding heart. My breath and heartbeat seemed to slow, or was it time that had slowed?

A bloodless face emerged in a patch of moonlight. It almost glowed. Against the darker horizon, it appeared to be a disembodied head floating in air.

I blinked, and it was before me, a foot from my face. A gleeful sneer tugged the corners of its mouth. The twisted thing seemed to savor the moment, to sense my weakness. I couldn't move. I didn't want to. It bared its fangs. I watched, frozen, helpless, a fly in a web awaiting my demise.

The vampire's smile widened. His unblinking eyes bulged while it closed the gap between us.

Wolf came barreling through the trees. His hindquarters bunched then straightened as he sprang. His front legs curled underneath, his jaw widened, aimed at the fasgadair's neck.

The bloodsucker's head pivoted toward Wolf.

As the creature crashed to the ground, with Wolf atop, the spell broke. My mind cleared. My perception returned. The grotesque din of chomping canines penetrated my psyche. Blood spewed from the monster's neck, decorating my dress with crimson splatters. I screamed.

Everyone came running. Cahal's eyes were wild, darting in every direction as if he anticipated more, though his words said otherwise. "Should be all of them."

"How many were there?" Declan doubled over and rested on his knees, panting, straining to regain his breath.

"Counting this one?" Cahal swung his huge axe over his head. As it began its swift descent, the fasgadair's eyes popped wide open. With a sickening thud, the head tumbled away, and Cahal answered, "Four."

The body and its head turned to dust.

I ran and puked—twice.

Declan came to comfort me. I hoped he hadn't seen my dinner spewing forth. The smell was bad enough. Sitting away from the contents of my stomach, head buried between my knees and arms wrapped around my legs, I attempted to purge the fasgadair's image from my mind. Its head—eyes wide open—rolling from its body, played over and over.

Declan settled beside me and rubbed my back. "Are you all right?"

"Let's see." I held up my fingers to count out my complaints. "I'm so far from home I might as well be in outer space. My mother's alive, and it's up to me to save her and everyone else. To do so, I have to kill my uncle, who, by the way, happens to be a vampire. I just witnessed the removal of a bloodsucker's head. Its blood is splattered all over me, and I have puke breath." Six, but I could go on. And on. If I had the breath.

Declan chuckled. "You're not like anyone I've known."

What an odd response. I raised an eyebrow. "Have you ever known any humans...or half humans?"

"Nay."

"That's probably why."

He laughed, and his whole body quaked. Its infectious quality took me by surprise. Despite my circumstances, I laughed with him.

Then my smile faded. "I froze. If Wolf hadn't rescued me..."

"Don't torture yourself worrying about what might have happened."

"But why couldn't I move?"

"The fasgadair have powers. Remember?"

"Did anyone else freeze?"

"Nay. I'm not sure about Wolf, but the rest of us are believers. God gives us strength, diminishing the fasgadair's power over us."

"But not over me."

We sat in silence. "Why didn't you tell me about Maili?" What prompted the words? As soon as they escaped, I wanted to stuff them back in.

He took a deep breath. "I never saw the point of mentioning it."

Of course he didn't. There was no point. I was a half-human who would return to my realm, or so I hoped. He was a gachen with responsibilities here. Besides, he might be in love with the girl. I had no way of knowing without asking, and I wasn't about to go there! I kicked myself for bringing it up. "Forget I mentioned it. Let's go."

When I attempted to stand, he grabbed my wrist, rooting me. An electrical charge surged up my arm from his touch. "Nay. Let me tell you."

"There's no need." I breathed deep, relieved he let go. Had he felt it too?

"I should have told you. She is the daughter of Eadbhard, an elder of the Arlen clan of Kylemore. As a gesture of good faith to unite the clans, they arranged our marriage when I was five years of age."

He sounded bitter. That answered my question.

"She's a nice enough girl. I've never had an issue with the arrangement..." He stared straight into my eyes, "...until now."

A ripple of heat rose to my face over the way he spoke the word *now* and gazed at me. At least the darkness veiled my blush. "Why are you telling me this?"

"I am telling you because I like you, Fallon. A lot. And I think you like me, too."

I stopped breathing and failed to respond.

"Am I wrong?"

I wanted to say yes. I knew I'd regret saying anything to the contrary. It was one of those moments when the right thing and the honest thing did not align. My brain shut down, and my heart took over. "No."

He pulled me close and wrapped his arms around me. I feared he would kiss me despite my pungent breath. I'd hate to have to push him away. For an absurd moment, I wondered if they had tooth-brushes approved by the American Dental Association in Ariboslia. I stifled a snicker.

He pulled away. "What's so funny?"

Great. Why did I have to have a knack for making myself laugh at the most inappropriate times? "Nothing." I stood. "We should get back to the others."

When we returned to camp, Ryann looked back and forth between us. Did she suspect something? I avoided her gaze and clutched myself with my arms, hoping I appeared freaked out over the fasgadair. It wasn't untrue. Yet my mind kept returning to Declan's admission of his feelings for me. My hearts' uncontrollable leaping trumped fear and disgust. I smiled and tried to make it wane, but probably didn't fool Ryann. She stared hard.

Cahal was more interested in Wolf. "What a godsend! He ripped out the throats of all but one." He patted Wolf on the head.

Wolf flinched and lowered his head with each ponderous touch.

"We made a good team." Cahal smiled—a couple of missing teeth added to his sinister appearance. His face darkened, and he eyed Declan and Ryann in turn. "We left Fallon. That can't happen again. Declan, make sure she's covered at all times." He knelt and packed his bedroll. "We must travel by night and sleep during the day when the fasgadair are weak. Pack up your things. We're moving out."

CHAPTER NINETEEN

The amulet led us along a dirt road consisting of two carriage ruts deepened over time. I walked with care, but the dim moonlight failed to illuminate my path enough to avoid tripping. We kept silent. Mild breezes carried subtle floral scents, reminding me of playing in the yard near the dryer vent. The night symphony included a tireless chorus of crickets and occasional croaks of frogs mingled with random pings of kicked stones and the crunch of twigs. I might've been lulled into sleepwalking if those were the only sounds.

Instead, my wild imagination kept me on edge. At every owl's screech or coyote's yowl, I latched onto Declan's arm. As my eyes darted about, searching for the source, he laughed at me.

By the time the sun rose, I was exhausted. I tripped over every root, stone, and twig underfoot. When I fell for the second time, Declan half carried me. My foot caught on the mildly uneven surface, and I nearly took him down with me. After a couple more hours of staggering, Cahal allowed us to make camp. He went to hunt, along with Declan and Wolf, while Ryann and I gathered firewood.

"Do you know how to build a fire?" Ryann asked.

"Ummm, I've done it before."

"Do you mind building one?"

"Ahhhh...Sure." I wanted nothing more than to lie down and rest. But I had to do my part. I found rocks to build a fire pit then filled it with kindling. I tried rubbing two sticks together, stopping on occasion to wipe sweat from my brow. I turned to Ryann. "You wouldn't happen to have a lighter, would you?"

She raised an eyebrow and tilted her head. "A ligh-ter?" Her lips matched the word.

"Never mind." I waved her off. Tired and irritated, I glowered at the kindling. When it sparked to life, I jerked as if a jack-in-the-box had sprung out of the sticks. How did that happen? I hadn't been rubbing the sticks together, had I? I must have. It was the only explanation.

I regained my bearings, leaned forward, held back my hair, and blew gently on the glowing embers.

"How did you do that?"

I almost fell into the fire. Ryann stood behind me. How long had she been standing there? "Oh! You scared me." I held my hand over my chest and took a deep breath.

"How did you start that fire?"

"I rubbed two sticks together."

"Nay. I saw you."

"Saw what?"

"I saw you with the sticks. But you stopped. You stared at the fire, and it lit. You have your mother's ability." A dreamlike quality softened her voice. She seemed to look through me. "Can you do it again?"

"I don't know."

Ryann reached for a stick from the nearby pile and thrust it into my hand. "Try."

"Ryann, this is dumb. I can't set it on fire by staring at it."

"Sure you can. Try. Stare at the end like you stared at the

kindling. What were you thinking about when it lit before? Do it again."

As silly as I felt, sitting there staring at a stick, I did my best. I stared at the tan twisted fibers at the tip, envisioning it burning. I concentrated so hard, the flame igniting the end startled me. "Oh!" I dropped the stick.

Ryann threw it into the fire and stamped the ground with her foot, her grin wide. "I knew it!"

"Knew what?" Declan emerged from the thick tree cover into the clearing, rabbits dangling from his hands.

"The blood flows in her veins. She has Cataleen and Aodan's ability to start fires."

I wanted to hide. Declan, Cahal, and even Wolf stared as though bugs streamed out of my mouth and crawled across my body. I was grateful when they went to work preparing supper. Their attention made me uncomfortable. I was already a freak in this world. I didn't need anything else making me stand out further. Besides, other than not needing matches, what purpose would such a so-called gift serve?

WITH A FULL STOMACH and my physical and mental fatigue, I expected to fall into a deep sleep despite the daylight. The sun peeked through the canopy of swaying trees, dappling my body in moving light like a mirror ball. The hot air dampened my skin with perspiration. The constant grasshopper hum called to mind summer days, sprawled on the living room floor under the ceiling fan. Bumpah, lounging in his recliner, flicked cold water from his glass on me, while Fiona carried on about damaging the wooden floors. Even so, when her back turned, droplets flew from his chair. I giggled at the memory, wishing he were here to cool me off.

I managed to doze, but I didn't sleep deep enough to dream. Part of me desperately wanted to know what Aodan was up to. Another part wanted to heed Sully's warning and stay away. Perhaps it was best that I couldn't dream, and the choice was taken from me.

An ear-piercing "tra-la-la-la-la" rang from an unusual bird in the branches overhead, jerking me awake. After it flew off, I slept again, but a couple of fighting chipmunks, squeaking at one another, woke me. I longed for a cozy bed and a dark, cool room.

WITH EACH UNEVENTFUL night on our journey, my anxiety lessened. I actually preferred walking in the cool of night. Each day, I managed to sleep a bit more, but still no dreams.

Almost a week passed. We followed the amulet in blind faith. Everyone took turns sprinkling Sully's dust. We plodded on, every ounce of my being sore from movement and insufficient bedding— why had I agreed to all of this? We would have made more progress on a treadmill.

Declan and I didn't talk like we used to. I felt as though he avoided me. What had happened? We were so close in Notirr. Countless possibilities bounced around my brain. Was it to keep Ryann from discovering our feelings? The lack of privacy? The need to keep quiet to avoid soliciting unwanted attention? The busyness of preparing meals? Was he tired? All possibilities, but I feared the real reason might be our last private conversation. I'd said too much. I kicked myself for bringing up Maili, and worse, for admitting I liked him.

I longed to end my self-torture and ask. But I couldn't risk coming across as desperate. What if his feelings for me had changed? What if he realized what a lost cause I was? I couldn't bear to hear him say it. Couldn't endure the humiliation.

Of all things, why couldn't I stop thinking about this?

Wolf seemed to sense my misery. When he wasn't hunting, he stayed by my side. Even so, the weight of everything closed in. My inadequacy, my aching body, exhaustion, and loss of my confidant welled up, threatening to destroy me.

While I contemplated dropping to the ground in defeat, a solid gray structure peaked above the tree line in the early morning light. After days of nothing but trees, something different made my breath catch.

"The Tower of Galore." Ryann pointed to it, and then turned to me. "No one goes near it. Giants lived there. It is thought to be uninhabited now, but no one risks getting close enough to find out."

"There are giants here too? Why didn't anyone mention them?"

"I have only heard tales of them. I've never seen one."

"Neither have I." Declan turned around and walked backward, facing me. "They're nothing but stories invented to frighten children. The older kids used to scare me senseless with tales of them when I was young."

"I hope you're prepared to face your fears." Cahal looked back at the amulet. "We seem to be headed right for it."

"They can't be worse than those bloodsuckers, can they?" I asked Declan, unable to look him in the eye, but hoping to keep him talking.

He shrugged, grown silent.

I sighed.

The vast size of the giant's tower amazed me. The trees thinned, clearing away to reveal the entire structure. The closer we drew, the larger and farther away it appeared. We spent another night walking toward it. When the sun rose, we remained a good distance away, and Cahal told us to make camp.

"This is not good," Cahal grumbled as we dropped our packs, scanning the open perimeter. "We need cover."

"Any attackers will be out in the open, too." Declan shrugged. "We will have plenty of warning."

"But if they're big enough to build that," I gestured to the gargantuan tower obstructing the sky, "they must be huge. How could we outrun them? Where could we hide?"

"Have no fear. As Declan said, they are mere stories to frighten children into staying away. God is our protection." Ryann threw Declan a warning look.

He widened his mouth and eyes innocently, lifting his hands in defense. "Cast your threatening gaze Cahal's way. He's the one who's concerned. Not me. Anyway"—he drummed his hands on his legs—"those stories have succeeded in keeping others away. We have that going for us too."

Cahal grunted, nodded, and sheathed his battle-axe, signaling his approval. The gesture had come to put me at ease. He only disarmed himself if he felt secure.

The only other issue with our being out in the open was lack of prey and wood. Cahal removed some dried meat from his satchel and distributed it to each of us. Exhausted, I laid on my bedding, chewed the jerky, and looked up at the sky. An occasional bird flew by the otherwise clear sky. The sun shone down, but the day was cooler and drier than most. A gentle breeze swept past.

I reached for another piece of jerky and realized it was gone. My stomach hungered for more. I sighed and closed my eyes. What I wouldn't give to get home. Or just give myself over to this evil uncle guy and get it over with. What if I dreamt of him? What if I talked to him? Perhaps I could convince him that I'm no threat. Perhaps he'd leave me alone.

I crossed the bizarre dreamland and stared at the woman on the shore before it occurred to me that I was in the dream. I turned, hoping to find the swirling light. The lights popped and fizzled as they had before. A blurry image became clear. Some sort of an ornate room full of red and gold. A large tapestry draped the wall.

"Bad form, Fallon."

"Huh?" I jumped and spun around. The woman was still staring at the shore far away. No, not her. I now recognized the masculine voice.

"You heard me. You've somehow figured out how to connect with the mind-link your mother and I share. How is it you're able to jump into my head, but I can't access yours?"

"I-I-I don't know." Even in the dream, every hair stood on end. Chills washed over my body for being caught spying by a murderous creature.

"It seems I've misjudged you. You have power. Come to me, Fallon. Come to Diabalta."

"Why would I? You want me dead."

He chuckled. An ominous sound. "Why would I kill someone with powers like myself? I could teach you, hone your abilities. Together we could be unstoppable. Come to me."

"And become a blood sucker? No way." My body quavered uncontrollably. I grasped my head and squeezed my eyes shut.

"Don't shut me out, Fallon. Come—"

"Go away!" My voice echoed within the confines of the dream world. Followed by merciful silence. I dared open my eyes. The light was gone. I turned to the woman and screamed. Her face was right before mine, teeth bared, lunging.

"Fallon!"

Something had a hold of my shoulders, shaking me.

"Fallon, wake up."

I opened my eyes.

Declan stared at me, his expression twisted with concern. "You were having a nightmare. Are you okay?"

I glanced around. Cahal, Ryann, and even Wolf had their eyes trained on me.

"I'm fine." I slipped out of Declan's grip and sat up.

"You're not fine, Fallon. You're shaking." He sat next to me and placed a protective arm around me. "What happened?"

"Nothing. It was just a dream. I'm fine." I set my jaw and fought the tears.

"Good," Cahal called from over Declan's shoulder. "Time to move out."

We packed our things in the shadow of the tower and resumed our trek.

Desperate to talk about anything to exorcise the loop of Aodan's conversation out of my head, I sidled up to Declan. "Why do you think the amulet would lead us to a tower where giants lived?"

A stupid question. One I didn't expect him to have an answer to.

He responded with a shrug.

"Aren't you worried?"

"A little. But this is God's plan. He has a reason for it, and I trust Him."

Swallowing the lump in my throat, I wished for such faith to help me face whatever resided in the monstrosity before us, and to rid myself of my impatience and the temptation to seek resolution with the very being who wished to kill me, despite his words.

CHAPTER TWENTY

By sunrise, we arrived at a stone threshold ten times my height. I searched for the top of the tower. This close, it wasn't visible, but I grew dizzy seeking it. I hugged my arms around my middle, definitely not eager to meet whatever created such a monstrous building —or required a door this size. But I welcomed the distraction. Anything to keep thoughts of Aodan and Declan out of my head.

As I studied the stone etchings, a loud clang next to me made me jump. Cahal banged on the door with the back of his battle-axe. I stepped back and held my breath, expecting something heinous to open the door. When nothing did, he banged again. By the fourth try, we grew impatient.

"It may be deserted." Declan turned to me. "The amulet points this way, right?"

The arrow aiming at the door remained aglow. I nodded.

"We should try to open it." Declan arched Cahal a glance.

When none of us located a doorknob or a notch, Cahal wedged his battle-axe into the seam to pry it open. Exertion twisted and reddened his face, and veins in his neck I hadn't known were there bulged and pulsated.

"Let's try pushing it in," I said. All of us, including Wolf, leaned against the door and pushed. It was hopeless. I turned, slid down the door, and sat on the stoop.

Declan's arms pressed against the entrance. Hanging his head between them, he stood there. "We can't give up." His flattened hands formed into fists and struck the door as if they could accomplish something Cahal's battle-axe couldn't. He took a few steps back to address us. "Drochaid points through this door, right?" He turned to me for confirmation.

I nodded.

"Then there must be a way." Declan picked up rocks and chucked them at the door.

"Stop! 'Tis no—"

A grinding sound, stone against stone, interrupted Ryann. But the door wasn't opening.

"Look." She pointed higher up on the door. A small square window budged. We backed up to peer inside, but it was too high.

"Who goes there?" a voice boomed.

"It is I," Ryann shouted, "Ryann Mughráin, daughter of Abracham Mughráin, descendent of the Mughráin clan, founders of Notirr. I travel with fellow clansmen Declan Cael and Cahal Fidhne with Fallon Webb of the human realm, to assist in her quest to defeat Aodan Tuama."

I glanced around certain all of Ariboslia heard her. What was she, the town crier? Why not just hand over her birth certificate and college transcripts? Shouldn't this quest involve some stealth? What if these creatures didn't want us to succeed?

"What leads you to the Tower of Galore?" The gravelly voice sounded like it came through a megaphone.

"A pechish amulet," Ryann said.

The window closed. Seconds ticked by. I glanced at my companions. "Why'd he leave? Do they have a problem with the pech?" My questions met blank stares, frowns, and shrugs.

"I wonder—"

Another noise, similar to the window opening but louder, closer, interrupted Ryann. On the bottom of the door, in the center, a small rectangle opened. The rock had been smooth before—seamless.

We all gasped. Stubby, sausage-like fingers emerged from the shadows, beckoning us. "Come quickly." The owner of the hand sounded like the voice from the window. "Not him," it said when Wolf stepped forward.

Wolf sat.

I hesitated, my eyes fixed on him. When he motioned toward the opening with his snout, I frowned, turned, and crawled through.

Once inside, I watched Cahal attempt to squeeze his mass through the small opening. His broad shoulders stuck. He twisted, kitty-corner, and pushed through it. The door shut, sealing us inside.

I stared at the little man who'd let us in. He stood about half my height, yet twice as wide. A long red ponytail and matching beard flowed over his shoulders. Past him, the door we'd come through was now virtually invisible. No handle, nothing, revealed its existence. But a small staircase off to the side led to a platform where something resembling a megaphone hung on the wall.

"You're pechish." Ryann voiced the surprise I'm sure we all felt.

The pech cleared his throat. "Eh hem. Well, yes. Now, let me see this amulet of which you speak."

I stepped toward him and got down on one knee, allowing him access to Drochaid while keeping it around my neck.

He grasped it in his chubby hand and studied it for a moment. "Drochaid. Hmph." His nose wrinkled as if he'd caught a whiff of something nasty.

Not the reaction I was expecting, not that I'd had enough time to process this little twist and expect much. I glanced at my friends. Concern masked their faces.

"Did you take this castle from the giants?" Declan asked.

"Giants?" The man let Drochaid fall. "No. We built this place to appear to be the work of giants, centuries ago when the gachen first arrived. We spread stories of giants so none would disturb us."

Eyebrows raised, we exchanged nods. I, for one, was impressed.

Ryann introduced us again with a slight bow, pounding her fist twice in rapid succession against her heart. When Declan and Cahal did the same, I followed suit.

"I am Tollak." He imitated Ryann's greeting. He looked each of us in the eye in turn. "The secret of the Tower of Galore must remain intact."

A chorus of "of course," "certainly," and "without a doubt" accompanied bobbing heads.

"Your word will not be enough. The secret you carry is trusted only among the pech. Before you will be allowed to leave, you will eat a *glemmestein*."

"What's that?" I asked.

"A mineral that melts on your tongue. You will be allowed to stay here twelve hours, no more. The glemmestein will erase any memories gained in that time."

"What if we refuse?" Ryann asked.

"Then you will not be allowed to leave. Come. I will lead you to Pepin."

When I searched my companion's faces, it appeared they were not pleased with having their memories erased either. But what choice did we have? How would we open a door without a handle, or seams?

We followed Tollak through several stone rooms. Intricate designs engraved in every surface. I'd expect it to be cold, but the temperature was perfect. The ceilings, supported by elaborate pillars in some of the larger rooms, high for the pech, allowed us to walk upright. Only Cahal had to stoop in entryways.

"You've come in time for the Turnering av Stryke," Tollak explained as we walked. "We hold competitions to separate the strongest males coming of age. It is an important rite of passage. Those who excel will be fit for the royal guard, as I am, or assigned to equally important work." His chest puffed. "Those who fail to perform well will bring much shame to their families."

When we came to a hall smaller than the entrance into the tower, I groaned. It was dark. No telling how long it was. We would have to crawl the entire distance.

"These halls are meant to be tight. Should the gachen choose to attack, they will find passage difficult." Tollak laughed. "It's too dark for you to see, but surprises line the tunnel."

Cahal planted his feet, arms ready. "What kind of surprises?"

Tollak clutched his hands behind his back and rocked on his heels. "Oh, spikes, barricades, things of such nature." His eyes sparkled. He lifted his palms. "Those are for intruders, not guests. For you, there will be no surprises. You have my word as an official of the royal guard."

Cahal went first, motioning us to join him. He had to lie sideways and shimmy along. I waited until he was through and a glimmer of light shone in the distance. The walls closed in around me. My chest tightened. I gulped for air and hurried toward the light. Once free, I faltered as I stood, gasping.

Declan rushed to me. "Are you all right?"

"I just...need...to catch...my breath." Doubled over, hands on my knees, I panted while Declan patted my back.

"Wow," Ryann gasped. "This is amazing."

Cahal grunted something like agreement.

Once I collected myself, I looked about the room. A wooden railing spanned the space across from where we now stood. I inched closer, noting the long drop. The railing, tall enough to prevent the pech from falling, wasn't sufficient for us. I kept a safe distance as I peered over the edge, backing up further when I began to swoon.

"The heart of the Tower." Tollak waved his hand, palm up, as though presenting something special. And it was. Openings such as the one we gazed through lined all four walls, revealing pech going about their business.

It must be like standing on the terrace of an inner-city apartment. Stairways lined the walls like fire escapes. But if this were the city, I'd see sky. I struggled to wrap my brain around it—I was not looking out but into the center of the tower.

"Incredible! You can't even see the top." Ryann leaned over the rail, and I clenched my hands, fighting the urge to pull her back.

"This way." Tollak gestured for us to follow through a section of railing he opened like a gate.

As I neared, my surroundings swam about. Declan put his arm around me to steady me, keeping me close to the inside wall. His protective touch sent a warm sensation coursing through my body, making his guidance all the more necessary. We descended a long stairway, passing many similar openings beyond the wall. When we reached the last set of stairs and the ground floor was a reasonable distance, my feet stabilized and Declan released me.

The four of us emerged into the center of the ground floor. Booths with jewelry, ceramics, tools, weapons, and food stood in clusters, forming a market. Pech stopped and stared, openmouthed, as we walked by, and I drew in my shoulders, wishing to shrink to their size. A small child took one look at Cahal and ran screaming for his mother, eliciting more attention from others. Wide eyes surveyed our group and traveled up and down Cahal's height.

I tried to hide as we crossed the marketplace, but it wasn't possible. We stood so much taller than everyone and everything around us. We stuck out like polar bears in Meer Kat Manor. I hunched over, failing miserably at making myself smaller as we ascended a staircase. We arrived in an empty room similar to the one we'd left. I relaxed slightly then tensed again when we approached yet another narrow hallway we would have to crawl through. It appeared we were returning to where we'd come without having turned around.

CHAPTER TWENTY-ONE

When we emerged from the tunnel, I recovered in another strange room. Smoke poured from a cauldron and various pots on a long counter. It reminded me of the smithy at the museum I went to in third grade. And a laboratory. A strange hybrid of the two. Another pech with long, red hair tied in a braid flitted about, tossing items into the pots.

"Pepin!" Tollak's booming voice almost knocked me over.

"Oh!" Pepin tipped over a pot. A small fire flared up. He extinguished it by throwing sandy material over it, but more pots toppled in the process.

Tollak turned toward us and rolled his eyes. "That runt is softer than a molting squashbug." He pointed at Pepin. "*This* is what happens to pech who fail to perform well at the Turnering av Stryke."

Pepin dropped the items he'd collected into a large basin and waved a dismissive hand toward it. "I'll clean it later." He neared us, wiping his fingers on his apron. He was clean shaven, unlike the bearded men I'd passed. With the apron and the braid, he more closely resembled the women, despite his furry unibrow and stout frame. "My apologies. Pepin at your service." He bowed and pounded his fist against his chest.

Ryann introduced us, and we imitated the greeting.

"Drochaid led them here," Tollak grumbled.

Pepin beamed, revealing sparkling white teeth. "Truly?"

Tollak rolled his eyes again. "I must return to my post. I leave you with Drochaid's creator." He waved his hand and bowed slightly in Pepin's direction in mock reverence. "Return to me within eleven hours. Fail, and you will not be allowed to leave." After bowing and pounding his chest, he clomped away, his rigid body swaying like a metronome—ahem, like a metro gnome. I laughed.

All eyes trained on me, eyebrows raised. Why must I find humor at the most inappropriate times! "Sorry." Must sober up.

Humor gone. Tollak's words hit me. What if we got stuck here? Perhaps we should leave now to avoid entrapment. I checked Drochaid. No glow. Nothing. Drochaid's dormant state must mean we were in the right place. For now.

"May I?" Pepin stepped forward with a hand out. "May I see Drochaid?" He spoke wistfully, as if it were a long lost family member.

"Sure." I removed the amulet and handed it to him. He ran a finger over the circular indent in the center. As soon as Declan began speaking, my mistake was clear. I couldn't understand a word. "Please." I reached for Drochaid. "I need it back."

Pepin cocked his head and wrinkled his bushy unibrow. The fuzzy caterpillar straightened and Pepin passed me the amulet. "You don't speak Ariboslian? You spoke it earlier. Did Drochaid enable you?" He reached his hand out. "May I?"

"Yes." He didn't know? I knelt, holding it out for his inspection.

"How is it you found me?"

"The arrows pointed us in this direction." I searched his face for understanding. Finding none, I added, "They glow."

Other than a couple slow blinks, his face remained unchanged. He didn't seem to know much about his invention. Why did it bring us here, to him? Was he to join us? How would *he* be helpful? He was puny, even by pech standards, shorter than Tollak and almost one-third his width.

For a moment neither of us moved. Then Pepin leaned in. "I must confess, I'm not entirely sure how it works."

I fought the impulse to say, "Duh."

"How is that?" Ryann asked. "You created it."

"I forged a transportation amulet to allow inter-realm travel. The only difference was the materials used and the design on the face."

"But the language translation and guidance?" Ryann asked. "You, the creator, are unaware of such features?"

He smiled up at us, hands clasped behind him. "Yes. I made what I knew how to make, an amulet allowing passage through the megalith, nothing more. I am unaware as to how Drochaid does more, other than my belief that the One True God made it so. The real mystery," Pepin lowered his voice, "is why it led you back to me."

I shrugged. "Maybe you're supposed to join us."

"Me?" His eyes grew bigger. He jabbed a stubby thumb toward himself. "Why should I join you?"

"Perhaps your task is incomplete," Ryann suggested. "Drochaid led us here. You are a believer. What is it you are currently doing for God?"

Pepin's face flushed, almost matching his hair. "You make a good point. I am not allowed to speak of God. But I should try."

"They know you are a believer?" Declan asked. "And they let you live?"

"Well." Pepin cleared his throat. "They had little choice. As with any who fail to bow down to Torsten, the god of stone, or worse, who profess belief in the One True God, I was sentenced to execution. They threw me in the bowels of the tower to be devoured by the uilebheist. But my God was with me and I prevailed." He held his right hand in a fist in front of his face, pinched the fingers of his left, pulled it back to his face, squinted one eye, and released his pinched fingers. He dropped his hands and smiled wide. "A well-aimed pebble, with the slingshot God helped me smuggle in, proved fatal to the beast."

"*You* defeated a uilebheist?" Declan's eyes traveled the short distance from Pepin's feet to his head.

"With a *pebble*?" Ryann added.

Cahal's eyebrows rose.

"All is possible with the One True God." Pepin beamed.

Though I had never heard of a uilebheist, Pepin didn't appear quite as small as he had a moment ago. His presence outweighed his body.

"They had to let you go." Ryann spoke as if entranced.

"Correct." Pepin grinned. "The law must prevail."

"You must join us on our quest," Cahal said.

"Aye," Ryann and Declan both agreed.

Somehow, I found their eagerness threatening. Did they think Pepin was worthier than I to partake in *my* quest? I tried to disentangle myself from the sudden jealousy snaring me. When all eyes aimed in my direction as if waiting for my approval, I nodded.

Pepin glanced at each of us in turn and sighed deeply. "I'd need to pack some things."

WE TOOK a nap while Pepin prepared for the journey. When he woke us, ready to go, I wanted to return to Tollak. But since no one else worried about being trapped here and Drochaid remained dormant, I was overruled. Instead, we followed Pepin to the gymnasium to watch the Turnering av Stryke.

We arrived for the boulder toss. Many young pech competed to determine who could throw a large boulder furthest. The pech with the least distance was taken out of the running. Those who fared better continued with larger boulders. Their faces grew crimson, contorting with effort as they released exaggerated grunts, groans, and growls. It struck me as hilarious. I doubled over, tears coursing down my face with laughter. When I sat back up, I found myself surrounded by disapproving eyes and grumbles. My smile faded, and I scooted toward Declan.

I tried to contain myself by averting my attention to the crowd. They went nuts no matter what the outcome. When a pech did well, they cheered. When they failed, they booed. Both sounded the same. Only the body language differed. Hands rose in the air for the cheers. For the boos, the hands rose to the mouth to amplify the sound.

Antsy, I squirmed in my seat. If only I had a watch, a clock, or even the sun to clue me in as to how much time had gone by. I needed to do something other than sit here. My stomach rumbled. "Can we get something to eat?"

Pepin nodded. "Follow me."

He led us through a sea of merchants. Since he was a slower guide than Tollak, I had more time to glance about. Behind the counter of one kiosk sat a female with white hair in a tight bun. She scowled at me as I passed. A sign I couldn't read hung in front. *What* was she selling? Nothing was there.

I scooted closer to our guide. "Pepin, what was that shop? There's nothing for sale."

"A reincarnation shop."

"What's that?"

"If someone wants to guarantee their station in the next life, they purchase it." He puffed his cheeks. "Most pech believe if we lead a good, strong life pleasing to the god of stone, he will bless us with strength and riches in our next life. If we haven't, we can buy it."

"Purchase your next life? That is the dumbest thing I've ever heard."

Pepin led us to a booth where we bought soup and bread. We found empty tables to sit nearby. The similarity to a mall food court reminded me of Stacy. Was she still searching for me, wondering where I'd gone, if I was still alive? She must've given up on ever seeing me again by now.

"Is something wrong?" Declan asked.

I shook my head and refocused on my food. I wasn't quite sure what the soup consisted of. Root vegetables and some type of meat, seasoned with enough salt to give it a nice flavor. Surprisingly delicious.

The thought of the food being "surprisingly delicious" amid short, red-haired creatures reminded me of a Lucky Charms cereal commercial. I chuckled aloud as the Lucky Charms leprechaun sang in my brain in his Irish lilt. I stopped laughing when I noticed all the eyes on me.

"We must go." Pepin rose to return his empty dishes. "We have a little over an hour left."

"How do you know how much time we have? Do you have a watch?"

The face everyone made in my direction when they hadn't a clue what I'd just said came over Pepin. "A watch? You mean a lookout? How is that related to time keeping?"

"No, a watch is a device that tells the time."

"Oh." Pepin scratched his head and winced as if attempting to make sense of it caused him physical pain. "The pech need no such device. We have an internal sense of passing time."

We followed Pepin through the tunnels to the main door where Tollak and a few others stood guard. Tollak gave all but Pepin a glemmestein. It looked and felt like an air gun pellet.

Tollak invaded Pepin's space and towered over him. "You know the rules, runt." He poked Pepin in the chest, pushing him back, then stepped forward to bridge the gap again. "Do not give away our secrets. Unless you care to test your luck with the uilebheist again."

Pepin stepped out of range, and his Adam's apple bobbed up and down.

Tollak turned toward the rest of us. His face, full of contempt, softened slightly. His shoulders raised and chest puffed out, he marched back and forth before us. "Take the glemmestein now. Place it on your tongue and let it melt."

I popped the silvery rocklike thing on my tongue. Cold and

smooth, it melted fast into a bitter, thick fluid which coated my tongue. I fought the urge to spit it out, gagging as I struggled to swallow. Then it was gone. Not even a lingering aftertaste remained.

Drochaid pointed toward the space on the wall where the door should be. Once we showed Tollak the glemmestein had melted, he waved his hand along the wall. The seam appeared, and the door slowly opened, scraping along the ground.

Tollak cleared his throat. "In a couple minutes you will have forgotten all you have seen here. Pech do not say goodbye, so forgive me for not doing so."

We squeezed our way out, and the hole in the door sealed, disappearing behind us.

Wolf lay by the door. He perked his head up when we came out. I hurled myself at him. He rose in time for me to throw my arms around him.

I let go of Wolf and faced the others, searching their expressions for evidence of memory loss.

Ryann was the first to question it. "Perhaps it did not work. Perhaps we will..." Confusion squinched her brow. "What was I saying?"

CHAPTER TWENTY-TWO

"W hat in the—" I'd been standing on the threshold. Now, without a step, I stood about twenty feet away on the grass, as though I'd been transported from one spot to another. And the sun —seconds before it hovered at our backs. Now, the tower blocked all but the lingering rays peeking out from behind.

Ryann held her hands out as though steadying herself. "What happened?"

"The sun." Declan pointed to where it had hung in the sky. "It was over there. And I"—He turned back to the Tower door—"was standing there."

Cahal's head shifted back and forth from where we'd been standing to where we now stood.

"Oh, my." An unfamiliar voice spoke behind me.

I jumped, and then looked down in its direction. My body jerked at the sight of the small man standing there.

"Who are you?" Ryann and I asked in high-pitched voices.

Cahal and Declan asked, "Where did you come from?"

"Oh, my," the gnome-like creature repeated, shaking his head.

I stared, waiting for an explanation. He had appeared as if by magic. His features, accompanied by his magical appearance, reminded me of the Lucky Charms leprechaun.

"I'm Pepin, the pech who made the amulet you wear." He motioned toward me.

Cahal unsheathed his battle-axe and bounded over to Pepin, shaking the ground as he went. He held the weapon low before Pepin's face. "I will not ask again. Where did you come from?"

Cahal, scary in his natural, relaxed state, truly frightened me now. I tensed, fearful for this poor little man, Pepin, whoever he was. Cahal's pants were longer than Pepin's entire body.

He shook his head and sighed. "I wish they hadn't given you a glemmestein."

"Glemmestein?" Our voices echoed the unfamiliar word in unison.

"Yes." The strange little man glanced at the tower. "To make you forget." He spoke in a hush. "Please, not here." He reached out a shaky hand to the axe before him and gently pushed it down. "I will tell you what I know, but not here. Where is Drochaid leading you now?"

"Wait." Cahal held up his hand as I was about to speak. "Who erased our memories?" His eyes narrowed as if it would better enable him to discern the truth.

Pepin groaned. "The pech, but—"

"Your people just erased our memories, and now you want us to follow you?" Ryann stood, hands on her hips.

I threw Wolf a sideways glance. He sat and licked his paw. His lack of concern put me at ease.

Pepin threw his hands up as if under arrest. "It was the only way they would allow you passage. Please, I promise you. I am who I say. I'm a believer in the One True God. If you don't believe me, check Drochaid. It pointed at the entrance before. It points another direction now. Am I right?"

"He's right. It's pointing that way." I motioned to the left of the tower. "We never even went inside."

"But you did," Pepin said. "That is why the direction has changed. You have fulfilled your mission here. I am with you. Please..." His eyes darted back to the tower as he hunched over, cowering. "This is treason. I will be prosecuted for this."

Cahal grunted. "Follow Drochaid. At the tree line, tell us what you know."

We marched in uncomfortable silence across the open field. Cahal followed Pepin closely, battle-axe in hand. The moment we reached the trees, with the weapon at Pepin's back, Cahal pushed him past the trees to block us from view. "Talk. Now."

Pepin explained what had occurred in the tower—what we'd forgotten. I'd done and said things I couldn't remember? An icky feeling spread over me, like spiders crawled up and down my back.

"I pray you are telling us the truth." Ryann said.

Declan put a hand on Pepin's shoulder. "Until we have reason to believe otherwise, we'll trust you. You have our word that the tower's secret and your disclosure with remain with us."

"Aye." Cahal grumbled, returning the battle-axe to his back.

Ryann and I both nodded.

Pepin's brow furrowed. The air trapped in his overextended cheeks escaped with a soft hiss. "There is more I must tell you. Drochaid is missing a jewel. See there?" He pointed to the center circle. "The angel told me it needed a jewel found undersea. But I couldn't get it. Pech can't swim. We sink like stone. I'm surprised Drochaid works at all..." His words trailed off, eyes downcast.

Ryann's face grew peaceful. "An angel visited you?"

"Yes. That is what prompted me to forge Drochaid. The angel told me to make an inter-realm travel amulet. The only difference between Drochaid and more ordinary ones was the materials used and the image engraved on its face."

"Angels are real?" I breathed the question as my mind attempted to wrap around the concept.

Ryann looked at me as if I were daft. "Of course. Angels are

God's army, carrying out His will. It is quite an honor to receive a visit from one. It means God has big plans for you."

If what she said was true, why hadn't I been visited by an angel? I'd say I had a pretty big part in His plans. None of *them* were chosen to overthrow Aodan.

Ryann placed a gentle hand on Pepin's shoulder. "Not to worry, my friend. Drochaid has gotten us this far. God will see us through. If we need the jewel to complete our mission, He will ensure we find it."

Pepin perked up a little, though he didn't seem convinced. Perhaps he was disappointed in himself. Sinking was a legitimate problem. Despite my love of the ocean, I was hopeful Drochaid wouldn't lead *me* under the sea unless it also proved to be an underwater breathing apparatus. I much preferred relaxing on its surface to testing my lung capacity underneath.

As we twisted our way around thorny brush, Pepin told us about his kind. "The pech have lived in Ariboslia longer than any other creature. We are the oldest race, but not the wisest." He pushed a large branch out of his way and let it fly as he passed. It smacked me in the stomach.

"Ow!" I cried. I peeled the thorny branch off me and inspected my in-desperate-need-of-a-wash dress to find a small tear toward the side. Scraped skin with tiny droplets of blood peeked through.

Declan rushed to my side. "Are you hurt?"

"I'm fine." I covered up the hole and pressed on, in front of Pepin.

Declan jumped in front of me, pushing branches out of the way, gently holding them for me to grab and safely walk past.

Pepin snorted. "I've never fit in with my kind. We celebrate our individual strength above all else. It's prideful." He cleared his throat. "I don't say this because I don't have the physical strength of most. It's the truth. Despite my defeat of the uilebheist, I was essentially shunned."

"You defeated a uilebheist?" Declan's eyes widened.

Pepin filled us in on the conversation we'd forgotten. The creepy bugs-crawling-on-my-skin sensation returned. What else happened that I couldn't remember? Where did the memories go? Did that thing they made us take extract part of our brain? Who knows what could happen in this bizarre world with flying toads and retracting grass. I shuddered, trying to focus.

"As I was saying...Despite my defeat of the uilebheist, I was shunned. Their laws would not allow them to kill me, but didn't require them to acknowledge my existence either."

"So you're the only one to succeed at such a feat?" Cahal asked.

Pepin nodded.

"I'm amazed they weren't impressed," Declan said.

"Nothing, not even our strength, is more important than the gods of the pech." His eyes widened. "I mean...to them. Not to me."

Ryann laughed. "It's all right, Pepin. We knew what you meant."

Pepin threw her a feeble smile. "As I was saying, I'd become invisible. But it was good. It allowed me to travel freely. No one concerned themselves with my whereabouts. In visiting other villages and cities, I learned about other cultures and religions. I saw how the gachen behaved compared to the pech. I compared the different villages. Notirr in particular showed me how it is to love—something pech know little of. In all I've learned, I've come to believe real love is only possible with the One True God."

I wished I had half Pepin's conviction. I wanted to believe in his God. Something tugged at my heart, urging me to have faith. I fought it. I wasn't worthy. Perhaps I would be, once I saved my mother. For now, I hoped to find her, as long as I didn't have to do anything heroic. Just get her and go home.

CHAPTER TWENTY-THREE

T he woods were dark and difficult to traverse over the felled trees, rocks, and uneven countryside. I missed the roads. It was probably safer out here though. Who in their right mind would wander this forest at night? Besides us.

Pepin told us we had taken a nap in the tower, but it didn't feel like it. I was exhausted and wanted nothing more than to lay down and sleep for a day or two. Judging from my friends' slow progress and occasional tripping, they felt the same. Still, Cahal insisted we press on. Surprise, surprise. He was probably right. We were not nocturnal beings by nature and risked losing ground if we allowed ourselves to fall into our natural routine, even for one night.

Pepin jogged along, panting.

I stepped closer to Declan. "Look at Pepin. He's so small. Are you sure it was a good idea to bring him?"

Declan shrugged. "Size isn't everything. He defeated the uileb-heist. And he says he's traveled a lot."

I shook my head. "Not at this pace. Look at him—he's a tad taller than Cahal's legs. He has to take about *twenty* steps to one of his."

Wolf must've overheard our conversation. He stopped in front of Pepin.

"Whoa. Sorry, friend. I nearly ran into you." Pepin attempted to sidestep Wolf.

He moved squarely in front of Pepin, blocking his path yet again, and lowered his front legs, offering Pepin a ride.

"Oh. Thank you, Wolf." Pepin showed no trace of embarrassment as he hopped aboard. With his naturally reddish skin tone and the darkness surrounding us, I could only guess if he blushed. But his voice sounded grateful, and he didn't hesitate to accept the ride.

Perhaps with the fasgadair attack so far behind us, or because we were in a heavily wooded area where others weren't likely to be, Declan wasn't as concerned about being quiet. Or maybe enough time had passed since our confession of feelings. But I was grateful he was loosening up around me again, talking. I didn't want to risk losing his companionship by asking what had changed. It didn't matter.

"Can you teach me...um...what language do you speak?" I asked. As difficult as it might be, it would be nice to know the language in case something ever happened to Drochaid. And it would offer a source of a never-ending supply of things for us to talk about. And I was bored.

"'Tis Ariboslian. But you'll have to give Drochaid to someone else."

I handed the amulet to Ryann.

Declan pointed to a large evergreen and said, "Craobh."

His accent obscured what he was saying. He trilled the R, which I loved, but struggled to understand. I repeated it to him, thinking I'd misheard, "Croove?"

He chuckled slightly and nodded, then pointed to a bush. "Dos."

Now it sounded like he was speaking Spanish. "Dos?"

We entertained ourselves in this manner as we traveled. We would then repeat some of the words I'd already learned to reinforce them. It helped break up the monotony.

By the time we got to the gachen word for water, I was tired and punchy. I couldn't get enough of Declan's accent, his true voice, but it sounded so funny, like "buuuu-r". I started laughing so hard tears came to my eyes. I tripped over myself as I walked. At first Declan stared at me as though I should be locked up, so I repeated the word, drawing it out. I loosed a guffaw, clutched my pained stomach, and almost toppled over. I looked back at Declan and tried to say the word again but could only squeak.

A smile tugged at his face. Then he laughed with me.

Cahal glanced back at us like he'd never met us before and had no idea why we were following him. Ryann shook her head as if we were beyond hope. Pepin chuckled.

Declan egged me on by telling me sillier sounding words. At that point, all hope of learning a language was gone. Everything sounded so funny we laughed, fighting to catch our breath.

Cahal stopped and dropped his satchel, his typical wordless way of saying, "Time to make camp." He wasn't much of a conversationalist.

Pepin dismounted.

Ryann returned Drochaid. "All right, *children*," she said. "Fallon, do you want to help me collect firewood?"

She phrased it like a question, but it sounded like a command. No doubt an attempt to keep a close eye on me.

"I was thinking about teaching her to hunt." Declan turned to me. "Would you like me to teach you?"

A multitude of tiny joy bubbles rose to the surface, popping like soda. I responded with a bit too much eagerness. "Yes!"

"Is that acceptable, Ryann?" Declan asked. "Pepin can help with firewood."

"Of course." Her disapproving expression contradicted her words. "Would you mind starting a flame first, Fallon? It's easier for you."

"Sure." I collected twigs while Ryann cleared vegetation and fallen leaves from an area until only dirt remained. As she lined it with rocks, I threw down the kindling. I gazed at the twigs, and they burst into flame.

"Can I go?" I asked.

Ryann nodded, frowning.

What was I waiting for? Why did I feel like I shouldn't go? I swallowed, trying to ignore it, and followed him.

Though I was more interested in time alone with Declan than learning to hunt, I tried to be a decent student. He showed me how to identify tracks, which direction they headed, and how fresh they were. He explained how to determine where animals were likely to be, near water sources and such.

"Here." He squatted then pulled me down for a closer look at rabbit tracks in the mud. His right arm rested on my shoulder as his left hand pointed.

I struggled to focus on his words. His touch had all my attention.

"The tracks head in this direction—there." He pointed to a hollow log. "But they do not come out the other side. The rabbit is still inside."

"What should we do?" I whispered, wishing to stay where we were.

"Walk slowly over to that end of the log. Step in front of it when I tell you."

I followed his instructions as he moved toward the middle.

"Go," he whispered.

I moved in front of the entrance as Declan kicked the middle. Claws scratched inside the log between kicks. The rabbit sounded like it headed my way. It must've seen me and turned in the other direction.

Just as the rabbit appeared from the opposite hole, Declan ran and grabbed it. I turned away as he twisted its neck. He laughed at me.

I couldn't look at the body dangling from his hand. It had been a living creature. I was an accomplice to murder.

When we returned, Declan handed the rabbit to Ryann and

nodded to the fire. "I'm amazed how easy it is for you to do that now, Fallon. Pepin, have you seen what she can do?"

Pepin's eyes glazed over as he stared into the flames. "No."

Declan handed me a stick. "Watch."

I concentrated on the tip and a flame erupted. Much easier than it used to be.

Pepin let out a long "Ooo" then glanced around as if to see if everyone else was as impressed. "Doesn't this impress you, Cahal?"

"Fire is a dangerous tool. God has His reasons for what He allows. But I've seen what happens when such powers are in the wrong hands. Aodan was banished from Notirr for starting a fire that killed a few and wounded many. The fire that took my father's life and did this to me." Cahal pulled up his tunic sleeve, revealing puckered skin covering his shoulder.

Never had I heard Cahal speak so many words at once.

Bellies full of rabbit and a soupy root concoction Pepin whipped up, we laid down to sleep. The day was overcast and cool. Perfect for sleeping.

I dreamt. The lights appeared quicker this time.

"Fallon." Relief lined Aodan's voice, as if he'd been waiting for me.

A tornado of emotions swirled inside me. Should I run? Should I talk to him? Sully warned me to run away, not to look at the light. But what if I could find out where he was, what he planned? What if he didn't intend to kill me? Would he turn me into the monster I feared I'd become? A cyclical debate raged, rooting me to the spot.

"Fallon!" Aodan commanded my attention.

"What?" I yelled, irritated, instantly regretting having responded at all. I should have thought this through before dreaming again, should have formed a plan. I knew I should run. What stopped me?

I couldn't see his face, but I sensed him smiling. His glee filled the space of this imaginary world.

"I'm glad you've returned. Have you given my offer any consideration?"

"What offer? To turn me into a monster?"

"A monster? Nay." He snickered. "I offer much more than that. I offer you power, control...immortality."

"Yeah. At the price of becoming a monster. Killing innocent people. Feeding off them. Enslaving them. Enslaving my mother."

"It's merely a means of survival, dear one. Is the lion evil for feeding on the lamb?"

"That's not the point." Was he trying to confuse me?

"I'm in your mind, Fallon. I know you. I sense your pain. The loss of your family. If you accept what I offer, you will have your mother. You can make her and others you care about immortal. They don't have to die...ever. You don't have to experience such pain. You can be in control of your destiny."

It took a moment to absorb his words. Someone understood my pain? All the death. The lack of family. Would it be possible to never face the loss of loved ones again? Would I be forever free of the desire to cut myself? Could I have real control? Isn't that what I'd been fighting for my whole life? Control? And family? He offered me both.

No. Something about this wasn't right. No one can cheat death. People have to die eventually. This offer was served on a platter of damnation. If you believed in such things. The monster. This is how I'd become the monster.

Did I care?

Aodan's delight mingled with my torment. A disconcerting sensation.

No. No. "*No!*" I squeezed my eyes shut.

The joy dissipated, replaced by rage. "You can't shut me out so easily, Fallon. You will join me. You know you want—"

His presence lifted. I opened my eyes. The light was gone. I turned to the woman for her merciful attack to wake me.

CHAPTER TWENTY-FOUR

After another week of traversing thick woods, we came to a slim dirt road, the only kind that seemed to exist in Ariboslia. No more brambles to slow us. I let out a sigh and rubbed the scratches along my arms, feeling freed by the open road compared to the cramped woods, but also tensing up. Roads were only laid where people or, in Ariboslia, some type of semi-intelligent creature traveled. I searched every direction, listening for movement, ready to retreat into the forest.

"Declan," I asked, "Shouldn't we keep to the woods? Under cover?"

"Nay. We're far off the path to Diabalta."

"So? Isn't it still dangerous?"

Ryann sidled up to me. "Aodan expects you to go to Diabalta to rescue your mother. Besides, this isn't his territory. Yet."

"Drochaid seems to be leading us to Gnuatthara," Declan said.

I looked at him. "You mean—"

He nodded. "To the Treasach."

I groaned, dropped my shoulders, and wrinkled my nose. I wanted nothing to do with those baby killers. "Really? Of all places?"

Declan laughed.

"What?"

"You." He shook his head, still chuckling. "Drochaid is unnecessary as a translator with you. You make your feelings known without speaking. They're written all over you."

Should I act indifferent to visiting a bunch of baby murderers? I wanted nothing to do with those barbarians. I didn't care if they were on our side. I was not on theirs. "Why would God want us to go there?"

"All will reveal itself in due time. For now, we must trust. Perhaps we can get supplies whilst we're there." Ryann looked down at her footwear. "And shoes."

I agreed on her point. Pebbles kept making their way into holes in mine. Every few steps, I had to shake my feet to free my shoes of rubble, like a cat walking through a puddle. It aggravated me enough to consider going barefoot.

The way grew steep, climbing a plateau, and my calves burned halfway to the top. When a twenty-five-foot-high wall came into view, Cahal reached his five-word-per-day quota. "Be on guard. Stick together."

"The wall surrounds the entire village on this plateau. They built it during the clan wars," Declan said. "With their size and strength, they had few worthy opponents. It went decades unguarded until the threats escalated a few years ago. Now, as the fasgadair grow stronger, the Treasach have heightened security." As we approached the entryway, he spoke out of the corner of his mouth in a hushed voice. "This is the only way in or out. They close the gate at dusk and will not raise it again until sunrise."

I gulped as my gaze ran up and down the enormous guards. My anger fizzled, and the old feeling I'd grown to expect settled in the pit of my stomach—fear. They must be eight feet tall, with biceps the size of basketballs and hands capable of picking me up by the head like a claw machine.

One glance at these supposed super beings, and I believed

Declan's parents told him the truth about his abandonment. It was his size alone. He was more muscular than most teenage boys, but his height was average, perhaps a smidge taller than most. I didn't get a good look at the Treasach children at Notirr, but no way was he half the mega-infant these guards must have been. Envisioning these monsters as babies, toddling around in tents for diapers, made me laugh.

Yet again, all eyes aimed at me as though I'd swallowed a bird and its tail feathers stuck out of my mouth. I stopped smiling.

A pungent odor—a cross between a locker room and low tide—hit me. I stepped back, brought my hand to my nose, and let out a strained, "Ugh." The smell strengthened with each step. What caused such a stink? It hung in the air like fog with no signs of lifting, making my eyes water, clouding my vision.

Wolf snorted multiple times. Pepin dismounted as Wolf paused to swipe at his nose with his foreleg. He continued blowing air out his snout.

A city with only one way out. Was I this desperate for new shoes? Perhaps I could get a few more miles out of the ragged pieces of leather dangling from my feet. But no. Drochaid insisted.

At the gate, face-to-stomach with the guards, I trembled, wrapping my arms across my rib cage. Even Cahal, reaching the shoulders of the shortest one, had to look up at them.

Ryann, our self-appointed speaker, shielded her eyes from the sun and spoke to the guards. I steeled myself for her over-disclosure, unsure what these people would think of a human in their midst. "We are travelers from Notirr. We seek a room for the night, food, and supplies. Have you room for us?"

They waved us by with undisguised impatience. Their distrustful eyes turned to me and narrowed. I clung to Declan, hurrying him past. Either their paranoia was contagious or my imagination was out of control.

I breathed easier once we were several feet away. That was it? Ryann wasn't going to offer blood samples? They didn't even bother to ask who we were or what our business was. They weren't very good at being paranoid.

I peeked back at Pepin. He must've felt like an ant in comparison. If he did, it didn't show. He walked through the gate with an air of confidence. The guards must pale in comparison to a uilebheist.

Beyond the thick walls, market stands littered a bustling courtyard. Merchants shouted to potential buyers. People hurried from place to place in a seemingly haphazard fashion. Stone and wood buildings lay beyond, lined by alleyways. With the wall so high, and the visible area within so wide, I couldn't possibly determine Gnuatthara's true size.

A monstrous horse startled me as it galloped past. With a massive Treasach astride, they blocked the sun, and the ground vibrated under their weight. I was about the height of the horse's leg. The animals must be bred for size and strength as well.

The further from the entrance we drew, the fainter the stench became, unless I was becoming desensitized to it. Since we were far enough from the guards, I asked, "What was the rank smell?"

Pepin scrunched his nose. "What smell?"

I scowled at him. "It smelled like sweat and bad fish."

"The Treasach line the wall with a compound made from decaying fish. The fasgadair are repulsed by the stench. I don't know what else you smell," Declan said.

"The sweat smell is the Treasach." Ryann wrinkled her nose. "I notice it too."

"Is anyone else bothered by the fish smell?"

No one responded.

"I guess it's only you." Declan smiled, elbowing me. "You must be a fasgadair."

"Ha. Ha. Very funny." I stuck my tongue out at him.

Ignoring our banter as usual, Cahal called over his shoulder, "The inn is this way."

We followed him across the courtyard like bugs on a sidewalk, attempting to avoid giant feet.

After Cahal secured a room, we headed to a pub across the alley. I would've much preferred take-out and retreat to the security of our private room, but I supposed fast food was a luxury the gachen were not accustomed to. We huddled together at a corner table. Pepin sat across from me. Nearly obscured by the table, he reminded me of pictures Bumpah used to draw of a cartoon man with a large nose and two eyes peeking over the edge of paper, napkins, envelopes, or whatever else Bumpah had available.

As more Treasach filed in, I wished we were closer to the exit. "'Tis better to have our backs to the walls," Cahal explained in his few-words-as-possible manner.

No one seemed to have any qualms about Wolf's presence. A large woman, her blonde hair woven into an intricate braid, bustled through the crowd. She carried a massive platter over her head, pausing now and again when the commotion threatened to tip it. Without asking, she placed the tray loaded with random meats onto the center of the table. She never uttered a word or smiled.

What? No menus? This was unquestionably the most bizarre dining experience of my life.

After everyone bowed their heads for a moment of silence, Cahal reached for two large T-bone steaks. He tore into one, tossing the other to Wolf. Ryann, Declan, and Pepin looked unconcerned as they, too, dug in. I gaped, dumbfounded. We ate like this without plates as we traveled. But this was a restaurant. What kind of restaurant failed to offer simple things like plates, silverware, menus —choices?

"Is something wrong?" Declan wiped juice off his mouth with his sleeve as I stared at the remaining mound of meat before us. Where were the eggs, bacon, and other breakfast foods?

"No," I mumbled, reaching for what appeared to be a chicken leg. It tasted charred, unseasoned. As I chewed, the waitress returned with a tray of heavy mugs. She placed all but one on the table—the other she put on the floor for Wolf.

Eager for something to drink, I lifted the cup to my lips. By the time the scent reached my nose, it was too late. I'd already taken a sip. The sour liquid touched my tongue. I spit the foul liquor out. "What is that?" I broke down and wiped my mouth on my sleeve, since napkins seemed nonexistent.

"Mead." Cahal drank it like water.

"It's nasty." I pushed the cup away. "They drink this stuff this early in the morning?"

Declan, Ryann, and Pepin passed on theirs too. Declan shrugged. "The Treasach enjoy fermented drink. The Cael prefer to avoid drinking too much. 'Tis better to be clear minded. Not to worry. We'll get water later."

"You'd think they'd want a clear mind too, especially if they're afraid of invasion." Nods met my comment.

As I sat, chewing my food, morbid fascination drew my attention to the Treasach. Scars and bruises peppered their arms, heads, and necks. Manners appeared as nonexistent as napkins. Male and female alike erupted in guttural, full belly laughs at any bodily noise. Half-chewed meat hung from their crooked, yellow teeth. The way they groped at each other made me drop my gaze. My appetite dissipated as my desire for a bath elevated to new levels.

I couldn't ignore the commotion at the next table. A male with a black beard separated into two braids leaned back in his chair and scratched his shaved head. A scar ran from the front of his ear to his chin. A low gurgle in his gut rose in volume as it ascended his esophagus. He unhinged his jaw as gastrointestinal fumes spewed forth accompanied by the sound of the sudden release of toxic gases. The noise reverberated throughout the pub above the din. His mates exploded with laughter as they feigned attempts to waft the noxious scent from their noses.

I shook my head. Giant six year olds.

A couple of tables away, seven loud, obnoxious males complained about nighttime guard duty. Our waitress dropped off heaping plates of grilled carcasses in front of them. As she turned to leave, one of the creeps swatted her behind.

Mouth agape, I stared, wanting to beat him senseless despite his stature.

The woman didn't hesitate to reply by clocking him, close-fisted, square in the jaw. *Yes!* She then walked off as the male, gazing at her with admiration, grasped his jaw and rammed it back in place without as much as a wince. He laughed with his buddies as they barraged him with congratulatory pats on the back and punches on the arm.

Neanderthals.

I scanned my companions' faces for their reaction to these grotesque beings. All but Cahal, who sat licking his fingers while ignoring the ruckus around him, appeared as uncomfortable as I.

Cahal paid, liberating me from a horrific place that should only exist in nightmares. I rushed through the crowd, dodging unwelcome advances, and burst out the door. Cahal set off for supplies as the rest of us returned to our room. The time had come I was most anxious for, an indoor bath and a real bed.

"The bathroom is down there." Ryann pointed at a door down the hall.

"We share it?"

"No need to look so scared." She smiled, placing a consolatory hand on my shoulder. "The door has a lock."

The shared bath didn't sit well, but the pool-sized tub did. I could swim in it. Once I soaped up, someone banged on the door, causing it to bulge with each strike. A gruff voice yelled, "Move along in there!"

Fearing an impatient Treasach might break down the door, I fled, soap residue clinging to my skin.

Cahal had not yet returned when I entered the room. "Was it me or was Cahal the only one not bothered by the Treasach at the pub?"

Declan shrugged as he walked past me out of the room.

"Cahal responds to things in his own way." Ryann sat on the bed by the door, brushing her hair. "'Tis not for us to judge him or to discuss him without his presence. If you have a question for him, you should ask him directly."

Her tone wasn't unkind. And she was right. Still, her correction stung. I retreated to the other bed.

Snoring made me stir. Dazed, I wiped my eyes and pulled myself up on my elbows. Thin strips of light streamed through the shutter slats. Cahal had returned, clean-shaven. He slept in a sitting position, slumped against the door. Ryann slept on the bed closest to the door. Wolf lay beside me in the one near the window, a paw slightly twitching. Declan, on the floor next to Pepin, must have shaved too. Without his scraggly beard, he looked much younger...and cuter.

Pepin was the guilty one. On his back, mouth open, he gargled air. As the air left his mouth, his moustache puffed out.

I groaned, draped a leg over the side of the bed, and kicked him.

He inhaled sharply, smacked his lips a few times, grunted, and rolled over.

The sleeping conditions weren't ideal, but I couldn't complain, now that the only noise was deep breathing. It had been too long since I slept in a dark room. Or on a bed. And I had Wolf. I lowered myself back onto the mattress and closed my eyes.

I gazed along the horizon to the woman on the shore.

"Fallon, I've been waiting for you."

My body jerked toward Aodan. It was happening much quicker now. How could I have been so careless? Was it too late to run now?

"Have you considered my offer?"

"I will never join you." I attempted to make my voice sound stronger than my will, but I was growing tired of this journey.

"Ah, how unfortunate. I'd hate to consider the alternative. You heard rumor of what I did to my dear sister, have you not? My twin. We shared a womb. Our minds, our very souls were connected." He quieted, probably for dramatic effect. "How much more might I torture you?" The phony compassion in his voice sent chills up my spine.

"Isn't that what you planned to do anyway?"

"Despite what you may have been told, I'm not as bad as I may seem. Notirr is still secure, is it not? They have their freedom."

"So it's not enough to kill me? You're threatening them now?"

"You don't have to die, Fallon. Neither do the Cael. Reconsider my offer, before it's too late."

A shrill, unceasing whistle pierced the air. I bolted upright in bed and scanned the room, trying to get a grip on reality.

Declan, looking groggy, rose to open the shutters. "Night has fallen." He pointed across the way. "Look at the wall."

We all crowded the window. The guards lining the wall had multiplied. How long had we slept?

Declan stiffened, "It might be a drill or..."

"Or what?" I breathed.

Cahal reached for his axe and moved toward the door. "Or we're under attack."

CHAPTER TWENTY-FIVE

"Check Drochaid," Cahal ordered me.

The amulet wobbled in my hands. "It's pointing out the door."

"We can't just walk out of here following that thing." Ryann gestured to Drochaid. "If someone sees it, they might figure out who she is."

Cahal nodded and opened the door. "Keep it hidden until I say."

Fingers shaking, I tucked it under my dress.

He led us, weapon in hand, to the main floor. The whistle wailed as we searched the inn's lower rooms. Not one person remained in the building, not even the innkeeper.

While Cahal, Ryann, Declan, and Pepin peered out the windows, I hung back with Wolf, cowering. Gooseflesh broke out all over my body. My stomach shriveled up. I had to get out. With no outsiders in sight, I didn't feel the need to wait for Cahal to give the word. I consulted Drochaid. "It's pointing this way."

I bolted down a hall toward the back of the inn. The others followed me to an external door.

"It's pointing outside." A sensation of being tethered to a cinder block and tossed into an ocean seeped over me. The cacophony muffled. My surroundings blurred, reminding me of my first encounter with the fasgadair.

"We should go back to the pub." Declan's speech was slow. "There might be people, and it is closer to the gate."

"Nay. We must follow Drochaid even if it goes against our judgment." Ryann spoke at a crawl too. "Besides, the chance of escaping out the main entrance is slim. Perhaps Drochaid will lead us to a place to hide."

Cahal looked out the window. "No sign of movement. It might be a drill. If this is an attack, we must protect Fallon. Ryann, lead with Wolf. Declan, stay with Fallon and Pepin. I'll cover your backs. See the alley?"

Heads nodded in slow motion.

Cahal's face turned to mine. His head tilted, and his brow furrowed in an unhurried fashion. He handed Declan the battle-axe then returned to me. His massive paws seized my shoulders and shook me. My brain rattled back and forth. He released his grip, and I looked about. The noise returned to its original deafening decibels as my vision cleared. My friends no longer moved in slow motion.

"All right now?" he asked.

"I think so." *What happened?*

Ryann grabbed my elbow, caught and held my gaze. "Fallon, something prompted you to be here, to help us. Hold onto it. Keep it in your mind. And no matter what happens, you are loved."

What an odd thing to say at such a time. I nodded so she would release her grip. But I had no idea what made me agree to all this. Family? My mother? Partly, but that wasn't all. The way they care for orphans? Their love for me? Never had I experienced such love, particularly as a stranger. That must be it.

"Head for the alley," Cahal barked orders. "Surround Fallon so she can check Drochaid. Move in the direction she points. Stay in formation. And keep quiet. We cannot afford to attract any attention. Go."

My heart skittered as we entered the open air. I scanned the landscape, like a kid on a diving board who'd never been in a pool. Ryann and Wolf were already out, so I hurried behind them. My eyes darted in every direction. The scent carried on swirling wind further put me on edge. What was it? It reminded me of the time I licked a nine-volt battery. It tasted metallic with an electrical bite. If such a taste had a scent, it permeated the air now.

Wolf's hackles rose. Did he smell it too? He lifted his snout in multiple directions skyward, sniffing.

The sensation of sinking washed over me again. I shook my head. Was this what Ryann meant? I'm doing this for them...the Cael...for love. Images of Ryann with Colleen, Declan with the orphan, my gran holding me after my nightmare. I tumbled those thoughts about my mind like balls in a bingo spinner.

Once we reached the alley, Declan shielded me while I looked at the amulet. It pointed to the right. We ran in that direction. We remained in formation, running, stopping to check the direction, delving deeper and deeper into the maze of homes, away from the entrance.

As we skulked about, advancing to the next break in our path, something hit my leg, hard. I shrieked as I shot into the air. Without checking to see if I was okay, my companions formed a circle around me, nearly blocking my view. I peeked over Wolf and Pepin to find a wall, nothing more.

Cahal turned to me. His eyes widened as he thumped his fingers against his breastbone.

When I got his meaning, I pointed in the direction Drochaid showed me.

He nodded and nudged Ryann and Wolf forward. Returning to formation, the rest of us followed.

Between two homes, in what appeared to be a dead end, lay a hole in the ground. A man in the hole, holding one end of a covering above his head, summoned us. He emerged, lifting the cover further, waving for us to enter.

Every ounce of my being wanted to run the other way, but since Wolf went, I followed.

Once inside, in full view, the man's height made it clear what he was—a Treasach. He lowered the hatch and latched it. Using a small lantern hanging from the ceiling, he lit a torch, and then put a finger to his mouth, motioning for us to remain silent. He handed the torch to Cahal and lit two more: one for Declan and another for himself. Then he blew out the lantern and led us down a long, crude tunnel.

The dank earth reeked of mold and decay like the time Stacy's mom decided to start composting, not realizing she wasn't supposed to add meat. But being built by the Treasach, the tunnel was big enough not to make me feel claustrophobic. Our guide stooped a bit. The rest of us, including Cahal, stood upright.

We walked in silence for what felt like miles. When Pepin fell behind, Wolf offered him a ride. The stranger kept a quick pace, his back to us. I dared to check on Drochaid, multiple times, sure it couldn't be right. Why would it lead us here, following him? A phantom imitation of the village whistle echoed in my mind making it hard to determine when it was no longer in earshot. An occasional drip of water and squishy footsteps from waterlogged shoes accompanied the sound, slowly overtaking it.

"What happened?" I asked Declan, keeping my voice low. "I couldn't see anything. Why'd we follow him?" I jerked my head in our tour guide's direction.

"He threw pebbles at us to get our attention. They made you jump."

"And we followed him?"

"Drochaid is leading us this way. Whether he's helping or not, it's part of God's plan. Besides, he's not a fasgadair. Would you rather have waited for them?"

Oh, great. So we were here because the other idea was worse...

worse than trusting a Treasach. Declan, without an ounce of guile, was no good at calming a girl's nerves.

The tunnel widened at a dead end where other Treasach men, women, and children huddled together near a hatch similar to the one we'd come through. The anonymous man unlatched and lifted it enough to peer out.

He secured the lid and turned to us. "You are now miles from Gnuatthara. The sun will be up shortly. When it rises, you will be safe from the fasgadair. I must return. There may be others in need of help."

When he turned to leave, Ryann asked, "Kind sir, who can I thank for rescuing us?"

"My name is of no consequence. I'm merely a servant of the One True God. You have Him to thank, no other." He retreated into the darkness, his torchlight disappearing after him.

"Thank You for sending Your servant, Lord. Bestow peace and blessings upon him."

I had to strain to hear Ryann's words.

"Amen," Cahal, Declan, and Pepin added.

Declan addressed the Treasach. "It was not a drill? Gnuatthara was attacked?"

One of the men, frowning, nodded. "The whistle alerts the village and hurts the fasgadair. We use their heightened senses against them." A sly smile emerged then disappeared. "It buys us time. Their powers are useless until they find it and shut it off. As long as it continues, we have a chance."

"That explains why we never saw one," Declan stated without looking at anyone. "They were disabled, searching for the alarm."

The man gave a weak nod. "And they have our guards to contend with. The fasgadair might not overtake us, but for the sake of our women and children, we vacate when we have the chance, leaving only the soldiers behind."

So *now* they value life.

I sat in the dank, musty tunnel with only dark thoughts to entertain me as we waited for sunrise. Declan put his arm around me. Ryann kept glancing at us, but I didn't care. After what we'd been through, I welcomed the comfort. His warm body calmed my nerves. Even Ryann said nothing. Perhaps, despite her tough demeanor, she would've liked someone to comfort her too.

As I surveyed the Treasach in the dim lighting, my hatred toward them petered out. Gargantuan children clung, wide-eyed, to anxious parents. Maybe if they weren't so fearful, they wouldn't be so quick to rid themselves of any perceived weakness.

"Momma, I'm hungry." A girl with long blonde hair tied in a braid sat across her mother's lap.

Her mother pushed loose strands out of her daughter's face. "Shhh...soon. Rest now." Wasn't she the waitress?

Ryann pulled a piece of jerky from her pack, shuffled across the floor to the little girl, and offered it to her. The mother shook her head while her daughter buried her face in her neck.

"Please take it. I have plenty more."

The woman reached out a tentative hand for the meat. She nudged her daughter, who studied the jerky, then her mom. When her mom nodded, the girl grabbed it and took a bite.

"I am called Ryann. What are you called?"

"Ta..." The child mumbled the rest under her breath.

Ryann let out a soft chuckle. "Could you say that again, sweetie?"

"She is called Tashaundra." Her mother spoke.

"What a beautiful name."

The woman and her child smiled.

"I had a friend with that name. Do you know what it means?" Ryann asked.

Tashaundra shook her head and looked at her mom.

"My grandmother was called by that name. I do not know its meaning," her mother said.

"It means God is gracious." Ryann turned back to Tashaundra. "Do you know what it means to have God's grace?"

The girl shook her head again.

"It means He loves you, no matter what. You are loved, dear Tashaundra. Never forget."

Tashaundra stroked her mother's neck with one hand, chewed the jerky in the other, and gazed with large, sparkling eyes at Ryann. Her mother's expression was harder to judge. She seemed to be surveying Ryann. The other Treasach stared at her as well. I couldn't read them, but something had changed in their eyes.

CHAPTER TWENTY-SIX

W e continued our quest at sunup, putting as much distance between us and the fasgadair as possible. Cahal wanted to travel at night, which meant we would forge ahead on little to no sleep—again.

With each uneventful day, Cahal allowed more time to rest. I stuck close to Declan.

Ryann didn't object to my clinginess aloud, but she watched us, rarely allowing us out of sight.

My life was in danger, but my mind kept returning to the memory of his arms around me. He felt the same, didn't he? What stopped us? A betrothal? How could someone he didn't love come between us and our chemistry? How could he let it?

I tried to push those thoughts out of my mind. How could I even continue to dwell on these things? I wasn't staying. I'd either find my way home or die trying. But Declan wouldn't leave my mind. Thoughts of him tormented me. Thousands of partial arguments chased each other around my mind as I attempted in vain to predict his responses.

Two nights after our escape from Gnuatthara, while we hunted for food, I broached the subject. "D-Declan."

"What?" A couple paces ahead of me, he scanned the ground for tracks.

I hadn't planned the conversation. My body trembled. Heat rose to my face as my heart hammered in my chest. The words hesitated to leave my mouth, because once they left, they could never return. "How do-do you feel about me?"

He stopped his search and turned to me. "You know how I feel about you, Fallon. But there's Maili and—"

"I know." The levy had broken; the words flowed easier now. "But isn't it a little barbaric to marry someone your parents choose for you? What about what you want?"

"'Tis not about me or what I want. 'Tis about what God wants."

"What do you mean, it's not about you? It's your life, isn't it? You're the one who has to spend the rest of it with a stranger. Don't you want to be with me?" My voice cracked. I feared I might be nearing, or worse, had already surpassed the pathetic line.

Seeming to sense my vulnerability, he reached out and grabbed my arm. Caressing my face, he gazed into my eyes. Then he pulled my face toward his.

My breath caught; my heart raced. His breath warmed me. He was about to kiss me when a loud bark startled us.

We both jumped back.

Wolf shifted his head to meet our eyes in turn.

Declan backed away, his eyes full of fear. "Sorry, Fallon. I don't know what I'm doing."

Before I could utter a word, he turned on his heels and ran toward our camp. Standing there, staring after him, I felt like the biggest loser on the face of the planet. He ran from me. I actually made a guy run away. They should bottle me and sell me as boy repellant.

Wolf licked my hand.

I yanked it away and walked back to camp, taking my time. I didn't want to face anyone.

Wolf followed a few paces behind.

When I arrived, Cahal occupied Declan by teasing him for failing to find meat. "Good thing Wolf is here, huh? He got enough meat for all of us." Cahal gave Wolf a pat on the head, then sat back against a tree, sighed, and folded his arms behind his head. "I could retire and let Wolf fetch our food." He closed his eyes, missing the unimpressed look Wolf threw at him.

I silently thanked God for Cahal's atypical chattiness just when I needed it. It allowed me to slink by to the opposite side of the fire, away from everyone. I sat, picked up a stick, and drew pictures in the dirt. Wolf settled beside me, resting his head on his paws. I was so ashamed, part of me wanted to push him away. He now knew first-hand how pathetic I was. But, another part, the needy, pride-less part wanted the comfort of his presence. I let him stay.

Ryann didn't question why we came back empty-handed. When I dared look up, I found her eyes flip-flopping between Declan and me as if she were watching a tennis match. I returned to my drawing, pretending it completely engrossed me.

Eager to avoid the disquiet, I ate little and excused myself to bathe in the lake. I took longer than usual and intended to go straight to sleep when I got back to abstain from any conversation.

Ryann intercepted me upon my return, foiling my plan. "Fallon, what is going on between you and Declan?"

Though she was not one to sidestep an issue, I wasn't prepared for such a pointed question. "I don't know what you're talking about." I turned to walk away.

She grasped my wrist. "Aye, you do." She took a deep breath. "I know something is going on." Her tone, gentler than it had been a moment before, seemed genuinely concerned. "It might help to talk about it. I promise not to judge either of you. I want to help."

I slumped to the ground. "I don't know what to do."

"Start by telling me what happened."

I cradled my head in my hand. "I told him I like him."

"Does he feel the same way?"

I nodded. "Well...he did." I wrapped my hands around my legs, locking them in place with clasped hands. "But he's going to marry Maili anyway." When I felt the oncoming rush of tears, I buried my face in my hands, annoyed at myself. These taboo public displays of emotion were becoming habitual. "He hates me now. I've ruined everything. We were such good friends, and now he won't even talk to me."

Ryann sat next to me and placed an arm around my shoulder. "It won't last. He'll talk to you again soon. But you must be careful. You can't allow your desires to control you."

I wished someone would tell me I was free to see Declan. I didn't understand their politics or customs. I didn't understand how marrying Maili was God's plan. Why would the Creator of the universe care who someone married?

"It's not wrong to be a friend to Declan," Ryann continued. "But it's wrong to desire something you're not entitled to. 'Tis worse to attempt to obtain it without regard for the outcome. And there are consequences, Fallon. Consequences neither you nor Declan should have to contend with. We may not understand them, but our rules are for our own protection."

I groaned. Why was life so complicated? "What should I do?"

Ryann smiled. "To keep Declan as a friend, you must maintain a respectable distance. And you must consider what he's going through."

"I've already lost his friendship."

"Nay, you haven't. He's doing as I advise you. Keeping a distance. He will speak with you again when he's ready. But you must abandon any notions of having a romantic relationship with him."

My shoulders sagged, but I nodded and followed her back to camp.

As EXPECTED, Declan treated me like a leper the next night while we followed glowing arrows south. Didn't I know this would happen? He'd done this once before, and I hated it. I finally had his friendship back, only to lose it again.

I spent miles tripping on tree roots, beating myself up internally, when a ray of light broke through the dark cloud in my mind: Ryann. I could talk to her without risking the friendship. It seemed nothing I said disturbed her. She had a way of cutting through the bull. A voice of reason. What my emotions jumbled, her logic simplified. I kicked myself for not entrusting my feelings to her long ago. She might have stopped me from making a mess of things.

Perhaps I should tell her about my conversations with Aodan.

I sensed the ocean before it came into view. The temperature dropped about ten degrees. The winds wafted salty air to my nose. A raucous din unique to seagulls then crashing waves filled my ears.

The treetops blazed with the morning light. The ground grew rocky. The vegetation thinned. A seemingly endless ocean spread before me. Water crashed against the rocky coast, sending sprays into the air, dousing the stone like rain. The sun peeked over the crimson horizon, casting a path of orange highlights along the crests rippling toward me.

I consulted Drochaid. "Now what? The arrow points *into* the sea."

"The Sea of Firinne." Ryann gazed at the water.

"Um." Pepin looked down and scuffed his feet as if kicking pebbles where none existed. "We're probably here to find Drochaid's missing jewel."

I loomed over him. "How are we supposed to find it?"

"I don't know." His shoulders and arms raised defensively as he backed away. "The angel told me it's in the sea."

"Then jump in and get it." I'd no right to take my bad mood out on Pepin. The varying degrees of disapproving glances aimed my way didn't surprise me. I deserved them. Still, I couldn't pull myself out of the funk.

"What?" I held my hands up as if surrendering. "Didn't the angel tell *him* to get it?"

"Please understand." Pepin's eyes pleaded for mercy. "Pech are like rocks in many ways, including our buoyancy. If I jump into the sea, I will sink to the bottom. God knows this. He created me this way. He could not have intended for me to go in there."

"Pepin." Declan spoke as if addressing a four-year-old. "This is very important. Can you remember exactly what the angel said to you?"

Pepin threw Declan a look indicating he did not appreciate being spoken to in such a manner. Then he narrowed his eyes and crossed his arms with a huff. "Of course, I remember. You don't forget a visit from an angel." His face cleared, and his arms returned to his side, his expression growing almost angelic, his voice singsong. "The angel said, 'Pepin, do not be afraid. I am an angel sent by God with a message. You are to create an inter-realm transport amulet of limestone, turquoise, and malachite. The face must bear this symbol.' The angel gave me this." Pepin pulled out a worn piece of parchment with a drawing matching Drochaid's markings. "Then the angel said, 'When it is complete, give it to the elders of Notirr. It will need a jewel which will be found in the Sea of Firinne.' I told the angel I would do as asked. That's all."

"So the angel didn't tell you to get the jewel, only that it was necessary and where to find it. And if your recollection is exact, the angel advised you to give it to the elders of Notirr first," Ryann said.

"Yes." Pepin nodded and straightened. All traces of worry left his face. "Pech have good memories."

"Well, look around." Ryann began searching among the rocks. "It may be in one of these tide pools."

I didn't consider the bottom of a tide pool to be undersea. Still, I wasn't eager to go deep-sea diving without proper equipment, so I went along with her suggestion. If anyone else disagreed, they didn't vocalize it. We fanned out among the rocks. I searched a couple of tide pools and crevices between rocks, continuing to advance toward the sea, when I came across an unusual tide pool. Its surface was smooth as glass. I knelt at the edge and attempted to peer past my reflection into the water. I couldn't. It was like trying to look through a mirror.

I peered at myself. Was it a trick? Despite random dirt smudges and tangled hair, I looked beautiful. My skin had darkened slightly, and pink tinged my cheeks. Not one trace of a blemish existed across my former pizza face. My eyes sparked with zeal.

The flat surface wavered, rippling out from the center evenly in all directions. As it stilled, my reflection contorted into the image that tormented me in my nightmares. My face, fangs bared, lunged at me. I lifted my arms to protect myself, lost balance, fell into the water, and hit my head on the rock on the opposite side. Eyes open, I sank. The sunlit surface drew further away and disappeared.

CHAPTER TWENTY-SEVEN

My head throbbed. I groaned and blinked. A beautiful face, framed in a cascade of golden hair, appeared before me. Eyes, as blue as the sea, shimmered like sunlight on waves. I twitched and pulled myself up on my elbows. *Where am I now?*

"Eat this."

I sat and looked from the seaweed-like substance in her hand to her eyes. Who was she? Could I trust her?

"It will take away the pain."

Searching her face, I found no evidence of malice. I reached for droopy, green leaves and took a tentative bite. It tasted like salty paper. The second, larger piece required quite a bit of chewing, but I managed to break it down enough to swallow. Within seconds, the pain dissipated. "Wow. My headache is gone. What was that stuff?"

Instead of answering, she draped a gown across the bed. "Get out of those wet clothes and put this on." She turned and started from the room.

"Wait? Who are you? Where am I?"

Without hesitating, she continued out and disappeared from view. Why hadn't those been my *first* questions? Had I grown so accustomed to the bizarreness of this place that I no longer questioned waking in odd places with strangers tending to me?

I picked up the dress wishing it were a little more...not a dress. Despite its efforts, Ariboslia would never convert me into a girly girl. Not if I had any say. *Nothing* would dash my dream for the glorious day when I could throw on a pair of jeans.

After changing, I had to admit the dress wasn't bad. Never had I worn anything so comfortable. It weighed next to nothing and swirled like air over my body. If not for the material's slight swish and adequate cover in the mirror, I'd wonder if I weren't wearing The Emperor's New Clothes. But no, the light aqua material hugged my torso and arms and fell at my waist.

While I awaited the mystery girl's return, I inspected the sea-blue and ivory room. A candle chandelier hung from the lofty ceiling. The canopy bed, bedecked in luxurious ivory bedding, nearly touched the ceiling. I wanted nothing more than to snuggle up on it and sleep for hours.

A fish swam past the window.

"What in the world?" I peeked out into what I had mistaken for a blue sky to find many multicolored fish in varying shapes and sizes. Was I under the sea? Was this one of those underwater cities? Was the girl a selkie? I opened the door she'd gone through and found a long empty hallway. Where had she gone?

The familiar warm sensation on my chest made me grab Drochaid. It pointed down the hall. I allowed it to lead me through the impressive grand hallway, down a flight of stairs, and another hall. When the arrow pointing to the right lit, I stopped and peered through the open doorway.

A dining hall. A long table stood in the center of the room. Numerous lidded, silver platters sat on the table as though prepared for a large dinner party. The glittery ceiling, which appeared to be made of some kind of metal, curved upward from all four corners. Another elaborate chandelier dangled from its highest point. Candlelight reflected off the shiny dome, bathing the room in light. Against the far wall, a school of large neon fish swam past an enormous window. I moved closer to watch them, but they'd gone. Nothing but blue water remained. As I neared, a large gray mass with an eye the size of my head raced by, and I jumped back.

"Fallon."

I leapt again at my name. A man sat at the table. Where had he come from? I turned to flee, but something rooted me to the spot. It wasn't just his knowing my name, but the way he said it—full of affection. Was he one of the selkie the others had warned me about?

As I stood, transfixed, immeasurable calm rained down on me. Something compelled me to turn and walk toward the stranger. Peace seeped deeper into my being with each step. How could he have such a profound effect on me? Judging from his short, dark hair with minimal flecks of gray, I guessed him to be in his thirties. His kind face was well groomed with trim facial hair masking his jawline and upper lip.

As I neared, he stood, revealing a long, white robe cinched by a gold belt. He held out his hand, and I placed mine in it. His warm skin sent peace radiating throughout my being. He guided me to a seat at the table, where, in one smooth movement, he pulled out a chair and motioned for me to sit.

"It is wonderful to meet you in person." His buttery voice melted in the air as he spoke. He seated himself beside me.

Something about him made me feel inferior yet ... loved. His amiable eyes were as I imagined Santa Claus's might be if I believed in such things. Somehow, he seemed to command respect and undying loyalty. I bowed. "The honor is mine."

His genuine smile dissolved all my troubles. He glanced at the table, and I followed his gaze to the numerous covered platters. "You must be hungry. Help yourself to anything you like."

I didn't hunger for food, but to learn more about this kindhearted man. To be polite, I selected a dish and spooned a small amount onto my plate. He poured red wine into a bejeweled goblet and set it before me. Then he reached for bread, broke it, and handed me a piece.

Being served by someone so enigmatic unnerved me. I should have served him.

"Thank you." I needed to know who this man was and how he knew me.

When I opened my mouth to ask, he spoke, "I have Drochaid's missing jewel. We have been saving it for you."

"For me? So it wasn't Pepin's job to get it?"

The man's hearty laugh filled the room with music, making me smile. I took a bite of the bread. Though it had no spread, it tasted like honey.

"No. Pepin was to advise you it was needed. And he did his task well. Here you are...in Saltinat."

"What's that?"

"An underwater selkie city."

My eyes widened. "Are you a selkie?" I hoped the attraction Garvey spoke of wasn't what captivated me. If that were the case, its effect surprised me. I expected a romantic attraction, but romance had nothing to do with what I felt. It didn't make me want to drop everything to stay with him, though I enjoyed his presence and wished to remain. Instead, it empowered me, made me feel as though I could accomplish anything he asked.

"No." He laughed again. It lit up everything around him, including me. "After we eat, I'll give you what you seek. You will need it to stop the fasgadair."

"Stop the fasgadair?" My hand, holding my next bite of bread, froze midair. "I thought my task was to rescue my mother from my uncle." I didn't care to remember the rest but added it under my breath. "And dethrone him."

"True, but it is only the beginning." His eyes seemed to penetrate my soul. "Why did you agree to this quest?"

I shrugged. "I guess I'm doing it for the Cael. And...I'd like to meet my mother."

"Do you feel nothing for your people?"

"Oh, no. I mean...yes. I mean...I care for those I've met so far."

"What do you think of the way they treat one another?"

What could I say? I envied their joy, their devotion. Any one of them would give their life for another. They saved the lives of so many Treasach. I had never witnessed such selfless acts. I wished I were as good.

"They are not good. Their flesh is bent toward evil, like yours. But something they have allows them to prevail over it. You can have it too. You can have the joy, strength, and love—all they possess."

Had he read my mind?

He pressed further. "What is your opinion of the God of Whom they speak?"

"I don't know. He seems to be the source of their generosity and kindness...their love. He is their purpose."

"Do you wish to live for a higher purpose?"

"I do. But who is this God?"

"He is Stacy's God."

How did he know about Stacy? She wasn't even in this realm. "Who are you?"

"I am The Way."

I'd heard that before—at church with Stacy. Did that mean...? Was this...? No, it couldn't be.

"I tell you the truth."

"What do I have to do?"

"Believe."

I wanted to believe. But doing so required me to peek into a place I much preferred to keep sealed shut. It meant searching my heart.

All at once, the weight of who I was came crashing down, nearly crushing me. Tears coursed down my cheeks. I'd been so selfish. I'd spent all my life angry, blaming everyone and everything but myself.

I'd felt entitled to my grandmother's love, parents, a so-called normal life. And I longed for things like Declan's embrace, though I knew it was wrong. People tried to reach out to me, but I didn't want their advice. I wanted to do things my way. To be in control. I didn't appreciate what I had. What made me think I deserved anything more?

I wanted to cry out to Him to find someone else. A less worthy person couldn't possibly exist. The ugliness within me oozed throughout my entire being, ensnaring me like a tar pit.

Desperate for this Man to pull me out, certain that only He could, I closed my eyes and cried, "I believe!" Though it rang like a shout within my heart, it came out a whisper. But my heart hadn't finished speaking. "I need You. Please forgive me."

He placed His hand under my chin, forcing me to peer into His eyes. There I found true empathy. With His other hand, He brought a handkerchief to my eyes and wiped away my tears.

"You are forgiven."

A tingling sensation swept over my body. I weighed nothing and might float away from the force of pure joy. It was true. I *was* forgiven. I would never allow myself to be consumed by the ugliness again. I would accept my mission. I would believe. I would do whatever God asked of me, whatever He empowered me to do. I would live for something greater than myself.

"Trust in God, not this." He let my chin go and tapped on Drochaid. "It is only a tool to be disposed of when you are ready."

He placed His hand on my head, and my eyes closed. A warm, electric tingle emanated from His hand. It flowed into my head and coursed throughout my being. Peace swept over me once more. For the first time in my life, I was content. I was loved.

When I opened my eyes, He was gone. I was no longer in the dining hall but back in the bedroom where I'd first awoken, lying on the bed. Had I dreamed the entire interlude? No. I felt different.

The girl who'd given me the dress returned. "Good. It fits you perfectly."

"What happened?" I asked. "Where'd He go?"

"He?" Appearing alarmed, she scanned the room. "You should not have come across any selkie men. They are strictly forbidden."

"He wasn't a selkie."

She relaxed slightly. "That would have been unfortunate." She reached to touch my head. "You hit your head pretty badly."

"I know what I saw. I didn't imagine Him." I looked down at Drochaid. A small aqua gemstone rested in its center. Funny, I didn't recall receiving it. Still, I had proof. "Ha! See? Here it is. He said He would give me a jewel and He did. How would I have this if I'd imagined Him?"

The selkie narrowed her eyes.

"Please," I begged, suddenly anxious to leave. "Now that I have the jewel, I need to get back."

"This way." She motioned for me to follow her into the same hall I'd walked earlier.

I paused as we passed the dining room entrance. It was empty. The table was bare. How had they cleared it so quickly? I shook my head and hurried to catch up with the selkie.

Confused by what I learned about the selkie from the gachen's stories, I asked as we walked, "I thought selkie preferred their seal form."

"Sometimes we do. Whatever form we take, our desire is to be in the ocean. That is why we have this city and others like it."

"Does anyone else live here? I haven't seen anyone." Except Him.

"When we rescued you from the water, we evacuated this area. It is standard procedure when gachen visit. If you met a selkie man, you would never leave."

"Oh, I'm not a gachen."

She stopped walking. Her eyes ran over me. "You're not? What are you?"

"I'm half-gachen and half-human. My mother is gachen. I'm from the human realm."

"You are gachen enough that we must keep selkie men away from you."

She turned and continued until we reached an empty room. It stunk of decaying seafood. Algae covered the floor, ceiling, and all four walls, leaving the floor slick. I slipped and caught myself against the far wall. My hand left an imprint in the muck and came away covered with green slime. Not wanting to soil my dress, I tried to flick it off.

After closing the door behind her, the selkie pulled a lever in the wall. Water poured in from spouts near the roof. The noise deafened me.

"What's happening?" I shouted.

"I need to fill the room," she yelled back. "If I opened the roof first, you would be crushed."

I strained to hear her words as I rinsed my hand in the rising flood. My breath caught— cool water encircled my waist.

As the space of air shrunk and I treaded water, I struggled to breathe. I loved the ocean, but not like this.

"Hold your breath." The roof opened, and the air pocket disappeared.

Underwater, I swam through the roof. My chest compressed. Fearing I might pass out, I kicked for the surface. When I broke through, I gasped for air, wiped hair from my face, and pulled myself out of the tide pool I'd fallen into. I lay down on the rocks, gazed at the sky, and breathed deeply, grateful for the open space.

When my breathing returned to normal, I stood gazing at the still water. Something compelled me to peer into it. Like before, I caught my reflection. This time, rather than mutating into my nightmare vision, a golden glow spread about me. The ugliness gone, I smiled. Time to look for my friends.

I spotted Ryann first and jogged toward her, eager to share the news. Ryann brought her hands to her mouth to amplify her voice, turned, and hollered, "She's over here!" She ran to hug me. "Where did you go? We searched everywhere for you."

Declan caught up. "Wow! What happened? You look radiant."

"Did you get the jewel?" Pepin asked.

"Yes." I smiled. "And you'll never believe Who I met."

CHAPTER TWENTY-EIGHT

I spent so much time in Saltinat, we had little time to rest. We ate and slept under a canopy of trees. Blanketed in cool, ocean air, the surf lulled me to sleep.

After what seemed only minutes, Cahal nudged my arm with his foot. "Time to move out."

I groaned. My body wanted more rest, but I followed, away from the coast. The land turned wet, and fog thickened the air. The trees, sparser in this part of the forest, grew wider and taller. Their branches fanned far above our heads.

Shoes in one hand, the length of my selkie dress gathered in the other, I trudged through muck. My feet disappeared, then reappeared, covered in grime that refused to let go. Then down, back into the mire, slime oozed between my toes, making me shudder.

"What is this place?" I asked.

"The Bog of Mulad. On the positive side, we will not be attacked here. All living things avoid this place." Ryann's body pitched forward. Her words came in spurts as she fought the mud.

"Gee. I wonder why."

"Except the Bogle," Declan said, apparently choosing to ignore my remark. "Oh, forget that. You said 'living'."

I looked back in time to catch his teasing smile. My breathing faltered. Would he talk to me again? "You said the Bogle isn't real."

"Not that I'm aware of." He shrugged, faltering when the ground tried keeping hold of his left foot. "But I've never looked for him either."

"Oh, stop." Ryann sounded exasperated, but snickered. "The Bogle isn't real. Don't listen to him."

I believed her, but couldn't help trembling as I surveyed my surroundings. Shapeless mounds of earth protruded from the ground with spindly stick arms and seemed to have eyes. *God, help me stop imagining things. Keep us safe.*

My mind returned to the daunting task, getting out of this place without falling into the mire.

The bog seemed endless. Wolf and Cahal took the lead. Ryann and I followed. Declan trudged along behind us with Pepin bringing up the rear, far behind.

Though Wolf was splattered with mud, his belly fur spiky with it, he had no trouble negotiating the terrain. He hopped back and forth from slimy felled trees to the sludge, skimming over its surface. He stopped every so often, turned our way, and waited for us to catch up. This time, he ran past us to Pepin and leaned forward, offering a ride.

Pepin, barefoot with his pant legs rolled above his knees, heaved a heavy sigh. "Thank you, friend."

The moment he straddled Wolf, they sank. Wolf's legs plunged into the muck past his hocks. He grunted and snorted as his head moved back and forth, tail flailing in the opposite direction. Pepin dismounted, but Wolf continued to struggle.

We all trudged back to help. Cahal stood in front of Wolf, Declan at his hindquarters. They reached into the squishy earth, grasped Wolf's middle, and tugged. Wolf came free with a wet sucking sound, like someone slurping saucy spaghetti.

Shoulders slumped, Pepin moved on. The rest of us slowed our pace.

Despite the slow going, my empathy for Pepin, and our depressing surroundings, I felt good—as though I'd shed a few hundred pounds. With the ever-tightening noose of anger and self-pity cast off, I looked forward more than ever to reconnecting with my mother, grateful for the opportunity to get to know her.

My childhood memories evoked sadness, but blaming everyone else was useless. My self-centeredness had poured out of my mouth, clouding my thoughts and vision. It must be shed for me to move on—to grow.

My biggest concern now was not Pepin, the mud, or the Bogle, but Declan. The way I had behaved with him was shameful. Part of me finally understood his desire to obey the ways of his clan over his own will. Another part of me still wanted him for myself. But after my experience in Saltinat, I had to live for something greater than myself as Declan attempted to do. I couldn't stand in his way.

I wanted to say something, to apologize, but I wasn't sure how. Despite his brief moment of speaking, he seemed impossible to approach. But I also didn't want to give him the wrong impression. Perhaps these were excuses, justifications to prevent further embarrassment. For now, it was better to say nothing.

He had joked with me. That was a good sign, and I didn't want to push it. Every once in a while he would turn our way, probably to check our progress. The first time he did, I smiled at him. His eyebrows pinched together, and he threw me a half-smile before turning to face forward.

Hours later, the trees grew closer together. The ground rose steeply and became more solid. *Thank you, God!* It felt strange, yet wonderful to walk freely, and I reveled in it. With my feet so mud-caked, I couldn't put my shoes back on, but I didn't care. The hard coating added a layer of protection from roots and pebbles.

Around midnight, under the glow of the waning crescent moon, we happened upon a hot spring. Though he grumbled, Cahal consented to us taking turns bathing. When my turn came, I sat at the edge and scrubbed my feet. Then I slipped from my clothes, lowered into the spring and sighed, content. The steam, barely visible, swirled and dissipated like little ghost tendrils. As warm water rolled around me, soothing my aching muscles, an impulsive hum of the Ariboslian hymn rose from my throat. I closed my eyes.

"Look what I found."

The unfamiliar voice yanked me from my momentary bliss. My eyes jerked open and turned in the voice's direction where a man stood. His menacing eyes fixed upon me. I wrapped my arms about myself.

His pale face illuminated in the moonlight as only a fasgadair's would. No matter what he was, his devilish smile as he admired me made me feel as if I bathed in a pool of snakes.

"What is that about your neck?"

I looked down. Without my high neckline to conceal it, Drochaid was partially in view. My stomach sank as he licked his protruding fangs.

"My, my. How pleased my master will be when I bring you to him."

I froze. My weapons were in the clearing with my friends. My clothes lay on the grassy bank beside the enemy. I couldn't fathom the humiliation of exposing my bare flesh to this smirking creature. Trapped like a bat in a sunlit room, knowing he could overtake me no matter which direction I ran, I studied him. Attempting to predict his intentions and next move. Would he walk into the water after me?

The familiar, sinking feeling began to sweep over me again. Now I recognized it. I was falling under the vampire's spell. My heart cried out. *God, help me!*

The answer didn't come from me, but it welled up within me. *Run!*

I jumped up and out of the water in a flash, which must've confused the vampire. I managed to run a few feet before its icy fingers snatched my neck. My feet lost contact with the ground.

Wolf's growl and gnashing teeth came from behind. The hand constricting my throat slipped. I stumbled back to the dirt. When I regained my footing, I ran without glancing back.

"She wears Drochaid."

I didn't chance a look back. I sensed more and bolted through the dense trees. I ran so fast I failed to notice the horizon.

I sailed straight off a cliff.

CHAPTER TWENTY-NINE

For a brief moment I felt as if I hung, suspended in midair. Then I fell. My stomach lurched, caught in my throat, and my body plummeted. The ground rushed toward me. I prayed, desperate, as I flailed my arms.

I sucked in my breath and held it. The advancing rocks stopped a few inches from my face, and then backed away in step with the beat of my arms flapping in the air. I exhaled with a whoosh. That was close. I'd almost become one with the jagged turf.

A gust of wind pushed me toward the chasm's opposite wall. I shifted my body to avoid another collision. My heart raced. What was going on?

I glanced about. My slender, lily-white arms were gone. Wide wings covered with dark spotted feathers replaced them. My chest tightened. I inhaled sharply through holes in my beak—beak? I turned into a bird?

So I was gachen enough to change into an animal after all. What kind of bird was I? I dipped my head to inspect my feet, catching a glimpse of yellow talons with sharp black nails and speckled underbelly before my body followed my gaze downward. I froze for a moment, unsure how to correct the unintentional dive. I righted my body and spread my wings, catching air like a parachute. So I was a bird of prey. I would have to let the others tell me which kind.

My friends...They could be in trouble. I needed to get back to them, but flying in the direction of my choosing proved difficult. The slightest change in the position of my tail feathers altered my direction and height. The breeze flung me about. It took maneuvering, but I understood how a baby bird learned by falling from the nest. Much of it came naturally, simply by wanting to stay afloat.

Free of the fissure, I soared above the tree line. Wind blasted past my feather-covered ear holes. The ground raced by. Everything beneath me shrunk as I glided out of reach of the tribulations below. Peace filled me.

My enhanced eyesight picked up the smallest detail from afar. Despite the speed of the ground rushing by, the trees blocking my view, and nothing but moonlight, I had no trouble spotting my companions. They stood over five headless bodies. I circled back, tucked my wings into a dive, and then released. What I wouldn't give to remain in this blissful state for eternity. But I had responsibilities, and my ever-increasing sense of duty wouldn't allow me to depart from them, so I dove.

I tried to land on Declan's shoulder, but misjudged my speed and the force necessary to slow my body. Instead, my flailing wing hit the back of his head and sent me spinning to the ground, hard. I ruffled the dust off my feathers.

Declan spoke to Wolf, but I didn't understand a word. *Man!* Drochaid must've fallen into the ravine when I transformed.

I attempted to talk, but my words came out a harsh "kak, kak, kak".

Ryann and Declan spoke to one another, throwing sideways glances in my direction. The inability to communicate infuriated me, as did trying to walk without sticking my claws in the ground. Frustration welled up and let loose with an ear piercing "kak!"

I had no choice but to return to the ravine for Drochaid. My audible complaints continued with an endless stream of "kak, kak, kak". I took a few leaps, flapped my wings, jumped, and fell to the ground in a heap. I gave it a couple more unsuccessful attempts before Cahal picked me up, folded my talons against my body, and heaved me into the air. Once released from his grip, I flapped like mad as I returned to the earth. Before crashing, I caught an air current and took off.

In the sky, calm swept over me again. I imagined it to be like an out-of-body experience, as if my spirit had shed its burden of flesh.

Fortunately, my bird-self had a keener sense of direction than my human side. I located the ravine with ease. Making out the amulet in the rubble proved simpler than expected. The jewel in the center glittered in the moonlight. I descended and settled on a boulder.

Drochaid was wedged between a few rocks. I pulled it free with my hooked beak, then clutched it in one foot, and hopped along gravel on the other. I failed to lift off. I hadn't dared swoop down and grab Drochaid in my talons without landing. What if I hurt myself on the rocks? No one was around to help.

I grasped the cord close to Drochaid, careful not to cut it with my tomial tooth. The stone dangled from one side, the cord on the other. Hoping it wouldn't trip me, I ran. An air current swept through, and I seized it, taking to the sky. The amulet in my mouth made me waver, so I let it go, swooped upon it as it fell, and grasped it in my talons.

Triumphant from my aerobatics, I returned to my friends. After dropping Drochaid on the ground, I landed and hopped to it. I flipped the amulet over my head with my neb and dragged it along behind me to my dress. Everyone stared as I shook my little bird head, bouncing from one foot to the next yelling, "kak, kak, kak!"

Ryann understood. She picked up my dress, motioned for me to follow, dropped it in a secluded area, and walked away.

How I changed back to human form, I haven't a clue. It seems I willed it so. When I emerged, everyone cheered.

"I guess you're enough gachen after all." Declan's lopsided grin and my euphoria sent my stomach into flips.

"A falcon." Cahal's face distorted into something resembling a smile, and he smacked me smartly on the back. "A good totem."

"It would be nice to be able to fly." Declan grinned.

A pang of guilt hit me. He longed for this to happen to him, fearing it never would, while I, someone who never expected to transform, surpassed him. How must that make him feel? "We're the same age. If it happened for me—"

Declan raised his eyebrows and looked into my eyes. "Fallon, I am happy for you."

I beamed, euphoric. "You should see everything from up there. It's amaz—" Shame settled upon me. I didn't know their totems. The pech didn't have a totem, and Declan hadn't found his yet. But I had no idea about Ryann and Cahal. Had I been so self-centered I never bothered learning about either of them?

I eyed Cahal and Ryann. "I don't know what your totems are. Why don't you ever change into them?"

"We are nothing as useful as a falcon." Ryann packed her satchel. "My totem is a puma."

"A puma? How's that not useful? They're fast...and fierce." I didn't give Ryann a chance to respond before turning to Cahal. "What about you?"

"Polar bear." He sheathed his weapon.

"There is no need to transfigure." Ryann threw her bag over her head so it draped across her body. "We can run faster in our totem form, but what would we do with you, Declan, and Pepin? Wolf or I can carry Pepin, but Cahal cannot carry both you and Declan. Besides, we are better fighters in human form. We don't spend enough time in our totem forms to become adequate fighters. Animals have instincts, but even they must practice their skills to improve them, as you have learned. But there is another problem you happened into."

I didn't hesitate. "Clothes."

"Aye. Our clothes fall off. Or in Cahal's case, rip."

"What if you packed the clothes and wore them on your back?

Now that I can change into a falcon, Cahal would only need to carry Declan." One glance at the tilt of Declan's head and the position of his eyebrows told me my suggestion didn't impress him.

"We could." Ryann sighed as if tiring of the conversation. "Or we could keep on as we have."

Cahal and Declan nodded in agreement.

Why did they want to keep going as is? In the air, I had the ability to scan the ground, providing more advance warning than Wolf. I could put a dress and Drochaid in a bag and tie it to my foot.

"Oh...and Fallon," Declan said. "I would appreciate it if you would not try to land on my shoulder again. Or anyone else."

"Why?"

"You do realize your talons are weapons, right?" He reached up to his shoulder. Dark, red stains spotted his tunic. He pulled his shirt neckline over his shoulder to show me the angry scratches and gaping hole my talons had left.

My vision grew fuzzy. He rushed toward me as I fell.

CHAPTER THIRTY

I traversed the rough terrain, dodging rocks and roots, climbing ever upward. At least the trees were larger and more spread apart here. I rubbed the egg on the side of my head. If only there was aspirin.

"How's your head," Declan asked.

"I'll be fine." I dropped my hand and attempted to ignore the pain.

"Sorry. I tried to get to you before you passed out."

"I know, Dec. You've apologized a million times already. It wasn't even your fault, unlike what I did to you." I dared look at his stained shirt and winced. "How's your shoulder."

"I'm well, Fal. Not to worry."

I caught his glance out of the corner of my eye and smiled. He called me Fal.

Pepin readjusted himself on Wolf's back and peered at the distant mountains. "Drochaid seems to be leading us to the City of Nica."

Cahal turned to us. "From here on, Wolf should lead. Ryann, Declan, stay on either side of Fallon. Pepin, pick a side, but stay close to her. I will follow. We must take care. Nica is an established fasgadair farm. We need to be cautious of anyone we meet, even gachen. Many are loyal to the fasgadair for their family's sake. Being under constant threat renders them untrustworthy."

"Farm?" I gulped.

"Remember what I told you?" Declan asked. "The fasgadair farm gachen for slave labor, blood, and more gachen."

Shivers coursed over me. "So what do we do?"

Ryann answered, "We must go where Drochaid leads."

"We must pray." Pepin swayed back and forth with Wolf's steps, a fistful of fur in each hand.

Declan glanced sideways at me. "Pepin is right. We must pray for safe passage and trust God. The amulet He provided has served us well. Though it goes against our judgment, we must continue."

"So we are walking straight into the lion's den?" I asked.

Cahal laughed. "Was that not the plan from the beginning?"

"What if it's time to let Drochaid go? Remember what I was told? I'm supposed to trust God, not the amulet." Even as I spoke the words, uncertainty overwhelmed me. Did I bring it up because I feared walking into a fasgadair's farm or because God was prompting me to stop following Drochaid? I wanted to trust God. I tried. I prayed for strength and faith. I waited to feel as though I had enough to carry me on. It hadn't come yet. I kept taking one step after the next, trying not to overthink it. Still, an echo of the warning resonated within the confines of my mind, "Trust in God, not this. It is only a tool to be disposed of when you are ready."

Ryann ended our debate. "Until God shows us it is time to stop following, we must continue."

WE FOUND a deep cavern to sleep in for the day. I tossed and turned as my mind raced. As much as I needed sleep, what if I dreamt? I didn't want to chance meeting Aodan. Not wanting to disturb my friends, I rose and sat close to the mouth of the cave.

I peered into the blue sky, wanting to escape into it and wondering what the coming days would bring, when shuffling feet startled me. I jerked toward it.

Declan sat beside me.

"Oh, it's you." I placed a hand over my chest. "You scared me." Breathing a sigh of relief, I laughed at myself for being so jumpy.

"Are you all right?"

"I don't know." On one hand, I was scared out of my mind. On the other, I was at peace. It didn't make sense. Part of me wanted to return to the safe, predictable life in my grandmother's house, despite my unhappiness there. Another part was thankful for the love I'd so longed for. The rest of me, the largest part, wanted to give back to God, to accomplish His purpose for me.

"We are close, Fallon. 'Tis natural to be afraid. But we need not be."

"I know, but it's not easy. I'm trying." I looked into his emerald eyes. What dwelled there now evoked comfort and fear—concern and something else.

"Fallon, I know I shouldn't..."

Uh oh. That didn't sound promising. With bated breath I contained myself, barely tolerating his lengthy pause.

"I think I'm falling in love with you."

My heart exploded in different directions. The goodness within me wanted to throttle the selfish side that danced joyfully. My gaze glued to his. I dredged every ounce of willpower to speak. "Declan—"

"I know, I know." He shook his head and stood. "Should I lie about my feelings for you? I want to be with you. I don't want to marry Maili."

"What about the clans? What about the promise your parents made?"

"What of it? It wasn't my decision. No one consulted me. Why should I suffer for it?" His voice grew louder.

I glanced in our sleeping friends' direction, afraid we might wake them.

Declan followed my gaze and dropped his voice. "What should I do, Fallon?" The pain in his eyes was as plain as the moon in the sky.

No. No. No. Not now. Not when I was finally ready to attempt to follow God's plan and be friends. What had I done? This wasn't Declan. It was me—the old me. I had poisoned him. My angry words spewed from his mouth. I didn't know how to fix the situation. I prayed silently before responding.

Though my heart broke to utter the words, though a part of me desperately wanted to grab his hand and run away with him, I said what I must. "You should do what God wants of you. Honor your parents." And then I spoke the final words not only to Declan, but also to God. "Please forgive me."

I MANAGED to avoid sleeping well enough to dream. We all headed out to complete our chores and eat before moving out. Declan was already gone. Somehow, he'd managed to sneak off without my notice.

As I gathered kindling for the fire, Ryann approached. "Are you well?"

Such an odd question. "I'm not sick, if that's what you mean."

"Nay." She smiled, her eyes full of concern. "You seem off. Declan is already gone, and you haven't asked about him."

"Oh that." I tried to wave it off, but my hands were full of twigs. I dropped a few in the process. I bent to pick them up. Then I stood and faced her. "Can I be honest with you?"

"Of course."

I walked to the fire pit we'd built, dropped the twigs inside, and sat. Ryann sat next to me and placed her larger sticks beside her.

"Declan wants to be with me."

"Oh." Ryann straightened. "Isn't that what you wanted?"

"I did, but...Things changed when I went to Saltinat. I understand why Declan wanted to obey his parents over his own desires. But I've made him abandon that. I made him like me...like I was."

"You no longer wish to be with him?"

"I do, but not like this. Not if it's not God's plan for us. I want him to be the person he was. Good."

"None of us are good, Fallon. Declan's heart is to do God's will. He's a bit sidetracked. It happens. But he'll return to it."

"You think so?"

"Aye." She smiled widely, put an arm around my shoulder, and squeezed. "I'm so proud of you, Fallon. You've come so far. God will bless it."

"So why is it so difficult?"

"Because life is difficult. But the closer you grow to God the easier it will be to deal with."

Relief swept over me. It felt so good to get this out, to talk to someone about it. "There's one more thing."

"What is it?"

I took a deep breath. "Aodan. I made a huge mistake. I tried finding out his plans and now I can't sleep. He knows about the link."

"Has he taken over your mind whilst you're awake, as Sully warned?" Ryann's voice sounded strained, like she was trying not to freak out.

"No. It's just in my dreams still."

She let out a heavy breath. "Good. If you see him again, run."

"It might be too late." I picked up a stick and drew in the dirt.

"It's never too late to turn things around. Just do your best. I'll pray for you. Just do one thing for me, will you?"

"What's that?"

"If you notice him take over your mind during the day, or if there are any gaps in your memory, will you please tell someone? We need to know if he's able to find out where we are, to be safe."

I nodded. "I will."

"Where's the fire?" Cahal tromped behind us with breakfast.

"Oh. Sorry." I looked at the kindling in the pit, and it ignited.

Ryann threw her larger sticks on top. Pepin emerged with a pile of sticks that concealed his face, blocking his vision. He dropped them next to the fire and brushed his hands.

Declan didn't return until the food was cooked. He grabbed a small piece and disappeared again. Pepin watched him as he went, and then eyed me for answers. I shrugged and turned to Ryann. She closed her eyes and nodded, silently letting me know it was okay.

God, thank you for her.

WE HIKED through a valley to the City of Nica. Declan avoided me for the thirteen thousandth time. Though he was supposed to flank me, he trailed behind. Far behind. I threw a quick glance at him. He faced the ground, scowling.

We kept to the woods, in sight of the river but avoiding the road. The fasgadair could be anywhere, not necessarily looking for us but happy for an unexpected treat nonetheless.

Wolf maneuvered through the thick branches with little difficulty since he no longer carried Pepin.

My night vision had improved, but some smaller limbs were tough to see. After being scratched on the cheek and poked in the eye, I kept my hands in front of my face to protect it.

Stopped in his tracks, Wolf raised his hackles, and lowered his head. A low growl radiated from his body.

I held my breath, listening. Not again.

Wolf took a few steps forward then looked at me as if warning me to stay back.

"Stop," I called out in a hushed voice.

Still facing me, Wolf nodded, and then dashed into the woods.

"Where is he going?" Ryann asked.

I shrugged. "I don't know. But he wants us to stay here."

"Is the arrow still pointing this way?" Cahal spoke over my shoulder.

I glanced at Drochaid. "Yes."

"We move on." Cahal walked ahead. "I will lead. Declan, follow behind."

Ryann, Declan, and Pepin resumed walking. I didn't.

Ryann placed a hand on my back, nudging me onward. "Wolf will catch up."

"No. We need to—"

Cahal growled, "Walk or I will carry you."

I followed.

True to Ryann's word, about an hour later, Wolf caught up. Someone with a pasty complexion that shone in the moonlight traveled behind him—a fasgadair.

CHAPTER THIRTY-ONE

"Aaaaaaarg!" Cahal snatched the battle-axe off his back and lunged at the bloodsucker. Wolf jumped between them, snarling. Cahal flung him aside.

"Stop!" I ran to place myself between the stranger and Cahal.

Cahal's chest heaved. His bulging eyes moved from me to the fasgadair before throwing Wolf a murderous look. "Traitor, I should have known better than to trust you." He returned his icy gaze to me. "Step aside or I will move you."

"Don't you dare touch him," I warned through clenched teeth.

"I mean it, Fallon."

"So do I. I told you. I trust Wolf. Besides, we might as well find out why the bloodsucker's here before we kill him." I softened my tone. "He hasn't made a move to kill us."

"If you stop Cahal, I'll do it for him." Declan raised a stake at the creature. "He's a demon, a monster. You don't reason with such beings. You rid the world of them." Never had I seen Declan's face so murderous. Was this always within him? Had I been the one to make this part of him surface?

"Please. He's outnumbered. Leave your weapons ready if you

204

must, but I have to know what he has to say for himself. If you feel you must kill him after he's spoken, I won't stop you."

Declan, his face still hideously disfigured with rage, lowered the stake to his side.

Cahal's face, devoid of emotion, left it impossible to ascertain his thoughts. He lowered his axe partway. "Tell us who you are and what you want before you die."

"I am what you say." The stranger spoke painfully slow, overemphasizing every syllable. "A fasgadair. But pleassss, understand. I am most ashamed. I thought it would save my family." He shook his head. "It does not matter what I thought. I am damned. I sold my soul to the Dark One. Unlessss..."

We all spoke at once, impatient. "Unless what?"

"About a fortnight ago, an angel spoke to me. He told me I would find a wolf in thesss woods tonight. I wasss to follow it, which I have done. He also said I would meet you."

Enlarged pupils surrounded by dull green with no whites stared at me, making me cold. I wrapped my arms around myself. When he tilted his head just right, catching the moon, they seemed to glow—yellow—like at the megalith. I gulped. "What do you want with me?"

"I am to tell you what I know about the celebration near Diabalta."

Our questions reverberated through the glen:

"Why are you telling me this?"

"Why would an angel visit you?"

"How do we know this isn't a trap?"

Cahal skewered Wolf with a stern stare. "Why would Wolf lead you to us?"

Only Pepin remained silent.

Our simultaneous questions seemed to baffle the fasgadair. His gaze shifted between us. "I only heard the angel's voiss. It will not appear to a creature such as I have become. Still, he came in response to my criesss to the One True God. I have denied my hunger and long for reconciliation with Him. If I do thisss, He will give me what I seek. I will not suffer for eternity in the underworld. That is His promisss."

The monster's serpentine hiss had the same effect on me as someone rubbing Styrofoam. But despite the fact that he made me want to vomit and had skimmed over Cahal's question, something inside told me he spoke truth. "I believe him."

Cahal growled. "Creatures such as this speak only lies! Give me one good reason why I should not strike him down."

"Something is telling me to listen to him, Cahal. We must listen," I pleaded. "He could be speaking the truth. Isn't everything possible with God? Might He use even a creature such as this for good?"

Cahal hesitated. His muscles twitched. Keeping a stern eye on the creeper, he lowered his arm. The weapon's massive head rested on the ground. Still, he did not return it to its sheath.

Declan muttered something under his breath. His knuckles around the stake went white.

I stepped closer to the vampire. "What is your name?"

"Le'Corenci."

Though the creature made me desire a scalding hot shower, I attempted to communicate with it. "What are you supposed to tell me?"

"In three daysss time, the fasgadair will hold a Gealach Lionadh to celebrate the new moon. It will be held in Ceasss Croi, a day'sss walk north of Diabalta."

"Lies!" Cahal's voice thundered. "I have never heard of this Ceas Croi."

"Not many know of it. Do not use the main entransss. There isss a secret entransss. But I cannot tell you where it isss. I do not know."

"But what of my mother?" I pressed. "Isn't she in Diabalta? My primary goal is to save her life."

"If you want to save her life, eliminate the fasgadair. At least kill Aodan. No one isss safe asss long asss the fasgadair continue to strengthen asss they have."

Something about conversing with this creature sucked the life out of me. Everything in my being screamed that such an ungodly being should not exist. It was an abomination.

I had difficulty digesting his message. I wanted to save my mother before venturing after my uncle. I hoped her presence would renew my strength. Now what? It seemed this entire journey consisted of nothing more than a maze with endless twists and turns. Just when I felt I began to make headway, I reached another dead end. I felt myself shutting down.

Le'Corenci must have sensed my withdrawal. He grew desperate, gazed deep into my eyes, and spoke more rapidly. "You *must* hear thisss! The angel said you are not to go to the City of Nica or Diabalta but straight to Ceasss Croi in your animal forms. If you continue northwest, you will have the cover of woodsss and will make it in time for the Gealach Lionadh. It is imperative you do exactly asss the angel instructed. Do you understand? Go no further toward Nica."

I nodded.

"One more thing. Escape through the secret passagesss. Trust those who will show you."

I nodded again, though his words barely penetrated the haze surrounding me. I needed sleep. I didn't listen to the rest of the conversation, barely registering when Le'Corenci returned to wher-ever he'd come from. I lost myself in my own mind—a jumbled web of confusion.

"Fallon." Cahal's sharp voice jolted me. "We must discuss this before moving on."

Declan got in my face. "Are we to follow Drochaid or that...that *thing?*"

I glanced at each of my friends in turn. All eyes were on me. Was this my decision? I groaned. "We go to Ceas Croi." The words escaped as if of their own accord, but it was right. I felt sure of it.

All but Wolf and I began talking at once.

Ryann shook her head and approached me. "Where does Drochaid point now?"

In my haze, I studied Drochaid. Dark. Nothing glowed. "It shows nothing."

"Does that mean we're to stay here?" Ryann asked.

My mind cleared slightly. "It means Drochaid isn't going to give us a specific answer. I'm going to Ceas Croi. Please don't make me try to find it without you," I said, more certain each time I stated that we must go.

"Le'Corenci lies. 'Tis a trap," Cahal said.

"A trap?" I asked. "Why would he bother? If Aodan's behind it, he knows where we are. Wouldn't it have been easier for him to send an army of fasgadair to attack us?"

Cahal shook his head. Feet spread, arms folded, he looked as immobile as a tree. "He might be leading us into an ambush."

"Cahal is right. We cannot trust Le'Corenci." Declan's eyes wouldn't meet mine. "Drochaid has not led us astray. If it's not showing us what to do, we must wait."

"No," I stated firmly. "When I was in Saltinat, He told me not to put faith in Drochaid but in here." I placed my hand on my heart.

"We are not to put our faith in ourselves!" Cahal erupted.

"No, not ourselves." *God, help me say this in a way that makes sense.* "We're to have faith in God and the wisdom He places within us, His believers. It does not come from us, but Him."

I didn't know how or why something as evil as Le'Corenci came under the reign of the God I'd come to know and love. It was further beyond my ability to fathom why He would choose to use such a creature. Then again, why did He choose me? However unlikely, I knew God used Le'Corenci as part of His plan. "I truly believe—no, I *know* Le'Corenci spoke the truth. We must go north-west, as the angel advised him. And we should go in our totem forms. Wolf can carry Pepin, and Cahal can carry Declan." I turned to Cahal. "I assume as a polar bear you could run with Declan on your back."

"We are weaker in our totem forms. And he will slow me down."

"But we will be faster, and I can alert you to danger on the ground. Even a polar bear with a man on his back is faster than a man, right?"

He nodded.

"Then it's settled."

"Nay, it's not." Ryann stepped forward. "What about getting into Ceas Croi? That thing said he didn't know the location of the secret entrance."

"I do." Pepin stepped forward. "Ceas Croi belonged to the pech. We abandoned it long ago." His stout shoulders shrugged. "Its identity was compromised. As you saw with the Tower of Galore, since the gachen arrived here, we've attempted to live in secret."

Cahal smacked Pepin on the back, knocking him forward. "I knew you would come in handy, little one!"

From the sideways glance Pepin threw Cahal, he clearly didn't appreciate the nickname. Still, he smiled.

We journeyed on until daybreak. Cahal found an area for us to sleep, concealed by shrubs with a ceiling of leafy tree branches. I moved in a daze as Cahal grumbled about being ripe for an attack, letting a fasgadair go, walking into a trap, and other complaints I couldn't quite make out. Never had I heard him speak so much, to himself or anyone else. No one attempted to calm him. I lay down, confident we'd made the right decision, but praying for God to strengthen and unite us, afraid to sleep. I didn't want to face Aodan, but I'd already given him a foothold. He would be there if I dreamed. I fought to keep my eyes open as I peered through the leaves to the moon.

The lights swirled, and I ran with all the energy I could summon away from it, toward the woman on the sandy beach. I didn't look back. As usual, the woman stayed the same distance away. Certain the swirling lights were expanding behind me, but afraid to look, I expected to hear Aodan's voice. But I didn't.

Another voice called to me from the opposite direction. "Well done, child."

I turned to the man from Saltinat, his white robe billowing in the breeze. "You are right to trust in God, not Drochaid. It is only a tool. Follow my prompting within you."

I wanted to run toward him and never leave, but I woke. Flying toads croaked in the trees above me. Peace swept over me like a breeze. Never had I woken feeling so refreshed, as though I had been in His presence. It gave me the strength to do what needed to be done, though I didn't comprehend what that was. I knew that all who were able must go to Ceas Croi in their animal form.

We traveled for two more nights without much trouble. With each passing day I grew more confident we'd made the right call. An intangible calm about the decision made it feel right. If the fasgadair were looking for us, they probably searched the City of Nica or Diabalta. And they'd be looking for a girl with an amulet, not a falcon. If an ambush awaited us in Ceas Croi, it must be part of God's plan.

Declan now only spoke to me when pertinent to the mission. An invisible wall had grown up between us, with neither of us able to penetrate it. So we avoided one another. It was probably for the best. My soaring high above him simplified the task.

On the third day, before the sun rose and we sought a suitable place to camp, I spied movement ahead of my friends on the ground. In the moonlight, I made out at least five human forms. Although they might not be fasgadair, I didn't take any chances. Circling overhead I squealed, "Kak, kak, kak!" repeatedly at the top of my lungs.

At my cry, all movement on the ground paused. Then everyone looked up before quickening their pace. They would be upon each other within moments. I dove, swooping over the possible attackers to determine who they were.

Fasgadair.

Remembering what Declan said about my talons being weapons, I took the opportunity to test them. After a quick, silent prayer, I landed on a fasgadair's head. With little effort, I squeezed my yellow, scaly, digits and the black nails pierced its scalp. The creature bellowed. As he attempted to grab me, I released, flailing my wings, retreating to the safety of the skies.

Chaos reigned below. The two bands had met while I fled to the air. On my return, I found one fasgadair down. Its body turned to dust and blew away in the wind. Wolf lunged at another's throat.

Cahal, still in polar bear form, standing on hind legs at a height of twelve feet or so, towered over a fasgadair. A deep, guttural sound emanated from his massive belly and projected from his snout.

Ryann, a puma, pounced on another bloodsucker. Her snarling scream and sharp fangs sent shivers up my puny spine.

Declan attacked another with his sword as Pepin, armed with my dagger, hacked away at its hamstrings from behind.

Another vampire sprang toward Cahal's back. I swooped down, piercing its scalp with my talons as before. This time, the middle talon on my right foot slid into something squishy, like a toothpick pierces a grape. I looked down at the eyeball on my claw.

Howling in pain, the creature sought to grab my wings.

After releasing my grip, I flapped with every ounce of my being, desperate to reach refuge in the air. Remembering from Gnuatthara that the fasgadair don't like loud, earsplitting noise, I screeched at the top of my lungs. As the creature grasped my right wing, and I feared he might rip it off, a menacing snarl rang from Ryann. The moment she liberated my wing from the vampire's grip, I took to the sky. From safety, I watched Ryann, on top of the fasgadair, bite its throat.

Howling, the fasgadair grasped Ryann's head and, with the flick of a wrist, twisted it.

Ryann's body fell limp.

CHAPTER THIRTY-TWO

"N o!" I screamed, though a kak came out of my beak.
The fasgadair didn't wait. It took off like a hummingbird through the woods.

I flew after it, hatred coursing through my feathered form. What I would do if I caught up to it, I didn't know. But I had to try. I kept it in sight for a couple of seconds before it disappeared. I took a few swipes across the horizon, scanning the ground for movement before giving up.

Circling my friends, I found the fallen fasgadair, some closer to their heads than others.

Everyone gathered around Ryann's lifeless puma form.

I dropped to a private spot on the ground to change. Upon landing, I nearly fainted when I found the fasgadair's eyeball still skewered on my talon. I tried to shake it off, but it stuck. Disgusted, yet eager to check on Ryann, I plucked it off with my bill and returned to my human form.

"Is she all right?" I already knew the answer, but a tiny piece of me wouldn't let go of the possibility a miracle had occurred.

Declan and Pepin parted to make room.

"Ryann is dead, Fallon." The pain in Declan's eyes pierced my heart.

"No! She can't be!"

"She's in a better place now." Cahal wiped his brow. "But we must bury her before we move on."

"This can't be. She can't die. She protected me. She has more right to live than I. She *can't* have died protecting me." I tried to run despite the tears blurring my vision. Declan grabbed me, but I squirmed and pried his arms off me. Once free from his grip, I ran into the thick woods, stopping only after tripping over a root.

"Why? Why? Why!" I yelled. "Why bring her into my life? Why get me to trust her just to take her away? You take everyone from me!"

Fury burned within me. I grabbed a branch and slammed it against a tree. I was a picture of ladylike grace—in an elegant gown, face twisted in rage, pounding on a tree with its own arm. I didn't care how I appeared. I whacked the tree until the stick broke to a useless nub. I flung the remains and slumped to the ground, sobbing.

Why did I feel so alone? I wasn't. Not anymore. God was with me, out of reach and silent, but present nonetheless.

"God, help me," I pleaded. "Take this anger from me, please."

Head buried between my knees, I sensed His presence. I imagined His arm around me. The anger subsided, replaced by profound sadness.

I leaned against the tree I'd taken my frustrations out on. Everyone around me died. This time, I'd been here to stop it but failed.

Am I being punished? Is everyone I care about destined to die?

Ryann's death was my fault. I'd been the one to suggest—no, *order* everyone into totem form. She told me they weren't adequate fighters as animals. If I'd been in human form, I might've been able to set the bloodsucker on fire. Why hadn't I thought of that? I might as well have been the one to twist her neck. I was as guilty.

I wanted nothing more than to kill the one-eyed fasgadair who had done this to her. She sacrificed herself for me, and for what? What was I doing here but leading my friends to their deaths?

Face in my palms, I choked on my sobs. "I'm so sorry. Forgive me. Forgive me for killing Ryann. I didn't mean to let it happen. Forgive me for wanting to murder the good-for-nothing monster. I can't help it. Why, God? Why did you choose me for this? I'm worthless. I'm—"

A surge of energy rushed through me. I took a deep breath and stared at the sky. Who was I to question God? Who was I to suggest to *my* Creator that I'm not capable of *His* purpose for me?

Fresh tears flowed. "I'm sorry, God. I don't mean to insult You. But how do I do what You're asking of me without losing more lives? I don't want anyone else to die because of me."

As I sat crying, wishing Ryann were here to talk to, pouring out the jumbled contents of my heart to an unseen Being, the answer came: go to Ceas Croi alone.

The solution itself didn't bring comfort, and I had no idea what I'd do when I arrived. But it was a definitive answer. And it hadn't come from me. I would never have suggested it. If it had been from me, I would question it. Instead, it strengthened me to face whatever lay ahead.

Once I'd calmed down and washed my face in the stream, I returned to my companions. Declan placed an arm around my shoulder and led me to a hole they'd dug. Ryann, in puma form, lay at the bottom. A lump formed in my throat. I wanted to see her face.

I will make it up to you, Ryann. Your death won't be for nothing.

Before covering her with earth, Declan spoke a few words. "Ryann lived a good, loving, selfless life in service to the One True God. She is now trouble free, celebrating her homecoming with Him and loved ones who have already joined Him. God, we are thankful Ryann is now with You. We will meet again when our time comes."

In a daze, I said goodbye and helped place the dirt over her. Dirt piled on top of the unfamiliar feline. The last piece of Ryann I would ever see was the pointy, sandy-brown ear. I'd been cheated. This cat wasn't her.

We made camp in silence, eyes downcast. Wolf, Cahal, and Declan hunted though I doubted anyone wanted to eat. It seemed we needed the normalcy more than anything. Pepin and I gathered firewood and kindling. As I picked up wood, despite my efforts to the contrary, my mind kept wandering to Ryann.

I would leave before my companions woke. It was the only way to ditch them. In bird form, I should be able to get to the entrance in the cliffs without difficulty. For now, I had to take advantage of my time alone with Pepin.

"So, Pepin. You say you know where the entrance to Ceas Croi is?" I shook my head over my pathetic attempt at being nonchalant.

"Mmmhmmm." He piled his short arms with sticks. He seemed too preoccupied with his grief to notice my pitiful act.

I relaxed a little. "Where is it?" I viewed him askance as I loaded up with kindling.

"Ceas Croi is a mountain range. The pech hollowed out tunnels, rooms, great gathering halls. I've never seen it, but the pech still talk about how wonderful it was..." He walked down into a gully full of broken limbs.

I followed. "I'm sure it was great, Pepin. But how do you get in?"

"It is full of mysteries, secret passageways, boulders to slow pursuers. I'm sure the fasgadair haven't learned all its secrets."

I shook my head. I definitely didn't need to concern myself with his suspecting my plan. I've never seen him so out of it. My gut twisted. I couldn't allow myself to think about what had put him in that state. "That's nice, Pepin. But where *is* the secret entrance?"

"A road climbs halfway up the tallest peak. At the end of the road is the main entrance. Guarded, I'm sure. Above it, on a ledge, there is what appears to be solid rock, but it is not. You can walk straight through." He tugged on a limb then dropped his armload to work it loose.

"What about the secret passageways?"

He yanked the stick free and broke it over his knee in thirds. "Hmmm?"

"Secret passageways. You said Ceas Croi has secret passageways."

His eyes, aimed at me, glazed over, looking through me.

"Pepin?"

His eyes cleared. "Ah, yes. Secret passageways..." He added three new sticks to his pile and gathered them.

"Yes." Something crunched behind me. I peeked over my shoulder to make sure we were still alone. "You and Le'Corenci said there were secret passageways. Do you know anything about them?"

Pepin shook his head and resumed his search. "No. I've never been to Ceas Croi. I hear it's wonderful though. The pech still talk about it..."

"You don't say." I gave up on getting anything more from him and added a couple extra twigs to my pile in silence.

CHAPTER THIRTY-THREE

Though my eyes drooped, I fought falling asleep. I needed to leave before they woke. Long after the others' breathing slowed, I glanced at Cahal. He sat facing the opposite direction, propped against a tree, keeping watch. I couldn't take my things, just a small cinch sack to carry my dress and Drochaid when I transfigured. I couldn't write a note in the dirt. They wouldn't be able to translate my writing. I sighed. Oh well. Hopefully they'd figure it out and not spend an eternity searching the nearby woods for me.

I grabbed the sack and, careful to step lightly, attempted to sneak away.

"Where are you going?" Cahal's hushed voice stopped me.

I turned to him, keeping the sack behind me so as not to raise his suspicions. "Umm, bathroom." They no longer argued that there was no room with a bath in the wilderness and understood my ultimate meaning. I almost added, "I'll be right back," but that would surely make me a liar. As it was, I'd have to take care of business before leaving. But perhaps I was still a liar by omission, for failing to tell him where I would be going after. It couldn't be helped. I had to do what I had to do.

Cahal eyed me suspiciously. What was taking him so long? He had no reason not to believe me. I'd left everything else behind. My bedding still lay mussed up on the ground.

Cahal finally waved me off. I headed deeper into the woods. When enough distance and trees separated us, I placed my dress and Drochaid in my pouch, and then considered my shoes. Ryann had carried them for me before. Though thin, they added too much weight and bulk. I would have to leave them and go barefoot when I returned to human form. Perhaps it was better this way. If they found the shoes, maybe they'd figure out what I'd done.

I flew off, taking to heights I'd never gone, staying above the cloud line for better invisibility. I imagined it must be like soaring above barren, frozen tundra. The wind pushed me forward, making travel easy. A few flaps, catch the wind, and coast. And repeat.

It didn't take long to find Ceas Croi. The peak jutted above the cloud line like an iceberg in the sea. I flew straight to the summit and landed on the rocky surface, the wind blasting me. Unable to see through the clouds, I pushed off, attempting to keep the mountain in view and not crash into it in the whiteout conditions.

Once I found my way through, I alighted on a lifeless branch. Finding nothing resembling an entrance below, I hopped off and flew to the opposite side. A road and a main entrance stood about halfway down the mountain. Didn't Pepin say the secret entryway was above the main entrance? Using my acute bird's-eye vision, I spotted a thin ledge. It wound around the mountain and disappeared about four hundred feet above the main entrance. It seemed like a path the pech might've used long ago.

Close to the mountain, I felt certain no one would spot me. The ledge lay right beneath me. I tucked myself into a dive and spread my wings in time for a smooth landing.

On the ledge, out of sight from those who might wander about below, I pulled Drochaid from my sack, taking care not to kick it over the edge. Unsure if I should keep using it, I prayed it might show me what I needed to know right now.

The arrow pointing into the mountain glowed. I danced, hopping from one foot to the other in a circle, unable to contain my excitement. So I wasn't being stupid after all. Was this the entrance Pepin spoke of? Could it be this easy?

I bounded over and pecked at the rock, stumbling as my beak went straight through. The rock was a mirage. I silently thanked Pepin and praised God while I returned to Drochaid and pushed it to the edge of the sack. I stuck my talons inside the pouch to hold down the bottom, pulled the top with my beak to open it, and pushed Drochaid in with my other foot. It took work and much fumbling, but I got it in the sack and dragged it along. Unable to see what lay before me other than solid rock, I inched forward with care.

On the other side of the wall, darkness engulfed me. A musty odor filled my nares. I stilled, attempting to check for movement with my other senses, to ensure I was alone. But as a falcon, my eyesight was my greatest strength.

I changed into human form and bumped my head. "Ow!" I covered my mouth. What if something else was in here and I'd just alerted it to my presence? I quieted, hoping my eyes would adjust. But that would require some amount of light. There was none. Never had I experienced such complete darkness, complete blindness. I reached out and groped the walls. Panic welled within me. What if I couldn't find anything? What if I couldn't find my way out? I touched something on the wall. Oh please be something useful! My fingers followed the protrusion. A candle? I circled it with my fingers, gliding toward the top. Yes, a wick!

But I couldn't see it. How would I light it?

"Please, God. Please." I begged softly. "I need light."

Flames erupted from the tips of candles in wall sconces. I held my breath, listening for signs of life, waiting for my eyes to adjust.

Firelight flickered. Did I do that? I shook my head. It didn't matter. I'd asked God, and He delivered. It came from Him. It's all from Him. *Thank You.*

I appeared to be in some type of tower. Candles lined the curved wall. Steps led to where I now stooped under the low roof. There was nothing else and nowhere to go but down.

I threw Drochaid and my dress on and descended the stairs. The glowing arrow pointed down the stairs. The smooth stone chilled my bare feet. Though I'd have preferred my shoes' protection, walking in silence was easier without them.

The staircase wound down forever. Sconces positioned every few feet on the wall cast flickering light. Constant fear of someone—or something—waiting around the perpetual bend slowed my progress. Then the stairs came to an abrupt end. No hallway, landing, another flight of stairs—nothing but a wall. I lifted my hand to the rock in my way. Rather than landing on the surface, my fingers slid right through.

Please let me make it through unseen.

Rather than step through and face whatever might be on the other side of the wall, I poked my head through, slowly. A hallway lay on the other side, lined with the same wall sconces, all lit. I checked both directions. It was abandoned—for the moment.

I breathed a sigh of relief and stepped through. Drochaid pointed to the right. Out in the open, I felt so exposed. The sconces were lit so this hallway was used. What if something found me? No. I couldn't worry about such things. Drochaid led the way. God was with me. This was His plan. I must trust Him.

The higher ceiling allowed me to walk without hunching over. I made it to the end of the hallway and peeked around the corner at another deserted passageway.

I didn't move toward it. My heart hammered in my chest. If I continued through this maze of hallways, I'd never find my way back. But then perhaps I wasn't meant to come back this way. *Trust, Fallon. Trust.*

I checked the amulet, held my breath, and dashed down the next hallway. I continued through an endless maze, panic increasing with each turn. I'd never find my way back. I stopped to catch my breath.

What was I doing here?

How stupid could I be? I had no plan other than to spare my friends whatever fate was sure to befall me—a fate Ryann already succumbed to. But how? What was I here for if not to give myself over to my uncle? It killed me to keep running around in the enemy's lair, fearing discovery. I was strangely tempted to yell at the top of my lungs and get my capture over with.

Marching feet advanced from the opposite end of the hallway, and I abandoned that foolish idea. I raced away down a long corridor, another flight of stairs, yet another hallway, and into a larger room.

Across from where I'd entered, a window in the wall allowed me to peer into another, much larger room. Long, stone tables and benches filled the lower area. Two rows of balconies, like the one I stood in, lined the four walls. A chandelier filled with hundreds of unlit candles hung from the ceiling's high center. The light in the dim room came from more wall sconces.

In my flight, I'd failed to consult Drochaid. I checked now. No glow. Nothing. Drochaid was dull.

I faced the heavens and mouthed, "Now what?"

Yet again, the answer came: *Give up.*

Though, deep-down, I hoped for something more miraculous, I'd expected as much. I was here, where I intentionally set out to be. How could I be content to stand in the shadows and avoid discovery now? I would never find my way back through the maze. A rock mirage hid the stairway leading to the tower. It would be impossible to find.

Perhaps my mission was to die. Wasn't I the one my uncle wanted? He hadn't begun to torture his sister until learning of me. Perhaps he would trade her for me.

No, I was already here. Why would he release her now?

I had to stop driving myself crazy overthinking this. God brought me here. He wanted me here. The rest didn't matter.

Resigned to await capture rather than seek it out, I sat on a cold, stone bench attached to the wall furthest from the opening. The stone sucked out whatever heat remained in me, and my mind wandered to territories best left uncharted. In a matter of minutes, images of torturous deaths plagued me while, in reality, I could only die once. Still, I couldn't help but mull over which was most distressing: the waiting or the dying?

My body was a bundle of nervous energy. My heart pounded like a drummer in a metal band. My hands clenched in a vain attempt to cease their shaking. My feet shook. Blood drained from my brain and flowed to my extremities in hopes that my body might do something... anything...other than remain seated. But I had to.

I must not allow my animalistic instincts to take over. I must stay in control. I must simply stay...despite what awaits me.

CHAPTER THIRTY-FOUR

I shivered, waiting for the fasgadair to capture me and lead me to
my demise. The wait was torture. I attempted to focus on those
I'd grown to love, the reason I was here. But my mind kept wandering
back to whatever horrendous end surely awaited me. Shuffling feet
startled me. My heartbeat quickened. I jumped to my feet. The thudding of my heart and the approaching footsteps grew louder. The
electric stench unique to the fasgadair filled my nose. An infinite
procession of them in long, hooded black cloaks filed into the auditorium, stuffing the lower level first, then the balconies.

I held my breath as the first fasgadair to enter my balcony locked
eyes with mine. They were like Le'Corenci's, but a sharper green
surrounded the engorged pupil. He partially blocked the other's path.
They filed in around and stopped also. Blobs of brown cloaks and
white faces lined my periphery, temporarily immobilized, their dead
eyes trained on me, but I couldn't tear my gaze from the first one. He
stood a head above the crowd still pouring in behind him.

"Who are you?" His icy, clipped words sent shivers down my
spine and my arms.

I released the trapped breath. With shaky hands, I revealed Drochaid.

The closest two blood guzzlers stared, wide-eyed. A few behind bumped into them. Random exclamations rang out behind them in confusion as to why the procession had stopped advancing.

The one who spoke before said, "Drochaid."

Murmurs erupted among them. Random exclamations including "Drochaid", "Fallon" and "prophecy" rose above the otherwise unintelligible muttering.

"Is she—?" asked the blue-eyed monster next to him.

"Aye."

The two who spoke moved toward me, each snatching an arm. Once in their frigid grasp, I was spun around and dragged through the crowd. The freakish onlookers surrounding me quieted, watching as I passed, but one further back in the crowd muttered something about a "missing eye". Was it talking about me? About the vampire I'd maimed? The bloodsucker responsible for Ryann's death?

I searched the grotesque faces, the nearly black eyes for a missing one. Murderous anger welled up within me. Somehow, the one-eyed vamp would pay for what he'd done.

We broke past the mutants and moved at incredible speed through the empty halls. My anger dissipated, and my gut churned as I fought against their ever-tightening grasps, my eyes darting everywhere. What had I done? Where were they taking me? What would they do to me once we got there?

God, help me!

A sense of being where I belonged washed over me. My mind quieted; my body relaxed. I wasn't alone. What was the worst they could do to me? Kill me? Then I'd be in paradise with my creator. Wasn't that actually the best-case scenario?

But how would I die? How badly would it hurt?

I shook my head and focused on my God, those I loved, even as I was pulled roughly by creatures who wanted me dead.

"What shall we do with her, my lord?" the short one asked. His spine bent in submission to the other, who stood erect.

"We shall take her to the slave chamber and advise Aodan. She shall not be harmed until Aodan's wishes are made clear."

"I understand, my lord."

I half wished they'd put an end to my apprehension.

They have my body, God. But You have my soul. I'm in Your hands. I trust You.

My captors continued to yank me down dark, winding halls and stairways, much like those I'd already traversed, but we continued downward when we reached stairways. After the twentieth or so descent my ears popped. We came to a guard blocking a door and stopped. The guard rose, threw open the lock with a clang, and stepped aside. They shoved me in and slammed the door behind me. The lock clicked as it slid back into place.

A pungent stench of decay and human waste hit me. I struggled to breathe. Tears sprang to my burning eyes. Gagging, I stared into the gloom—many others shared my cell.

Skeletal beings sat in the shadows around the barren stone room, huddled together on heaps of hay, staring at me. None of them made a move.

The raspy sound of coughs and labored breathing joined my pounding heart. I strained my eyes to determine who they were, but didn't dare move closer. Were they fasgadair, hungry for blood? Their pale faces and the whites of their eyes reflected the limited light.

I took a deep breath. Against the far wall lay pools of what could only be excrement and urine. Ah, now I understood why everyone huddled together. Even as my brain made the connection, I spun toward the door and emptied the meager contents of my stomach.

Once I'd recovered, a boy with matted, brown hair and sunken cheeks pulled himself off his moldy bed with great effort and approached me. His arm outstretched in my direction, moving at a zombie pace.

I inhaled through my mouth to avoid the stench and backed against the locked door.

"Is that...?" The boy spoke aloud, but not to me. His eyes were not on mine but on my neck. He reached to grab me.

He couldn't be a vampire. His eyes were human. Dirty and emaciated, but human. Or did zombies exist in this realm too? I held my breath as he approached, unsure what he wanted or how to respond.

He didn't grab me but the amulet. "It is." Hopefulness infused his raspy voice.

I slumped against the door, releasing the breath I'd been holding.

The boy called to the others. "She wears Drochaid." His hoarse voice sounded as though it must be painful to speak.

Several gasps emerged. One woman stood. Her movements slow and careful, she made her way toward me. Her matted blonde hair formed dreadlocks in places. Beyond the grime on her face, her eyes resembled my grandmother's and mine and, despite the lack of energy, shone with excitement and fear. "Fallon?"

"Yes?" My voice was barely audible. Could it be?

"I am called Cataleen. Do you know who I am?"

I nodded. "My mother."

She opened her arms. I closed the distance between us and hugged her. Her body trembled. Two drips landed on my shoulder.

I had so longed for this moment, envisioning it in so many scenarios, none under circumstances such as this. Now that it had arrived, it seemed surreal. I'd hoped her presence would evoke repressed memories. It didn't. We were strangers connected by lineage and nothing more. I awkwardly held a woman who, I assumed, cried for the baby she'd lost. Still, being united with her thrilled me, though it saddened me we would not have the opportunity to get to know one another. Not now anyway. Perhaps later...in heaven.

I backed out of her embrace to look in her eyes. "I must get you out of here."

"No. I must get *you* out of here. How did you wind up in here? You are meant to save us."

"I know." I dropped my head. What had I done? Why had I abandoned my protectors to come here on my own? And for what? To get myself captured and fail all of us? As soon as the doubt and despair crept over me, they dissipated, replaced by the certainty that had brought me here.

I couldn't tell her I'd come here to die. "It doesn't make sense, but I believe this is where I need to be right now. Have faith." My own words shocked me, and yet to the core of my being I knew they were true. A renewed confidence and strength beyond my own capacity came over me.

My mother grasped my arm. Horror froze on her face. "He knows you're here. He's coming for you."

The boy who'd been standing near me returned to his group. They huddled tighter together as if their closeness would make their individual bodies an indistinguishable wall.

Cataleen's eyes changed. Arrogant glee replaced the joy and fear. She held herself straighter and circled me, walking with a confident swagger. She laughed. "Aye, he knows you're here. What kept you, niece?"

I backed against the wall, my stomach in my throat, not breathing. So this is what the full-blown mind-link looked like? Aodan took her over completely? Thank God it hadn't come to that for me. Yet.

My uncle in my mother's body approached me. The sickening delight in my mother's eyes made me want to dry heave since I'd already lost my last meal. He reached out her hand toward my face. Gentle fingers pushed back stray strands of hair. The spot where he touched my forehead burned. I desperately wished to brush the icky feeling he'd left away.

Cataleen's hand hovered before my face. Her eyes peered into mine. But it wasn't her staring into my soul, it was Aodan—studying me as if he could know everything about me with just a look.

He stepped back. His lips, Cataleen's lips, twitched in the

corners and grew wide like the Grinch when he got a grinchy idea. Everything within me shuddered in response. What sick thoughts were transpiring in his mind?

Footsteps approached and the latch rattled, distracting. He glanced at the door then returned his attention to me. "My guards are right on time. I leave you now, for but a moment. I look forward to meeting you in the flesh...my flesh." He grinned wickedly.

Cataleen's body slumped. She picked her head back up. Fear filled her eyes. "He was here."

The door flew open.

I nodded. "That's why I'm here. It will be okay."

A couple of fasgadair clamped their icy hands on my arms. They didn't appear to be the same ones who'd dumped me here. At least, one of them wasn't. They were closer to the same height. But who could tell with those cloaks and those similar, undead eyes?

As they dragged me out the door, one said, "Our master wishes to see you."

I summoned up the most confident face I could and gazed at my mother to give her hope before the door closed between us.

CHAPTER THIRTY-FIVE

Yet again they pulled me through a maze of halls and staircases. This time we headed higher up. Again, my ears popped with the change in altitude. Even if I miraculously managed to escape these bloodsuckers, how would I ever get out of here?

We slowed our pace outside massive double doors. Guards opened them as we approached. We entered a gaudy room bedecked in gold and red velvet: the room from one of my visions. The giant tapestry of a bloody war hung on the far wall. A vampire, dressed in a black shirt and pants resembling something from my realm rather than the cloaks of the clones, lounged on a fainting couch. My captors threw me at his feet.

"As you requested, my lord."

Without rising, the fasgadair I assumed to be Aodan waved his hand. The two underlings bowed and retreated, closing the doors behind them.

Aodan went from completely relaxed to sitting upright, leaning forward eagerly. My eyes hadn't even perceived the motion. He was just in one position, then the other.

That grin. That evil, grinchy grin spread across his face. "Please. Have a seat." He motioned me to a similar chair opposite him.

I did so while keeping a wary eye on him.

Despite his pasty skin, when he closed his eyes, he was handsome with sandy blond hair. A bit of my grandmother's features—full lips and high cheekbones, flattered his masculine face. Not an imperfection, wrinkle, or other sign of aging existed. Flawless...aside from that pesky demon problem.

When he opened his eyes, a chill ran through my soul. Like Le'Corenci and all the other fasgadair, his enlarged pupils and irises took over the whole eye, leaving no room for whites. But Aodan's irises were bright purple, as if they'd been like mine before fasgadair blood infected his veins. He chuckled as his gaze roamed my body.

My cheeks warmed. I fought to keep my clenched fists by my side.

"Well, it appears we have captured the infamous Fallon at last." His eyes traveled to my feet and back to my face again. "You're not what I expected. You're just a little girl—puny." He chuckled and aimed his gaze at the heavens. "Is this who the Almighty brought forth to save the gachen?" His laughter grew louder, shaking his entire body.

I said nothing. I was no one to be feared, but the One who sent me was a power none of us could fathom. I didn't bother saying so. I glanced at him with feigned disinterest.

"You surprise me." He stood and walked around my seat as if he were on a Sunday stroll, arms clasped behind his back, gazing at grotesque battle paintings in golden frames on the walls.

Though I was interested in this uncle of mine and curious as to how I surprised him, I didn't dare give him the satisfaction. I remained silent.

"You came all this way to save people you don't even know." He motioned toward me as he appeared on the other side of the couch. "And look at you...The fate of the gachen rests with you? You're weak and small. You can't stand against me."

No but my God can. Even as the words coursed through me, I refused to take his bait and speak, confident my silence weakened him somehow.

"Have you nothing to say?" He sat down and crossed his legs.

I stared in his direction, but through him, as though he didn't exist.

"You're not in the least bit curious about your uncle?" He laughed again. This time, a nervous quality infused it. He waited, his creepy eyes on me. "But we had such a wonderful time getting to know each other in your dreams."

He sighed. "I'll admit. I'm impressed you somehow kept me from breaking through the mind-link. You confounded my soldiers. Even Morrigan with all her magic. She expected you in Diabalta. However did you manage to fool her?" He clicked his tongue and shook his head. "She will not be pleased. We have guards posted from there to Notirr. Where in Ariboslia did you go? How you managed to avoid them is of the utmost interest to me. And how did you know about this place?"

His confusion comforted me. If Le'Corenci had led me astray, we would not be having this conversation. Rather, I wouldn't be listening to this monologue. I shifted my gaze to the stone wall behind him, focusing on its spider web-like cracks. He didn't appear accustomed to being treated in this manner. He clenched his jaw, and a vein resembling the Mississippi river pulsed in his forehead. I fought the urge to smile.

"No matter." He jumped up. "It seems the guards wasted their efforts. How you got here is irrelevant, and the timing couldn't be better. Tonight is the Gealach Lionadh." He moved in front of me and stooped to gaze into my eyes, making him difficult to avoid. He lifted his hand to my face.

I forced myself not to react to the frigid finger he trailed down my cheek.

"Morrigan will not be angry long. How happy my mistress will be when I kill you in her presence, in the presence of all the fasgadair in

231

attendance." His fingers moved down to my neck and lingered. "So warm, so tender. How I will savor the sweet moment when I sink my teeth into that supple skin and drain your blood before the entire assembly." He licked his lips, his words a whisper. "How luscious your blood will taste."

He straightened and paced about the room. "Tonight, the hopes of the fasgadair will be reborn, all threats against me abolished. What a celebration this will be." He grinned back toward me.

A twinge of fear penetrated my resolve. I pushed it away. What-ever happened tonight, though I had no idea how, the prophecy would come true, even though it meant my death.

"Unless..." Aodan's tone became thoughtful. "You reconsidered my offer?"

I remained immobile, barely breathing.

"Immortality. Power. Control. You have gifts, Fallon." He cycled me and placed his hands on my shoulders. I lowered myself away from his touch. He grasped my shoulders harder, crouched down, and whispered in my ear, "A pity to waste them."

He released me, stood, and resumed pacing. He brought a finger to his lips and scrunched his eyes as if deep in thought. "I could release your mother."

My eyes flew to his. It had to be a trick. He wouldn't release her, would he? The one serious mistake I'd made, the one thing I regretted missing—leverage.

"Ah. That caught your attention, did it?" His eyes flashed. "You would like me to release her?"

For this, I dared break silence. "Yes."

"What price would you pay for such a gift?"

"I have nothing."

"But you do. You have something quite valuable."

"What's that?"

"I would release your mother and all the gachen locked up with her."

"In exchange for...?" I asked, growing tired of him.

"For your life."

My hopes deflated, and my gaze returned to the spider-web cracks in the wall. What game was he playing? I already planned on giving it as he intended to take it.

"I could make you powerful, Fallon. You could live forever. All you would need to do is become a fasgadair, like me...to bow before me as your king."

I hadn't considered the possibility of joining them. Nor would I. "Clearly you don't know me very well. That's not even slightly tempting," I spat, though it wasn't entirely true. The old me might've cared for those things. But I wasn't the same person who'd arrived in Ariboslia just months before. I didn't need the control I'd once needed. I had the love I craved. I cared nothing for power. I would do anything to avoid an eternity of damnation. Nor would I ever submit to him as my king. But the release of my mother and the others...

By accepting his offer, I would ensure their release, assuming he kept his word. At least I'd be alive, or...in some sort of conscious state...to see their freedom and know it was done. How could I come all this way, hand myself over to Aodan, and leave my mother and the others as captives? How could I leave Aodan in power when my purpose was to bring about the end of his rule? Now that I was here, in his presence, the concept seemed more ridiculous than ever.

But what about God? Could I take this into my hands and turn my back on Him?

But what if this was His plan? What if I was supposed to sacrifice my soul? As a fasgadair with a mind-link to Aodan, I'd have a better chance of destroying him. Wouldn't I?

"Oh, come now." Aodan's voice interrupted my thoughts. "Would it be all that bad? Living forever with others under your control?"

I returned to my stoic state.

"Or I could torture her. Like this..."

An uncomfortable prickling sensation made the skin on my arm itch. Then it burned. Horror filled my veins as the hairs flamed into tiny little fires. I smacked them out with my hand, but they flared up again.

Aodan cackled manically, and they stopped. The stench of burned hair filled my nose. What hairs remained had frizzled and blackened.

I wanted to smack the arrogant smirk off his face. I stared at his head, anger burning inside me.

His sandy brown hair burst into red and orange flames. The smile disappeared. He howled in agony as he smacked himself to put out the fire. Small clumps of scorched hair remained. The rest of his head was bald and charred.

He rushed me, cinched my neck in his vice-grip, and squeezed. Gurgling sounds escaped as I struggled to breathe. I grabbed his hand to pry him off. He was too strong. I stared at the tendons protruding from his neck. My vision grew blurry.

Not like this, God. Please don't let me die like this.

Aodan released me, and I took in lungs full of air. My hands rose to my burning throat as I glared at him.

"Never try that again, or the hairs on your arm will not be the only thing to catch fire. Besides..." He brushed the dead hair off his head. His skin whitened as new growth sprouted to the exact length it had been. He swept the fallen strands from his shoulders. His rage subsided, he smiled. "It's useless." He dropped before me again and touched my singed arm. "Somehow, I don't think you would fare so well. Not in your present state."

I pulled away.

"But I'm impressed. I thought Cataleen and I were the only ones with the ability to start fires with our minds. But there's the mink-link. Why shouldn't you have our other gift as well? You are her daughter after all. Imagine what a team we would make! With our abilities, nothing could stop us." He let out a high-pitched, girly giggle unbecoming of a villain.

"Why didn't you pair up with your sister?"

He pinched his eyebrows together. "Cataleen? She's too... too...*good*."

"What makes you think I'm not?"

A slow smile spread over his face. "Cataleen would *never* have set my head on fire."

I swallowed.

He stood, ran his fingers through his new locks, and dreamed aloud about a world with us ruling. As he blathered, he diminished his power. In all the books I'd read and movies I'd seen, villains shared a fatal flaw—their need to disclose every intricate detail of their evil plan as though to impress us with their genius. Or perhaps he hoped his irrational dreams would somehow infect me. If villains followed through without talking so much, they might be more successful. As it was, they gave their victim ample time to devise an escape. But Aodan needn't concern himself. No such schemes brewed in my mind.

God, I sure wish You'd let me in on Your *plan.*

CHAPTER THIRTY-SIX

"This is your last chance to change your mind. I can give you immortality." Aodan secured my hands behind my back. "Or you will die today."

For the first time in my life, puking seemed like a good idea, if only to release the pressure in my gut. What was I doing? Part of me wished my friends would come storming in to rescue me. Another portion wanted to accept Aodan's offer and free my mother. I tried to force those thoughts away, focusing instead on my God.

But doubt seeped in. What if I'd been tricked? What if I had failed a test? Hadn't I already taken things into my own hands by abandoning my friends and coming here alone? They told me not to listen to Le'Corenci. I'd believed the words of one of those demonic beings and a silly dream over my friends—believers. Then Ryann died. Because of me. My choices. I had no way to rescue my mother. Were those parts of God's plan or proof of my error? And I had trusted Wolf. What if he'd been using me all along just to get me to this point? To die?

I had to stop torturing myself. Right or wrong, nothing could change the choices I'd made. It was too late.

As of this moment, I already had immortality, maybe not in this life, but who'd want to stay here, with Aodan and his irrational mood swings, for eternity? And who knew how long he actually had to rule here, to treat this world as his personal playground. There were only two places people went for all of eternity. I'd choose paradise. To forever be with my Creator...Love. He could have the absence of all that is good, permanent torture. Not me. No thanks.

And who was I to take these matters into my own hands anyway? God had a plan. I didn't understand it, but He had one. I would trust Him. I would entrust my mother and the other captives with Him too. They were better off in His hands than mine any day.

"If it is God's plan, I will be with Him today." The binding kept my hands from shaking. But my voice wavered.

God, I hope I did the right thing. Give me strength...Give me strength.

Aodan growled. "Stubborn child." He shoved me toward the double doors, which opened as if on cue.

My knee banged against the hard stone, sending shooting pain up my leg that had never been right since I'd hurt it upon arriving in Ariboslia.

The two guards reappeared. They stood at the same height. In their cloaks, with all but their faces covered, only their blue eyes differed. The blueness of one was dull, while the other shone bright —sharp.

Aodan turned his gaze to his minions. "Take her to the bloigh rùm. Make sure she is not seen." A crooked smile crept over his face. "I want her appearance to be a surprise."

"We shall use the secret passages," the bright-eyed one said.

"Very well, De'Rahn. But be sure no one witnesses you walking through stone."

"We will take care, my lord." De'Rahn bowed his head.

Aodan materialized in front of De'Rahn. I turned back to where he'd been standing, then to where his body now appeared. How had he done that? I hadn't seen him move.

Again, faster than my eye could perceive, Aodan cinched De'Rahn's neck in his hands. "You do not like fire, do you?"

De'Rahn's eyes bulged out of their sockets. Still, no whites appeared—as if the entire eye was blue. Freaky. He gurgled an unintelligible response.

"Morrigan almost saw you once before, remember? If she learns of the passages through your carelessness, I will ensure you spend an eternity recovering from burns. Am I understood?"

De'Rahn managed a weak nod in Aodan's firm grasp. His mouth was wide like a fish out of water, desperate for air, struggling in silence.

"Good. Do not fail me. Go." Aodan released his grip.

De'Rahn's hand flew to his throat as he gasped for air.

I cringed at the red welts my demonic uncle's fingers left behind.

The guards bowed, though De'Rahn kept hateful eyes on Aodan as he dipped his head. The red, warped skin on his neck regenerated to its former pale, smooth surface. Both guards grasped me by an upper arm, lifting me off the ground.

As their painful grips cut off the circulation, my fingers went numb. I flinched as we ploughed through seemingly impenetrable stone.

After emerging from a moment of darkness, they continued without pause. The dimly lit maze of halls and stairs passed in a blur, only the bloodsuckers latched onto my arms remained in focus.

"One of these days, Be'Norr." De'Rahn coughed. "One of these days, I will have his head on a platter."

"Hush, brother. Be careful what you say in front of the girl."

"Oh, come now. Even Aodan doesn't understand Cianese." De'Rahn slowed for a moment.

I pretended to be clueless as he scrutinized me. They weren't aware of Drochaid's abilities? De'Rahn nodded, seemingly satisfied. "She doesn't know our language."

They resumed their fast pace.

"Don't be foolish." Be'Norr continued the conversation. "Someday we'll escape. Until then, we must do as Aodan wishes."

"I want more than my freedom." Pure hatred laced De'Rahn's words. "I want vengeance."

Another wall appeared before us. They stopped. De'Rahn tipped his head toward Be'Norr. "I'll hold the girl. Inspect the hall."

Be'Norr poked his head through the rock and back. "All is clear."

So they pushed me through and carried on as before, slowing upon arriving at a room full of cloaked monsters. They stood shoulder-to-shoulder, forming a wall, turning their pale faces in our direction as my guards pushed our way through. Those who noticed me cocked their heads listlessly to one side. Their enlarged pupils roamed to my neck, resting on Drochaid. The phlegmatic expressions on their faces remained unchanged.

"Let us through or Aodan will have your heads!" De'Rahn waved his arms.

The fiends turned their attention to De'Rahn. Some flinched, but they all parted like a vile Red Sea. I passed countless veiled bodies with ghastly, waxen faces, leering at me. Some licked their lips, making me shudder more visibly. My stomach lurched. This was what hell must be like. All it was missing was a bit of fire.

But no. God was still here. Even here. With me. True hell won't have His presence at all.

God, help me. Get me out of here...away from these wicked beasts.

De'Rahn and Be'Norr led me through the sickening bloodsuckers, to one of the balconies like the one where I'd been discovered. They didn't bring me to the opening, but remained a few feet back. The crowd was thin enough here that, despite the dim lighting and the cloaks blocking my way, I could see past them to the lower room and balconies—in the sea of cloaks the faces appeared as disembodied heads floating on its surface.

For a group of such a considerable size, everything was eerily quiet. None spoke. Swishing cloaks and the blood rushing past my ears was all I heard. And that smell. The electric smell permeated the place. I gagged on it.

I focused on the chandelier, trying to ignore the smirks around me.

Give me strength, God...Give me strength.

An eerie flute sound filled the hall. Bagpipe-like blows joined in followed by stringed instruments. Drums accompanied the creepy melody, giving it a more tribal quality. Finally the cloaked clones began to chant. The haunting music created a cross between the Celtic CDs Bumpah listened to, Gregorian Chants, and Godsmack.

The chanting rose—every voice in the hall and the balconies in perfect timing with one another. It surrounded me. Something about it made every muscle in my body twitch. I squirmed, desperately wishing to escape this demonic ritual.

Bumpah, if the worst happens today, we'll be together soon.

Aodan appeared on the balcony with a woman on his arm. They were only two besides myself without a cloak. Neither was chanting, but the chanters surrounding them cleared a path without missing a word.

The attractive woman's lustrous black hair sparkled in the candlelight. Her small, feminine features were what most women craved. From afar, with her eyes barely visible and partially closed, she looked like a model. But upon closer inspection, she appeared as old as time, despite no physical signs of aging. She carried herself as if time didn't matter and she hurried for nothing. And the light vanished in her completely black eyes.

Morrigan stood before me.

I shivered as every hair on my body raised, alert. Before me stood evil in its purest form. Even Aodan didn't fill me with such cold dread —draining my body of any joy from a mere look.

Her head moved in a strange jerky motion. Her intense, animal-like eyes roamed slower than a slug down my body and narrowed when they returned to my face. Her dainty nostrils flared.

If pure evil were a perfume she was bathed in it. It secreted from her like pheromones only I seemed to pick up. I almost wished myself dead rather than within such a close proximity.

Cheers replaced the chanting. The music stopped as cries rose from those who witnessed their approach and grew to a mighty tumult when more turned their way. The rulers brushed past us to the window and stood before the crowd on the balcony, soaking in the applause.

When the cacophony showed signs of dying down, Aodan raised his hands. The moment his hands reached the sky, the candles in the chandelier burst into flames. One by one along the walls, more candles lit. Light flooded the auditorium as the crowd renewed their applause, reaching a new high.

Aodan lowered his hands. Once the audience quieted down, he addressed them. "My fellow fasgadair!" The clamor revived. Aodan straightened, a smile of pure ecstasy curving his face. He signaled for silence once more. "I have the most spectacular news! We have more reason to celebrate this Gealach Lionadh. I have in my possession, from the human realm, my own dear sister's child. The long-awaited Fallon!"

The crowd hollered, shaking triumphant fists. And I was the object of their mocking derision.

"Fallon." Aodan summoned me forth as the cheering subsided, and the guards released me, shoving me to the railing between Aodan and Morrigan, refueling the audience's frenzy. "Fasgadair will speak of this night for centuries to come." He projected his voice over the din. "Tonight we crush the hopes of the gachen forever—all of Ariboslia will be ours!"

Aodan waited, sliding his words into breaks during the tumult. "Tonight, the lies of the false prophecy come to an end. Tonight Fallon dies!" His face contorted, revealing needlelike fangs. He took his time leaning over me as if savoring the moment.

Silence reigned. Not one dared breathe.

His frosty fingers swept my hair away from my shoulder. He sank closer. His hair tickled my ear. I fought the temptation to scratch or puke. A soft breath, loud in my ear, warmed my neck, and an overwhelming calm swept over me. The sharp points of his teeth rested above my collar. Before they penetrated my neck, I said, "I forgive you."

I meant it. I didn't understand everything. I didn't need to. I only knew what I must do, and I did it. I barely noticed the tips of his teeth sinking into my skin or the rush of blood escaping my body as he sucked. I felt love—undeniable love for this creature in the process of killing me.

So this is what it's like to die.

CHAPTER THIRTY-SEVEN

A odan released his hold and staggered back. His mouth opened in a silent scream. Pain bulged his eyes. Was he in emotional or physical pain? Perhaps both. Something tormented him. His mouth moved as though attempting to speak. Then he dropped to the ground.

The crowd hushed.

Tremors racked Aodan's body as if in a seizure. Then he stilled as if the life had left his body.

No one stirred. Not a sound was audible. All seemed frozen as we waited with bated breath for something to happen.

Morrigan bent over him. "He has no breath." She spoke slowly, as if in a trance, her hand gently caressing Aodan's face. Though my eyes failed to see her move, her face now turned up at me, her eyes angry slits. "What is the meaning of this?"

My body trembled, struggling to focus on the events transpiring before me. Aodan somehow failed to murder me. But the savage look in Morrigan's eyes could surely strike me dead. My head swooned. I nearly fell.

De'Rahn and Be'Norr gripped me on either side, holding me upright.

Aodan sucked in a breath, arching his back. We all jumped back. Morrigan pulled her hand away. It remained suspended in midair as her wide eyes stared. Morbid fascination filled me as he writhed.

Morrigan backed from him as though he might infect her. "What have you done?"

I took a deep breath, trying to still my trembling, and shook my head.

Aodan opened his eyes, groaned, and attempted to stand. Once on his feet, he swayed and looked at me.

I gasped. His eyes had changed. They looked like mine. His pale face held a tinge of pink.

"What have you done to me?" His voice had changed, stripped of its earlier arrogance.

"I don't—" I tried backing away, but the guards held me firm. "I don't know."

"I feel different. What did you do?" His eyes searched me. "I bit you. I drank your blood. Yet you aren't hurt."

Morrigan materialized in front of me as a gust of wind swirled my hair. She pushed Aodan aside and glared at me. "I demand to know what you've done." She stood, inches within my face. My body pushed back without my willing it to do so, with no visible force, moving my guards along with me. It was as if invisible force fields surrounded us. She, like a polar opposite magnet, repelled me within too close a proximity.

My mouth hung open as I shook my head. Clueless. What should have taken place here tonight, other than their intent to kill me, which had backfired?

Morrigan's face twisted into something more primal, more heinous. She let out an animalistic high-pitched scream full of pure rage. Something glinted in the candlelight next to her cloak—a blade.

Aodan stepped between us and grunted as the blade found its mark. He clutched his stomach and faltered backward into me.

Over his shoulder, Morrigan stared. She brought bloody hands up to her mouth.

Aodan slumped to the ground, landing on his back, his eyes wide.

Morrigan knelt beside him. "What trickery is this? Get up, Aodan. You are a fasgadair."

"I'm-I'm dying, Morrigan." He sputtered blood.

She released a nervous laugh. "You cannot die, foolish one. You are immortal. I made you immortal."

Aodan turned from her and cast his gaze upward. "Forgive me." Blood pooled in his open mouth and spilled down its sides. His dead eyes stared at the ceiling. The hilt of a blade protruded at an upward angle under his rib cage.

Morrigan pulled the dagger from Aodan's gut, and blood gushed from the wound. She opened the cloak, tore the tunic underneath, and touched the laceration. She turned her attention to his head. Her fingers glided down the side of his face and neck, leaving a trail of blood. Bending over him, she placed her cheek over his mouth as if seeking breath. Then she returned to the wound.

"He isn't turning to dust." Morrigan spoke to no one in particular. "But he isn't regenerating." Her emotionless voice seemed to be trying to sort it out. "He cannot be dead. 'Tis not possible. A knife to the chest would not kill a fasgadair." She looked up, her wide eyes blinked once in my direction. "You changed him."

Those within earshot sucked in their breath. A frenzy of activity buzzed. I stared, trying to make sense of what I'd witnessed. The guards holding me whisked me away.

Morrigan screeched. "Stop her!"

But flames erupted in the entryway, blocking the path, without wood or kindling to ignite. Had I done that?

My guards dragged me backward with inhuman speed, into the hallway, through stone, back into the hidden passageways.

One question pinged around my head like a bouncy ball with an endless supply of energy: *What* happened in there?

De'Rahn and Be'Norr released my arms. De'Rahn narrowed his

eyes. "Is it true? Did you change Aodan back into a gachen? Is it possible?"

"I'm not sure what happened." When I faltered, Be'Norr caught me.

They gazed at me as if they hadn't eaten in years. I feared they might attempt to bite me, as Aodan had, just to see what would happen. But I needed their help if I had any chance of escaping.

Be'Norr moved closer. He swept aside my hair and bent over my neck. His breath warmed me. As he prepared to pierce my skin, I stepped back. "Wait!"

He paused, stood, and stared at me.

"I let Aodan bite me. What if you try without my permission and it kills you?" I had no idea where those words came from. But they seemed my only hope of getting my mother out alive.

"Will you allow us then?"

"I don't know what I did or if I can do it again. But I promise to try if you'll help rescue my mother and the gachen with her."

The two looked at each other.

"If there ever was a good time, brother, 'tis now. Aodan is dead," De'Rahn said.

"But Morrigan..." Be'Norr adjusted the hood on his cloak, revealing dark hair for a brief moment. "And the others."

"Right now there is confusion. And the fire." De'Rahn turned to me. "How long will it last?"

I shrugged. "I've never done that before. I'm not even sure it was me."

The two cocked their heads in confusion then faced one another. As though reading each other's minds, they nodded.

Be'Norr waved me toward him. "We will risk it. The chance to return to our former beings will be payment enough. We'll help you."

The vamp brothers escorted me to the room holding my mother and the others. The same guard sat by the door, rising as we approached.

"Open up," De'Rahn commanded.

The guard had opened the door without question before. This time, he raised an eyebrow. "Why aren't you at the Gealach Lionadh? And why is she here?" He motioned toward me. "Didn't Aodan plan to kill her?"

"Ask Aodan what he plans. We are delivering her here, per his request."

Shaking his head, the guard turned to open the door.

The moment the lock clicked free, De'Rahn grasped the guard's head and snapped his neck like a twig. Once released, the guard dropped to the floor.

"Quickly," Be'Norr called to the captives, in a hushed voice. "We must leave before his body regenerates."

I ran to my mother. With renewed strength, I helped her to her feet.

She leaned on me as I assisted her out the door. "What happened to Aodan? Something within him changed. I felt it. Now I feel nothing."

"Come. We must go. Now. Aodan is dead."

She gasped and fell against me. Perhaps I shouldn't have told her yet.

I struggled to hold her up, despite her small, emaciated frame. "Are you all right?"

She straightened, bearing more of her own weight again. "I just... I always hoped..."

"Shhh. We can discuss it later. We need to get out of here."

De'Rahn took the lead. The gachen followed. Their bare feet padded on the stone, slipping on loose hay as they hurried along. I counted gachen as I turned back to make sure everyone got out—thirty-seven in all.

Be'Norr nudged me to follow the group, his gaze darting in every direction.

De'Rahn stopped at the end of a hallway, holding his hand up to us. He peered around the corner, down the hall to the right, then the left. Rather than take either passage, he scurried across to the far wall and walked partway through, motioning us to follow. He glanced down the other passages again. "This way. Quickly."

Once we all made it through, I breathed a sigh of relief. We'd gotten this far—praise God! Perhaps we'd make it out alive. Aodan was dead, through no plan of my own. One part of the prophecy was complete. Perhaps I hadn't chosen incorrectly after all.

CHAPTER THIRTY-EIGHT

O ur group followed De'Rahn and Be'Norr through the tunnels
for what felt like forever. Many of the slaves were malnour-
ished, and their muscles had atrophied, slowing our progress. When
we came to a stairway leading down, De'Rahn addressed us. "This
stairwell spirals for a mile or so, to a hidden entrance at the base of
the mountain, far from the main entrance."

I glanced at the tired faces. "Can we take a break first?"

De'Rahn hesitated then nodded. "It will be a while before sunrise
anyway."

The temporary surge of energy drained, and every muscle in my
body ached with fatigue. I leaned against the wall and slid to a sitting
position. Something tickled my arm. I touched it, and my fingers
came away with slime. I pulled what I could gather of the back of my
dress to find it covered with whatever coated the walls. "Ugh."

My mother sat beside me. "Are you all right?"

"I'll be fine."

"What happened? How did Aodan die?"

"I don't know. He bit me." I pushed my hair to show her.

She gasped and inspected it, then let out a relieved breath. "Two small punctures. Scabs have already formed. He was in no hurry, at least. You'll be fine." She peered into my eyes. "Then what happened?"

"Well, he-he fell. When he got up, he looked...different."

"In what way?"

"He looked human."

Cataleen covered her mouth with her hand, her eyes moist. She lowered her hand to speak. "How'd he die?"

"Morrigan stuck a dagger in him. She meant to kill me. He protected me."

"He protected you?" She straightened and tilted her head slightly, her eyebrows pinched together. "How can this be?"

I shrugged.

"We don't know either, but we're curious to find out. Aren't we, brother?" Be'Norr turned to De'Rahn.

"More than I can say." De'Rahn crossed his arms. "It's fortunate for you that we happened to be your guards. No others could have helped you escape."

"No, brother. It's fortunate she's helping us," Be'Norr corrected him.

"She better." De'Rahn threw an icy glare my way. "I'm getting hungry."

Be'Norr shook his head. "Settle yourself. Aodan is dead. You're getting what you want." He returned his attention to me. "What my brother means is that, aside from Aodan, we're the only ones who know about these hidden passages.

"Some of them," De'Rahn interrupted.

"Right. Years ago, we discovered a secret path. I leaned against a wall and fell through the rock. It led to a path, and we followed it. We have spent years tapping on walls, finding secret passages, following them, and mapping them. If anyone can get you all out of Ceas Croi unnoticed, it's us."

"Praise God!" My mother exclaimed, as did others who'd over-heard. They leaned toward those who hadn't heard to explain.

Excited chatter echoed through the tunnel. I hoped the news would renew their strength and quicken their pace—and not bring unwanted company.

We stood and resumed our trek. We needed food and water.

About ten minutes into our descent, Be'Norr stopped. "None will follow us here. But to be safe..." He moved toward a stone protruding from the wall and pushed it. A large circular stone embedded in the wall rolled across the stairwell, blocking the path behind us. "The pech installed these defenses. We might as well use them." He shrugged. "Keep going. De'Rahn and I will catch up."

Every few feet, Be'Norr and De'Rahn stayed behind to add another barricade until the stairs came to a halt, as they had in the tower.

"This is the way out. It comes out on the far side of the mountain, in a heavily wooded area. No one knows about it, and no roads traverse nearby. Still, we need to remain hidden until daylight." De'Rahn turned to me. "We will need to check for the sun, but Be'Norr and I are not able to in our current condition. Now is the time to change us."

"We have fulfilled your request, have we not?" Be'Norr said.

My heart pounded. Dare I let them try now? What if it didn't work? What if they killed me in the process? I'd already lost blood. And now I had two who needed to take more from me? How much could I afford to lose?

I glanced at the onlookers, so close to their escape. A promise was a promise. I would not go back on my word. *God, help me.* "I'm ready."

My mother turned to me. "Wait. Ready for what?"

"They want to see if-if what happened to Aodan could happen for them."

Her eyes grew large. "You mean—?"

I nodded.

"But what if it doesn't work? What if they—?"

"It's the deal I made. I can't go back on my word."

"But—"

I laid a hand on her shoulder. "I must do this. If you want to help, pray."

She stared for a moment, then nodded and backed away. She sat with the other gachen lining the stairwell, eyes wide as if watching a suspenseful movie.

A wicked smile tugged at De'Rahn's lips. He turned to Be'Norr. "You first, little brother."

Be'Norr studied his brother. "You're afraid it won't work."

De'Rahn laughed. "Don't be foolish. We'll both have a turn."

"But not if I die."

De'Rahn shrugged.

Be'Norr shook his head. "Fine." He took me in his arms. His teeth didn't hurt much more than a mosquito bite. Still, I had to resist the impulse to swat at him. The same sensation I felt with Aodan came over me again as he sipped—peace and an inexplicable love for him. Was it was possible to love someone you didn't even know, even a fasgadair?

Be'Norr released his hold and staggered back throwing me a pained, quizzical look before falling to the ground, writhing in agony. Then he stilled.

De'Rahn grabbed my arm. "What have you done to him?"

"I don't know, but you were there. You saw. This is what happened with Aodan." I shrank from the unpredictable anger in his creepy eyes.

Like before, we all waited, scarcely breathing.

Be'Norr sucked in a breath as he arched his back, startling us all.

"See?" I let out a relieved breath. "Just like with Aodan."

Be'Norr writhed, and then stilled, his breathing returning to normal. He moaned and blinked, glancing about the room as if trying to remember what had happened. He faltered as he tried to stand.

De'Rahn rushed to help him. "How do you feel?"

Between each exaggerated blink, normal bright blue eyes made an appearance. His skin darkened.

"It worked." De'Rahn didn't seem to believe his own words.

"What happened?" Be'Norr rubbed his head.

"You drank from Fallon, remember? How do you feel?"

Be'Norr looked himself over. "It hurts a little. Remember when you were a gachen and your leg would fall asleep if you sat on it too long? 'Tis like that." He held his arms out, inspecting each, one at a time, wiggling his fingers as if he'd never seen them before, and then returned his gaze to his brother. His eyes widened. "She did it. She cured me. I am no longer a fasgadair! I can feel it."

Gasps and praises rushed like a wave from the gachen along the wall.

De'Rahn gazed at me. His lips moved as if he wanted to say something. I expected him to demand I change him right away. His hesitation prompted me to ask, "Do you want to be healed?"

He turned from me to his brother and back, biting his lip. His fang drew blood. He licked it and nodded.

My confidence in changing him grew with two successful transitions, but so much blood loss at once...And something about De'Rahn in particular worried me, panging my gut. Despite my fears, I moved toward him.

De'Rahn gripped me tight. His breath warmed my neck as his conflicted moan amplified so close to my ear. He sank his teeth in —deep.

I cried out.

"Stop!" My mother moved toward us.

De'Rahn blocked her from view. Her voice sounded far away. "You're hurting her!"

I tried to push De'Rahn, but he didn't budge. I fought to cry out, but only a gurgling noise escaped. I needed air, but my breath came up short.

God, help me!

De'Rahn released me and stepped back as I slumped to the ground.

My mother rushed to me and cradled my head in her arms. I took deep breaths and struggled to focus. De'Rahn appeared to be choking. Blood spurted out of his mouth. He bent over, spit it out, and fell. His mouth opened and closed like a fish out of water, then stilled. Life left his bulging, unchanged eyes.

Be'Norr knelt beside his brother and jostled him. He then placed his cheek by his mouth and nose. "He's dead." Be'Norr turned to me. A dreamlike quality, as though in a trance, softened his voice. "You killed a fasgadair."

"We don't know that. You and Aodan stopped breathing too." *Please, God, let him be alive.*

The veins in De'Rahn's face turned gray with an almost imperceptible crackling sound. The gray fanned out to the capillaries, then the rest of his skin. Dust.

"I-I didn't mean to. I tried to help him, like you."

Be'Norr gently touched his brother's face, and De'Rahn crumbled like a disturbed sandcastle. Be'Norr remained, gazing at the pile of dust and flattened clothes, his face full of remorse. Then he straightened and moved toward me. "I know. 'Tis all right. Here." He yanked off his cloak, tore fabric from the tunic underneath, pushed my aside hair, and cleaned the wound from De'Rahn. "Let me help you."

"She's lost a lot of blood." My mother wiped my damp forehead. "She's cold. Look how pale she is."

"I'm okay," I insisted, despite the spinning faces and my throbbing weakness. "I'm sorry, Be'Norr. I-I didn't mean to kill your brother."

"Call me Evan. Be'Norr was my fasgadair name." Evan solidified into one collective vision. His soft, blue eyes, exotic against his dark skin, peered into mine. "Listen to me, Fallon. You did not kill him. I do not pretend to understand what you are or what you have done. But he bit you. He made the choice. He could have killed you, but did he concern himself with that possibility? No. Do not concern yourself with my brother's death. He deserved it." His shoulder's drooped as he applied pressure to the cloth. "I did too."

The difference in him overwhelmed me. He seemed so...
so...*human*. As a monster, he seemed ageless. But now...he couldn't
be more than a year or two older than me.

His eyes glistened with tears as a smile crossed his face. "Do not
think on the lost life, but the saved one. You fought for both. You gave
me back my life—another chance to get it right. I can't thank you
enough."

Murmurs coursed through the witnesses. One of them cried,
"Praise Fallon!"

I twisted in the direction of the cry. "No." I strained to be heard,
but my voice came out weak. I coughed. "The praise goes to God. I
am merely His servant."

"Praise be to God!" someone called out.

I smiled and closed my eyes.

CHAPTER THIRTY-NINE

"Fallon, wake up."
I moaned and blinked. Concerned faces surrounded my view.

Evan gazed at me, smoothing my hair. "Can you walk?"

"I'm not sure." I tried to stand. My mother grasped one arm. Evan took the other. Together, they lifted me. The stairs spun beneath me, and I faltered. "Whoa."

I tried to catch myself, but I leaned on my mother. She buckled beneath my weight, and we both nearly fell. Evan grabbed me, and Cataleen caught herself.

"We have to get out of here. Cataleen, you're weak too. I've got her." Evan stooped, threw my arm over his shoulder, and gathered me into his arms. Had I ever been carried like this, even as a baby? He walked me through the façade of a wall into the daylight.

Despite the canopy of trees blocking us from direct sunlight, my eyes burned. I buried my face in Evan's shoulder. I had no idea how long he carried me.

"You must be getting tired." I looked up at him. "I think I can try walking."

"You lost so much blood, Fallon. Let me carry you a little further."

Tears welled up in my eyes. What had caused the sudden rush of emotion? I blinked the tears away and rested against Evan.

The boy who first greeted me in the slave's chamber stopped up ahead and turned. "I think I hear running water."

"Find it," Evan called. "We'll follow you."

When we reached the brook, he eased me down. I lay prostrate, dipped my hand into the cool water, and brought it to my lips. When I'd had my fill, I pushed myself away from the bank and rolled onto my back. I stared into the sky as a giant brown bird swept close by, carrying something in its talons—a satchel? My heart thumped. I pulled myself up, looked to the others along the bank, and pointed skyward. "Look. The sky." My disjointed words came out in gasps.

The bird flew by again releasing a shivery cry.

"A golden eagle. Come." Evan helped me up. "'Tis probably a fasgadair and will alert the others. We must keep moving."

Before we got far, the eagle returned with something in its beak. Evan and I fell over as it swooped past us, released its satchel, and skidded across the ground to an ungraceful stop. It stood, ruffled its feathers, hopped over to me, and deposited a bunch of grapes at my feet.

Confused, I studied the strange bird and picked up the grapes.

It nodded, snatched the satchel, and hopped into the woods.

Evan scooped the grapes from me to inspect them. "A present from a friend of yours, Fallon?" He took a tentative bite. "They're good. Here. Everyone take one." He plucked one from the stem and handed it to me. He then stood to pass them out to the rest of the gachen.

I popped a grape into my mouth, its juicy sweetness ecstasy to my taste buds. Water. Now food. *How great you are, Father!*

My attention returned to where the bird vanished into the woods. Declan appeared from around a tree, and I sucked in my breath. "I knew it!" I managed to stand, but swayed once upright.

Evan grasped my arm as Declan ran to help support me.

I stared at Declan. Pure joy surged through me. "You-You're a bird, too."

His grin overcame his entire face as he nodded, green eyes sparkling. Then he grew serious. "When you disappeared, I knew right away what you had done." His once joyous eyes now flashed at me. "You're so stubborn." Despite his scolding, a smile tugged at the left corner of his mouth, sending waves rippling through my stomach. He seemed different—more confident. An attractive quality.

"Yes, but look at you. You have a totem." I pushed at him playfully.

"I guess coming to your rescue was the motivation I needed." He frowned. "What were you thinking?"

"I was thinking I didn't want anyone else to die on account of me."

Declan shook his head. "What happened? How did you—"

"It's a long story."

Evan handed me the rest of the grapes. "Eat these."

I turned toward the others. "But what about—"

"Eat." He ordered and faced Declan. "We can explain later. She's suffered some blood loss and needs food." He waved toward the others lining the bank. "They all need food. Are there more of those nearby?" He pointed toward the grapes.

Declan's brows furrowed as he studied me. "Follow me. There are more this way."

I walked a little better now, but Declan and Evan wouldn't allow me to try on my own. They each took an arm and half carried me along. How had I ended up with two guys doting on me? What a strange, unexpected turn of events.

OUR TROOP LOUNGED on the grass near the grapevines, gorging ourselves. "Where are Wolf, Cahal, Pepin, and Ry—" I brought my hand to my mouth. I blinked back the tears and swallowed the lump forming in my throat. It didn't make up for the loss, but at least I'd saved others. And it was clearly God's plan. I couldn't have worked things out the way He had. If things had gone according to my own power, we'd all be dead.

Declan caught my blunder. His eyes moistened. "They aren't far. I must go back and tell them where we are." He handed me his water bag. "Is Drochaid showing the direction?"

I shrugged as I drank. After returning the water to him, I checked Drochaid. "It's not doing anything at the moment."

"Good." He nodded. "It should be safe for you to stay and rest then. I'll locate the others and bring them here."

"I'll go with you."

"Nay." His eyes pleading, he looked to Evan then back at me. "Stay. Rest. You need your strength."

"I'm much stronger already."

Evan placed his hand on my arm. "Fallon, he will be faster alone. Let him go."

I sighed and rolled my eyes. "Fine. But be quick about it, would you?"

With a smile, Declan gave me a quick hug. "Keep an eye on Drochaid. Go ahead without us if it shows you where to go."

"But—"

He hurried away before I could ask how we'd find one another. Oh well...just another thing I'd have to trust God with.

I lay on my back, closed my eyes, and rested. Every once in a while I checked Drochaid, grateful each time it revealed nothing. I didn't want to face the possibility of having to leave without them and wonder if they'd find us. They wouldn't know what direction we'd be headed.

I had no idea how long I lay there, overthinking things yet again, when Evan prodded me.

"Fallon, your friends are here."

I jolted upright. Declan and the others emerged from the forest.

When I ran to greet them, Declan laughed. "Looks like you're feeling better."

Pepin cleared his throat. The sides of his beard rose with his broad smile. "Declan told us your story along the way. Incredible. I knew God had big plans for you."

I leaned down when he reached to hug me. The strength behind his tight embrace surprised me.

When Pepin and I disentangled, I ran into Cahal's open arms, and all but disappeared in a massive bear hug.

Before I passed out from lack of oxygen, Cahal let me go. "As did I."

Wolf sauntered up behind, looking sheepish. He glanced at the escapees and his eyes widened. He sprinted into the woods.

"Wolf!" I cried and turned to see what had spooked him. Was he afraid of emaciated gachen? That's all I could see over there. If there was some kind of danger, Wolf would save us. He wasn't one to turn tail and run. Then again, he'd been different since Le'Corenci. I eyed Declan. "What was that about?"

He shrugged, "Does Drochaid have anything yet to say?"

"It's pointing that way." I motioned ahead of us and wiped my mouth with the back of my hand.

"North. I didn't think we should return to Notirr. After what you told me, I fear Morrigan will have the fasgadair track you down. It will likely be the first place they search."

"As wonderful as it is to see you alive," Cahal interrupted, "we must put more distance between us and Ceas Croi."

Typical Cahal, pushing us ever onward. I shook my head, smiled, and followed—glad to have my friends back. But what was going on with Wolf? Would he come back?

CHAPTER FORTY

The food and water strengthened our bodies, but the feat of escaping Ceas Croi with our souls intact strengthened our spirits. We moved at a faster pace, which was still considerably slower than Cahal would have liked. He kept to the lead, glancing back periodically, stopping, waiting for the rest to catch up. But we still didn't have our full strength, and the way wasn't easy.

There was no path. Drochaid led us through thick woods overgrown with briers. Wolf returned, but kept his distance, far behind us. Still he hadn't greeted me. And he usually took the lead. He shouldn't have any issues traversing this terrain. Why was he acting this way? This was a good day. We defeated Aodan and rescued my mother plus some. He should be triumphant. Instead, he behaved as one who was pouting...or guilty. My stomach sank as doubt settled in. Should I have trusted him? The others hadn't wanted me to. Had he tried sending me to my death and it backfired? He didn't seem to notice me watching him. His eyes followed something, and he looked sad. I followed his gaze—my mother. Did he know her?

We came to a clearing, and Drochaid pointed us across a raging river. Where was He leading us? He didn't do anything without purpose. Was this to keep the fasgadair from following, thinking no one in their right mind would ever come this way?

Cahal, Declan, and Evan took turns carrying the rest of us across. Now we'd have to walk with dripping wet clothes. My lightweight selkie dress would dry quickly. With the sun still fairly high in the sky, the day was warm. Hopefully, everyone would dry off soon. Knowing Cahal, he'd make us continue through the night despite our weariness.

Wolf remained in the shadows only crossing after the rest of us resumed our trek away from the opposite bank. He shook, sending water shooting like a sprinkler. If only the rest of us could dry off so easily.

We crossed rocky ground. Our weary bodies stumbled. Declan and Evan both hovered over me while others fell. "Help them."

They looked at each other, and then back at me.

"Please. I'm okay. They need the help more."

Declan picked up an older woman who was falling behind. She slumped against his shoulder and closed her eyes. Evan put his arm around an old man who leaned on him and said, "Bless you."

I blinked back tears and pushed closer to Cahal. "When can we make camp?"

He scanned at the sky. The sun hadn't completed its descent. "We need to keep moving. It's not safe to sleep at night, remember?"

"How could I forget? But we can't continue like this without rest."

He stared ahead as he marched, probably envisioning countless ways his charges might be overtaken, depending on our choices.

Perhaps I could add another scenario. "Just a short break. A quick snack and a nap. Even a little sleep can help us move faster. We'll head out again before the sun sets."

Cahal surveyed our faltering troop, trudging along like sleepwalkers. He groaned and dropped his pack. "I'll keep watch. No fire."

"No problem." I relaxed. "We can do that. Thank you." I threw my arms around him. Well, part of him anyway.

He grunted, bringing a smile to my face. How I'd come to love this grumpy giant.

We sat and devoured the grapes we brought with us. My gaze kept roaming to Wolf, distanced from the rest of us. Crouching low, he crept to where Declan had left his things. He peeked at me a couple of times and must've caught me staring. I didn't try to hide it.

I crossed to him and reached to pet him. He lowered his head and backed away, leaving my hand suspended in midair, denied. "What are you doing, Wolf? What's the matter?"

He snatched Declan's pack lying in the grass, and hurried away.

I followed. But he was so fast, even with a pouch dangling from his mouth. I'd never catch up. At the tree line, he disappeared. What happened? Was he mad at me—or himself?

I cupped my hands together and yelled, "I forgive you!"

Quiet, I searched the forest for movement. Something skittered and squeaked in a tree above me. Birds twittered and leaves rustled in the breeze. Wolf was gone.

I blinked back the pooling tears and swallowed. If he'd done something, I didn't care. It was all part of God's plan anyway. We each played a part. But I couldn't tell him. Not if he wouldn't listen. My shoulders sloped. I'd never felt so tired. I ducked under a thick branch and headed back to the group.

An unfamiliar voice called me.

Had I heard correctly? I didn't move.

"Fallon."

I'd heard that. I swung around. A dark-haired fasgadair with dull, hazel eyes stood staring. My breath caught. I fought my natural inclination to run. Should I? It didn't appear he could harm me through the usual tactics. Would this one know that? Still, he could kill me. I wasn't invincible. But wait. "How do you know my name?"

"'Tis me." He slumped his shoulders and dropped his head. "Wolf."

"Wolf?" I nearly choked.

He nodded.

"How could you..." I couldn't form the words. "All this time...You were one of *them*?"

He raised his arms, open, as if in surrender. "In all the time that I've been with you, have I ever hurt you?"

I couldn't think. My mind reeled. This was too much. This was Wolf. He'd protected me, hadn't me? "What about Le'Corenci. You brought him to me. Did you intend to have me killed?"

"Of course not. I've been with you all this time, Fallon. I was with you in your realm, watching over you, keeping you safe."

"For how long?"

"Since you were three. After your father died and your mother was captured."

I gasped. "Did you have anything to do with that?"

His freaky eyes bulged. "Nay! I knew, without your parents, you'd need protection. So I came to watch over you."

"Why?"

"Because I knew your mother would want me to." His eyes held mine, pleading.

"It was you, wasn't it? You chased me through the woods. You brought me here."

"It was part of the plan."

"Who's plan? Your plan? What were you hoping to get out of it if you weren't trying to kill me?"

"Redemption." He took a deep breath. "I was hoping...I know you have no reason to... Will you return me to my former self, Fallon? Will you make me a gachen again?"

I stepped backward. "You knew?"

"Nay. Not then. An angel visited me and only told me what I needed to do to be redeemed. I had no idea how it would come about. I only knew that if I trusted and obeyed, God would fulfill His promise."

I groaned. I'd barely recuperated from changing the others...and killing one. Was this how it was going to be from now on? No, with Aodan dead and my mother free, I'd fulfilled the prophecy. Wasn't that all? Now what? Would I go home, or stay and help eliminate the fasgadair?

"I understand if you refuse...and if you don't trust me. I'm not worthy of redemption."

I hung my head and mumbled. "No one is." Not even myself. Yet God saved me.

Wolf silently closed the gap between us. "I never wanted any of this. There was no other way. I've denied my thirst, watched over you, and prayed to a God I thought would never hear me. But He did. He sent an angel to show me the way."

"So you did it all to save yourself."

"I became a fasgadair to save my people. I returned to you to keep you safe. I brought you back here and led Le'Corenci to you because the angel told me to. It was God's will."

"You might die. I tried to change one fasgadair and he died. I don't know why. I can't control it."

"'Tis a chance I'm willing to take."

"Okay." I nodded and moved my hair away from my neck.

His eyes widened. He approached me with a tenderness the others had not. He was so gentle, I barely felt a thing, except love. I swooned with love for him.

Please, God, let him be saved.

His faced twisted in pain as he fell to the ground. He thrashed about in agony, his head coming close to a rock. I stepped between his head and the rock and watched, helpless. But this was how the two survivors had reacted. It was a good sign. Who was he anyway? What was his name?

Finally his body spasms stopped. His breathing came easier, and color returned to his face. I sat on the ground, studying him. His shoulder-length hair, poufy from being tossed about in his fit, reminded me of the Wolf I'd loved. But the multicolored fur was gone, leaving this mystery man with black hair. He looked young, early twenties maybe.

His hazel eyes blinked, full of pain at first, found me, and sparkled. A smile tugged at his lips. He winced as he pulled himself up to sit with me. "Thank you, Fallon. I am indebted to you."

I shook my head. "No. Like you, I did as I was told. I did my part. The thanks should go to God."

"And I thank Him as well. Still, if you hadn't done your part, where would I be?"

"I could ask the same of you. I wouldn't have been able to accomplish any of this if you hadn't done your part too."

"Agreed." His smile warmed my soul. Something about his presence comforted me. He put his arm around me. I responded by leaning against him.

"Is that the difference between you, Le'Corenci, and the other fasgadair?" I asked.

"What difference?"

"Le'Corenci said he denied his hunger. You said you denied your thirst. I assume that means the same thing. Weren't you tempted to kill us?"

"It was easier as a wolf. And I had to. It wasn't a choice. I'd become a fasgadair to spare the lives of others, not kill them. God knew that. Le'Corenci did the same. He changed to keep his family safe. God knew our hearts."

"What's your name?"

"My fasgadair name was De'Mere."

"But what about—"

"There you are, Fallon. We've been looking for..." My mother stopped in her tracks staring at Wolf.

"Faolan!" she gasped.

"Cataleen." Wolf—I mean, Faolan—spoke her name slowly as he removed his arm from my shoulders and stood to greet her. "It's been a long time."

He trembled.

My mother flung herself into Faolan's arms, erasing the worry lines from his brow. He sighed, closed his eyes, and smiled. His arms wrapped about her as though never wanting to let go, gently rocking her from side to side, and she melted in his arms.

Cataleen pushed back to look at him. "You haven't aged."

"No." Faolan dropped his gaze. Shame crossed his face. "Fasgadair blood does that."

My mother looked confused. "You were—But then—How?"

Faolan tipped his head toward me. "Fallon changed me back."

"Oh, thank God." She hugged him again, and then pulled away. "Aodan is dead."

"I know." He pushed her hair behind her right ear.

"I should've—"

"Shhh. There was nothing you could do. He made his own choices."

"Fallon's blood changed him back." She gazed at him, her eyes moist. Tears followed twin paths down her cheeks. "He could've been saved. Morrigan killed him."

"Accidently," I interrupted their tender moment. "She was trying to kill me, not him."

Neither eye turned toward me. They were lost in each other.

"He might've been saved. We don't know. We can always hope. He could be with God right now." Faolan's eyes searched hers as he smoothed her hair. "I miss him too."

Wait a minute. Faolan. How did I know that name? Sully. Hadn't Sully told me about him? Yes. Faolan was the friend who helped my mother escape to my realm. But how—

Noticing I was still there, both my mother and Faolan freed one arm and held them out to me. I accepted their invitation and locked myself in their embrace.

Thank you, God...for everything.

CHAPTER FORTY-ONE

T he sound of a sharp inhale woke me. I lifted my head.
Pepin sat upright on his bedroll, staring at me, his eyes
wide. "Get up. Now." He leaped to his feet, rolled his bedding, and
shouted to the others. "Everyone. Pack your things. We must go."

Dread pooled in my gut, reminding me of all the times I'd
wakened before a test and realized I hadn't studied. Without word, I
hurried to pack.

Cahal armed himself with his battle-axe, threw his belongings
over his back, and roused those our commotion hadn't disturbed.
"Prepare to move out."

We were perilously close to Ceas Croi...and nightfall. The sun
was no longer visible behind the mountains. Its fading light cast
shadows on those in different stages of waking. Grumblings and questions shot into the air.

Pepin paused for a moment to scan the group. "I had a dream—a
vision. A large pack of fasgadair will track us if we don't move now."
He threw his belongings onto his back and focused on me. "Do you
still have Sully's dust?"

My stomach plummeted. How could I have forgotten? I found

the pouch and opened it. "A little." I held it up, sheepish. I had failed to cover our tracks. We'd crossed a river, but the fasgadair could easily pick up the scent on the other side. How could I have been so stupid? And I'd been the one to suggest resting so close to dusk. Stupid... stupid...stupid...

Pepin grabbed it and peered inside. "It will have to do. I'll spread this around."

I stuffed my things into my bag.

Pepin sprinkled the dust and shouted, "Go. I will go back a ways to cover our tracks and catch up later."

"Go back? No. It's too dangerous." I blinked back tears. Not another death because of my stupidity. I couldn't handle it.

Faolan laid a hand on my shoulder. "I'll make sure he returns."

Not Faolan too. "But—"

"It will be okay." Pepin softened his voice. "I have seen this. We will find you. But you must leave now, or we will all die."

"Come, Fallon." Evan grasped my arm and tugged, his eyes pleading.

Declan placed a hand on my back and pushed. "Now."

Between the two of them, my feet moved then quickened.

No one challenged Pepin further. We raced to the trees. I used my left hand to push branches out of my path. My right arm, bent before my face, protected my eyes. When we slowed to regain our breath, Pepin emerged from the brush behind us astride Wolf.

Cahal was the first to question him. "What did you dream?"

"An angel told me Fallon isn't safe. Morrigan has sent packs of fasgadair in all directions. She wants her dead." Green dust flew from Pepin's dangling hands. He lifted the pouch with the remains of Sully's powder. "This will confuse them. And as long as we stay on course to the north, they will not find us. But we must split up. At sunup, I will build a megalith. Wolf and I will travel to Fallon's realm and take her home."

Home? I was going home?

"The rest of you will continue north to the Ain-Dìleas through the Cnatan Mountains. Except you." Pepin stopped, dismounted Wolf like an expert rider, and pointed to the young boy who had touched Drochaid in the cell.

The boy almost ran into him. His eyes widened as he motioned to himself and mouthed a word that I assumed meant "me" in English.

"Yes, you." Pepin gestured him closer. "Your totem form is a cheetah, correct?"

When the boy nodded, Pepin continued, "You are to run as fast as you can to Notirr. Warn them to leave, immediately. Fasgadair are on their way to search for Fallon. They are to travel first to the Arlen in Kylemore, then to the Ain-Dìleas in Bandia. You are not to remain more than a day. They must pack and escape right away. There's no time for the elders to discuss this, only to tell everyone to gather their things. They must leave before the sun sets. Understood?" Pepin's eyes narrowed at the cheetah boy as if pushing the direness of the situation into his head.

The boy, face solemn, nodded as if entranced.

"Good." Pepin gave a quick nod. "The Arlen can arrange for transportation."

"The Cnatan Mountains?" asked an emaciated woman. "We will never survive. Strong, able-bodied men die passing through."

My mother frowned. "And if we do make it, are we to stay with our enemies? They worship false gods. They started this. They're responsible for Morrigan's existence in this realm."

Pepin glanced at each of the women and then to the boy. "You must go, now. Warn the Cael."

The boy nodded. His arms and legs slimmed. His body pitched forward and landed on all fours. A light orange fur with black spots sprouted. His head elongated and whiskers protruded until the boy disappeared and a cheetah wearing his clothes stood before us.

Declan helped him disentangle from his attire.

Pepin grabbed his satchel, removed a rope, threw the remaining contents at Cahal, and stuffed the boy's clothing inside. He secured it around the cheetah's front legs and across his back, like a backpack. "I pray it won't fall or trip you. Go. God be with you."

The cheetah nodded, let loose a birdlike chirping sound, turned east, and shot off through the woods.

Pepin returned his attention to the women and the rest of the crowd that had gathered, belongings in hand. He grunted as he threw his pack over his shoulder. "Come, I'll answer your questions as we travel. We will not be caught if we continue." He hopped onto Wolf's back.

Wolf kept a steady pace, but not as fast as typical, allowing the woman fearful of the journey ahead to walk alongside so Pepin could answer their questions. Cahal was already far ahead, but still within sight. Declan, Evan, and I followed, attempting to listen to whatever Pepin might say.

Pepin swayed on Wolf's back, tufts of fur protruding from each hand. He addressed the woman who'd asked about the mountains. "Summer has not yet ended. The mountains are still passable. God is with you. It will not be easy, but He will see you through."

He twisted to my mother. "As for the Ain-Dìleas...right now, the fasgadair are a common enemy. That makes them our allies." He paused for a moment, as if deep in thought. "Do you believe God could use anyone for His purposes, even those who don't believe?"

Cataleen nodded. "Of course."

"Remain faithful to our God, and all will be well," Pepin said.

"What about the Arlen?" Declan yelled at Pepin's back. "Are they in danger too? Should we warn them? Should they travel with our people to the Ain-Dìleas?"

Pepin nearly fell off Wolf trying to look back at Declan. He righted himself and called over his shoulder. "They will receive ample warning from your people when they arrange transportation to Bandia. A small pack of fasgadair will search for the Cael there. All but one will die. That one will return to Morrigan with news that neither the Cael nor Fallon is among them."

What had happened to Pepin in that dream? Suddenly he

seemed to know the future of all of Ariboslia. Declan, Evan, and I picked up the pace to hear him better. The woman, her question answered, dipped her head slightly, gave a shy smile, and moved out of our way.

"What about the megalith?" Declan gazed at Pepin, brows lifted. "Can you build one wherever you choose?"

"I can." Pepin sighed. "Not according to pechish law, but I can."

"You're going to anyway?" I asked. "Even though it's illegal?"

Pepin nodded. "That I will. There is little time to deal with pechish courts. And as an outcast, my request would be denied. They don't need to know. Besides, Cahal will knock it down once we're through."

Cahal acknowledged the request with a grunt and a slight tip of his head.

"So, why the three of us?" I asked.

"Wolf can help us find our way to your home. He knows your realm. He will remain with you until the time of your return as he did before, for protection."

I tried to gauge how Wolf felt about this, but he kept his head low as he trudged on with Pepin on his back. I couldn't even imagine. They'd just found one another again. And now they would be separated. Again. Because of me.

Tears moistened my eyes. All these people, family, finding one another only to be broken apart again. I'd be going home. Just what I wanted. I swallowed hard. Everything was happening so fast. I wasn't sure I wanted to leave. Then it dawned on me. I'd return. "I'll be back?"

"Yes. On the eighteenth anniversary of your birth, I will return for you. You may return with me then if you choose."

"Why go home at all? Why wouldn't I just stay?"

"I don't know. But it doesn't appear to be part of God's plan for you to stay."

"We'll need to gather forces, build an army against Morrigan," Evan said.

"You'll be safer in your realm whilst we regroup," Cataleen said.

I sighed. They were probably right. I could go home, resolve things there, let Stacy and my grandmother know I'm still alive, and then return, ready to face whatever lay before me. At least, I hoped I'd be ready.

Declan cleared his throat. "How will you choose?"

"Choose what?" I asked.

"Will you choose to return?" He glanced at me quickly out of the corner of his eye.

Did I really have a choice? How could I start all this, then leave them to deal with it alone? Could I return to my old life, knowing what I knew? I couldn't even imagine returning at all, going back to school. How dull and inconsequential it all seemed now. Then again, real danger existed here. "Did you see the future?" I asked Pepin. "Did you see what will become of me?"

Pepin shook his head. "I only know that you have been gifted with the power to save the fasgadair with repentant hearts from damnation...and kill those without."

I took a deep breath and slowly deflated. Why was I hesitating? I already knew the answer. I stared at the side of Declan's face. "Of course I'll be back."

The corner of Declan's mouth twitched, and his eyes softened.

My mother kept glancing to Wolf and me. A tear slipped down her cheek.

My heart ached for her. A lump formed in my throat. I stepped behind Wolf to come up by her side and lay a hand on her shoulder. "We will see you again." I spoke with confidence, hoping my doubts wouldn't reveal themselves, half waiting for Pepin to speak up and correct me if I was wrong.

She wiped the wetness from her face, gave a faint snuffle, and smiled. "You will. I'm grateful for the time God already gave me."

The conviction behind her words strengthened me. The doubts fizzled.

We continued until sunup. True to Pepin's word, we didn't

encounter any fasgadair. The Cnatan Mountains loomed before us, stretching as far as I could see, seeming like an impenetrable force field. I didn't envy the others their journey.

We came to a brook. Everyone rushed to the edge for a drink and to wash their faces. Declan and Cahal refilled their water bags. Pepin dismounted Wolf and headed toward a large boulder on the opposite bank. His foot slipped and came up wet as he crossed. He grumbled the rest of the way.

Wolf grabbed Declan's sack in his mouth, crossed the brook, and disappeared behind a clump of tall bushes. He reemerged in Declan's tunic and slacks, a little tight on his larger frame, and knelt beside my mother for a drink. They shared a quick smile before going for more water.

The water felt wonderful on my dry throat. How much I'd come to appreciate the little things, which were actually quite big.

Water bags full, Cahal turned to Declan and Evan. "Come. Let's hunt."

Declan and Evan followed Cahal into the woods after our dinner. Even the idea of rabbit made me salivate. Meat. We all needed some sort of protein.

Grunting, Pepin lifted the boulder and tipped it on its end so the length pointed toward the sky. I hopped along rocks in the water and made it across without slipping. I circled the balancing stone. How could it remain upright?

Pepin returned with another, equally large rock. Veins popped out on his crimson face, the corners of his mouth pulled down with effort. He grunted and released it a couple feet from the first. He raised the second stone so it stood parallel with the other.

"Need help?" Cahal asked, dropping the rabbit he'd caught, his eyes following the small man. Cahal, always so difficult to read, rarely changed his tone and didn't possess a wide variety of facial expressions. Even so, he seemed amazed and impressed. Perhaps it was simply that he gave Pepin notice and offered assistance.

The others took the opportunity to rest. I did the same as I watched Pepin carry another, larger boulder and place it atop the two. How did he get them to stand on end without toppling?

Pepin brushed his hands. "It's done." He looked at me. "We'll have one last meal before we return. We still have a considerable distance to travel to get you home. Will you build us a fire?"

"Sure." My body ached as I stood, but I gathered rocks and twigs. Plenty littered the near vicinity.

Evan and Declan returned to a full fire with more rodents to add to the spit. Everyone gathered around the fire and ate their fill. Laughter and merry chatter filled the space. My mother sang the Ariboslian hymn. Those who were still awake joined her. I drifted off to sleep with a full stomach and a smile.

"Ready?" Pepin nudged me.

"What?" I wiped my eyes. It took a moment to return to reality. "Already? Don't you have to cast a spell or something?"

He tipped his head back and laughed. I took that as a no.

"Cast a spell?" He chortled. "It's not magic."

"What is it then? How do you do it?"

"How do you change to a falcon? How does a bee make a hive? How does a spider spin a web? How—"

"Okay, I get your point."

"We do what our Creator designed us to do. That is all." He smiled and motioned toward the megalith. "When you're ready."

I glanced at my bizarre new family, still rousing from sleep. I didn't know most of the former prisoners, but they were still my people. My mother was the first to step forward for a hug. "A year may seem a long time, but 'tis nothing compared to fourteen."

Her bones protruded through her skin. It felt like hugging a skeleton. But she looked much healthier than she had, despite the conditions. "I know."

She let me go and smiled.

Cahal pulled me into his suffocating bear hug. "God be with you, little one."

Evan approached next. With his crooked smile and his short, black hair tousled from sleep, he looked adorable. I buried my face in his neck. He smelled like pine. His muscular arms enveloped me. "I hope we will meet again. I will never forget that you gave me another chance."

I backed up. "I don't have such power. God does."

His blue eyes flashed as he smiled. "But He chose to use you. And you could have said no."

I shrugged and returned the smile.

Declan stood before me, gazing into my eyes. I didn't know what to do. Should I hug him? As I tried to think of what to say, he pulled me into his embrace.

My head rested on his shoulder. I hated that his arms felt so good. But I was leaving for an entire year. Surely, a goodbye hug was acceptable. I squeezed him back and tried to memorize the moment— the feel of his strong arms, his musky scent. The ends of his brown hair flipping up, tickling my cheek. The tingle of my skin against his, and the flutter of my stomach.

"I'll miss you," I said. My voice cracked, and I blinked back tears.

"I will miss you too. Remember, you are loved."

EPILOGUE

S itting in the familiar purple moon chair in Stacy's bedroom felt strange. Comfortable, yet different. Stacy looked the same as she always did at the end of summer—her skin slightly darker so her freckles were less visible, but they had multiplied, covering almost every available space with a higher concentration on her cheeks. She sat on the edge of her bed, staring at me. Slack-jawed, her head jutted forward with eyes so wide, white was visible all around.

"You can't tell anyone." I hated disobeying Pepin and telling Stacy about Ariboslia. But I couldn't contain myself. I had to tell her. Besides, she wasn't just anyone. She was my best friend. She'd keep the secret safe.

Eyes still bulging, she shook her head, and then nodded.

Clearly, she needed time to process all this. I smiled slightly. How I'd missed her.

She exhaled sharply through her nose. "I just can't get over this. We thought you were dead." She closed her eyes and shook her head. "When Fiona showed up here crying..." A tear slid down her cheek.

I crossed the distance between us, sat next to her on the bed, and wrapped my arm around her. Part of me wanted to take the bunny trail down to my amazement at Fiona's ability to shed tears, particularly over me. But we could ponder that miracle later. We had three seasons to do so. "I wish I could've let you know where I was. There was nothing I could do. I was trapped. And it's not like there's cell service between realms. Not that I had a cell phone even if there was."

"I know." She sniffed and reached to her bedside table for a tissue.

"I have to go back," I whispered.

"What?" Her eyes went buggy once again over the tissue against her nose. She blew, gave a quick wipe, and scrunched it up in her hand. "You're going back there. With all those vampires? On purpose?"

"How can I not?" I got up to get her wastebasket and brought it to her. She threw the tissue inside. "God gave me the ability to save them...at least...some of them." I put the can back and plopped on the bed again. "I don't know why He chose to use me, but He did, and I can't turn my back on that."

Stacy took a deep breath. "I wish I could go with you."

"I wish you could, too. But you can't tell your parents, and they'd miss you. Besides, you have a scholarship. You have a great life and future here."

She nodded solemnly.

"And it will be dangerous. Some fasgadair will want me to help them; others want me dead. I'm not going to know the difference. But I must help those I can."

"That's so not helpful, Fal. Don't say stuff like that. I'll worry about you...always wondering if you're all right or not. If you're...If you're..."

"Hey. Don't think like that. We're not supposed to worry. About anything. Trust Him with it. I'm doing God's work, Stace. How could I not be all right? Even if I'm killed, we'll be together again...in heaven."

She scowled at me. "That doesn't make me feel better. I trust

Him, but...it's the not knowing. How can I handle wondering, not knowing if anything happens to you?" Her voice cracked, her green eyes glassy with unshed tears.

"I'll tell you what." I stared into her eyes, willing the severity of what I was about to say to sink in. "I'll make sure Wolf or Pepin gets word to you somehow if anything happens to me. Okay?"

She rolled her eyes and shrugged. "I wish there was some way I could get through, just to visit sometimes."

"That would be awesome. But there's no way. You'd need a megalith, an amulet, and you'd need to know how to use both. Could you imagine if anyone could get through at any time?" Disturbing images of people pushing gachen off their land, claiming it for themselves, selling it for profit, raising hotels and amusement parks, placing all the wondrous creatures I'd encountered behind bars for a small viewing fee. Houses would line the oceans. Laws about shape-shifting would be enacted, assuming shape-shifters would be allowed to live somewhat freely. I shuddered at the thought of humanity and the destruction that would be sure to follow. Traffic. Congestion. Smog. Commercialism. Disease. Humans would cause greater devastation than the fasgadair could ever dream.

I shook off the images. Thank God that would never happen. I longed to return all the more. "You know I have to go, Stace. Would you say no to God?"

Stacy groaned. "No." She sat back on her bed, slumping against the wall. "At least, I hope I wouldn't." She kicked at my thigh.

I pushed her leg away, toward the headboard, causing her to tip over. "Okay, then."

She righted, grabbed her pillow, and whacked me with it, then held it against her chest and part of her face protectively. Her smile wasn't visible behind the pillow, but the crinkles at the sides of her eyes gave it away as she peeked above it. "I'm glad you're back."

"Me too." A big part of me wanted desperately to return to Ariboslia, but I was glad. I needed to be here, to explain, to spend time with her and ease her mind. And I needed rest, time to prepare for whatever awaited me there.

Stacy threw the pillow next to her and leaned against it. "You're just in time for school." A devious grin spread across her face. "Your favorite."

I groaned. School bored me before. How would I survive another year after so much excitement? "Lovely."

"And it's senior year. Prom." She bounced the bed.

How could I possibly date a high school boy after meeting Declan? "For you maybe. Good luck with that."

"Seriously?" Stacy's jaw dropped, her eyes full of hurt. So dramatic.

"My word, Stace. Do we have to worry about this now? It's months and months away." And even longer until I return to Ariboslia. I sighed. "Maybe I'll go solo, but I am *not* bringing a date."

"As you said, it's months and months away. You never know what could happen between now and then." She raised her eyebrows as if she knew something I didn't.

She was wrong. There was absolutely no way I would bother with anyone here. My heart was in Ariboslia.

She deflated a bit, as if disappointed by the lack of fight. "At least we'll be together, right? You're waiting until after graduation to return?" Her eyes glimmered with hope.

"Of course. I'm not returning until my birthday. And, first thing Sunday morning, I'm coming with you to church."

Stacy smiled.

ADRIFT

Be'Thorr perched in the trees—trapped. Wind parted the leaves, threatening to expose him. If Fallon caught him now...

Fallon sat in her bedroom window seat. Her black hair hung down, concealing her face. She appeared to be reading, sometimes writing. Was she doing schoolwork? From what he understood of her world, her formal education should be complete.

What was she doing?

He ruffled his feathers, eager to escape.

Why wouldn't she leave?

Fallon glanced out the window, the tip of her writing utensil in her mouth, her purple eyes shifted his way. Be'Thorr ducked, then shook his head at his paranoia. She'd never spot him in this tree. As long as he stayed put.

She resumed her writing. Should he risk fleeing now? No. She'd look up the moment he took flight.

That would be his luck.

What a fool he'd been. What else did he expect her to do today of all days? Sleep it away? Go out somewhere? No. She'd be up waiting for someone to take her back to Ariboslia. How could he be so daft? He should have left hours ago. But he lingered, both eager for and dreading what was to come. And Fallon had risen earlier than expected and planted herself in that blasted window. And now her friend was awake too.

He wished *he* could take her back to Ariboslia. But that wasn't possible. Not now.

The sun was rising. Birds began their morning chatter. As they flew near his perch, they scattered, chirping warnings to others who might venture too close. But they needn't have worried. Be'Thorr wouldn't risk exposing himself for a meal. Despite his growing hunger.

A cool summer breeze rustled the leaves, exposing him. He held his breath. His cover settled back into place, and he breathed easier. Somewhat.

His stomach felt heavy and uneasy, like a thick sludge churned within.

Ah, Fallon. So clueless as to the truth about to be revealed. How much could her heart take? He wanted to protect her. But he needed his distance. And she was tough. Tougher than she realized.

His heart ached, to the extent his heart could hurt in its present condition. There she sat. So anxious she never left that spot...or went longer than five seconds without peering out the window. Waiting. How many hours would she sit there?

Something grunted below him. A huge boulder moved along the ground, through the woods, and into Fallon's backyard. The stone pitched forward, slamming one end into the ground with a loud thud, shaking everything within earshot. Be'Thorr shifted his grip and unfurled his wings to regain his balance, staring at whatever had thrown the rock. A small person with a red braid brushed his hands. Pepin.

Fallon and her friend pressed their faces against the window. A finger pointed at Pepin strolling down the path, probably to fetch another boulder. The girls disappeared from the window.

This was his chance.

Be'Thorr secured the amulet cord with his beak, careful not to snip it. He flew deeper into the woods, landed high in the trees, and listened for footsteps. Nothing followed. No shouts. He relaxed.

Was Pepin building a new megalith?

No matter. Be'Thorr leaped from his perch and flew toward the megalith from which he'd come. He'd catch up with them in Kylemore.

ADRIFT CHAPTER 1

Propped in the window seat, clutching my journal, I stared into the backyard where I'd sometimes glimpse Wolf watching over me. He was gone now. Nothing but the overgrown lawn, the dilapidated tree house, and the woods.

Today was the day.

Stacy flopped on my bed, flipped a page in her magazine, and gasped. Instead of taking the bait, I browsed earlier entries in my journal.

October 29. My memories of Ariboslia dim with the ever-darkening New England days. So depressing. Nothing compares with those heart-elevating, adrenaline-pumping months. This world is so bland. Like a plain, over-boiled potato. Going to school and pretending all I experienced hadn't happened is like watching television in black and white, trying to convince myself color never existed. However boring this world seemed before my adventures was now multiplied a hundredfold. School: a jail full of immature, shallow students who live for themselves, raising themselves above all others, and ignorant teachers who speak with authority on subjects they don't understand.

I've seen an invisible world! What I've seen would awaken

people to unimaginable possibilities beyond their nearsighted-
ness. But I'm denied, forced to answer science exams incorrectly
for a decent grade. Muted. Unable to speak about reality for fear
of being imprisoned, trapped in a padded cell, wrapped in a love-
me jacket.

Stacy let out another gasp. Louder. I flipped ahead a few pages.

January 17. Stacy, our church, periodic visits from Wolf, brief trips
to the sky in falcon form (when I dare), and the promise of
returning to Ariboslia sustain me during these dark days. The new
calendar and increasing sunlight renew my hope. The day is
growing closer.

I returned to my latest entry.

June 21. My eighteenth birthday has finally arrived. A year ago
today, I was dragged to Ariboslia. Was it all a dream? I have
nothing to prove it. Only this journal…something the world would
assume to be the ramblings of a psychopath.

But there was Wolf. And I'm able to transform into a falcon
and fly. There is no doubt about that…. Today, if I'm given the
choice to return as promised, I'll know.

My heart flipped. I glanced down at Drochaid for the gazillionth
time, hoping for one of the arrows to light up, showing me where to
go. My mother's amulet guided me every step of the way last year.
Still, I kept checking. But who was I kidding? I'd feel its warmth first.
I pulled my pencil from my mouth and continued writing.

This day, more than any other, I expect Drochaid's glow.
But I'm torn. On one hand, I want nothing more than to
return to the mysterious, untamed land where I received new life.
I want to do God's will and save lives…my family. I don't want to

waste my life in this house with my grandmother. On the other hand, I hate to leave Stacy. But more than that, I'm afraid. My life will be in constant danger. I won't know who to help. Those I'm meant to save and those who want me dead are the same—the fasgadair.

Then there's Declan....

Ah, Declan. Was it wrong that my heart did a little somersault? He's betrothed. Unavailable. And yet...those eyes. Those intense green eyes always penetrated my soul. So many memories of Ariboslia had faded, but those eyes were burned into my psyche.

I took a deep breath. This wasn't about Declan. It was about God's plans and my part in them. I must remember....

I tapped the pencil against the notebook, unsure what to add.

Didn't I have to do what God called me to do? How else would I live with myself? And how could I stay here? Bored out of my mind. I would regret it forever. I crisscrossed my legs and glanced in irritation at the dull amulet around my neck.

"You're obsessing, Fal. Stop thinking about it." Stacy peeked out over the magazine as she lounged on my pillows and a few overly loved stuffed animals from Bumpah.

"I can't help it." The notebook slid off my lap. "It's supposed to be today. What if Pepin was wrong? What if they decide they don't want me to return? What if something happened to them?"

Stacy lowered the magazine onto her chest and raised an eyebrow. "Are you serious right now? It's only six a.m. What time do you expect this to happen?"

Okay. She had me there.

"Wasn't it much later last time?"

Another good point.

"You still have the entire day. Besides, would it be so bad if you stayed a little longer? You have me. And it's not so bad to live with your grandmother anymore, right?"

"That's because *I've* changed." It started with little things:

cleaning dishes left sitting in the sink, taking out the overflowing trash, and responding in a pleasant tone.

"That's all it takes. One person to take the high road." Stacy rolled the magazine into a log. "And I'm telling you. She was a wreck when you were gone."

"Yeah. She seemed happy to see me.... For a few minutes anyway." I bent to pick up the journal. "The scrapbook made a huge difference too." What a project—sorting through the massive piles of postcards from Bumpah stashed all over the house, mapping them in a scrapbook with the few pictures I found of him.

"I so wish I'd seen her face when you gave it to her." She drummed the magazine against her leg. "You got her to stop sending herself more postcards."

"True. I curbed the insanity a bit."

"And she likes you a lot more now. So...I repeat: Would it be so bad if you stayed?"

Yes, yes, it would be. "It's funny. I keep thinking I have a choice. But I never applied to any colleges. I've never considered staying."

Stacy gripped the magazine and bit her lip.

"I'm not eager to leave *you*, ya know."

She fiddled with something invisible on her right knee.

"I don't belong here."

"None of us do, Fal."

"It's more than what awaits us after this life. There's unfinished business in Ariboslia. There's so much more I need to do—to learn."

"Well, I'm in no hurry for you to leave." Her frown deepened. Then she smiled, her eyes mischievous. "And I don't think Jeremy is either."

I rolled my eyes and groaned. "Oh please." There was one guy for me, and it wasn't any high-school boy...or recent grad. Not from this realm.

"What? He likes you."

Her singsong, teasing tone invoked my pillow-throwing reflex.

"Hey." She laughed, peeling the pillow from her face.

High-school boys. Nothing brought forth a more pronounced groan than their mention. Stacy knew this...and that I'd take the bait. "I would rather—"

She bolted upright and shushed me.

"What?"

"Shhh!" She held her hand up to silence me as she leaned her ear toward the left. "Did you hear that?"

"Hear what?" My un-hushed voice met more shushing. Her hand, still upright, waved at me.

A heavy thud shook the house. I twisted to peer outside. She slammed into me and pressed her face against the window.

"Dude, a *dwarf*!"

KEEP READING...

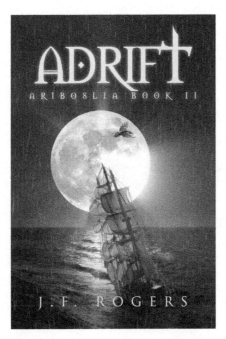

SHAMELESS REQUEST FOR REVIEWS

Authors need reviews! They help books get noticed and I love to know what readers think of my stories. So, if you enjoyed this story, pease consider leaving a review wherever you purchased the book or anywhere you think a review might be helpful. I'm forever grateful!

You are loved,
J F Rogers

ABOUT THE AUTHOR

J.F. Rogers lives in Southern Maine with her husband, daughter, pets, and an imaginary friend or two. She has a degree in Behavioral Science and teaches 5th-6th Grade Sunday School. When she's not entertaining Tuki the Mega Mutt, her constant companion and greatest distraction, she's likely tap tap tapping away at her keyboard, praying the words will miraculously align just so. Above all, she's a believer in the One True God and can say with certainty—you are loved. Connect with her at jfrogers.com.

BB bookbub.com/authors/j-f-rogers

f facebook.com/jfrogerswrites

g goodreads.com/JFRogers

⊙ instagram.com/jfrogers925

℗ pinterest.com/jfrogers925

y twitter.com/jfrogers5

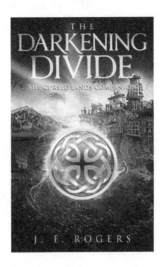

A jaded elf. A feisty dragon. And a deadly curse that threatens them all.

Samu would do anything to be bonded to a dragon, even serve a king he doesn't trust. But when a strange mist falls over his city and the humans massacre the elves, the last thing he wants is to come to the king's rescue.

Then the dragon eggs are threatened, and the Divide grows dark.

This was no ordinary curse.

Someone... or something... is staging an extinction-level attack against the elves and their dragons.

But Samu won't let that happen. He can't. He'll rescue the dragons or die trying.

The Darkening Divide is the action-packed prequel to *The Cursed Lands* Christian fantasy adventure. If you enjoy mixing up genres with elves and dragons in a steampunk world infested with humans, download *The Darkening Divide* today! You'll love this intro to J F Rogers's exciting new series.

http://jfrogers.com/free-book/

THE ARIBOSLIA SERIES

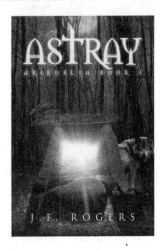

Astray - Book 1

A mysterious amulet leads Fallon to everything she's ever wanted...and possibly her death.

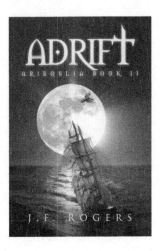

Adrift - Book 2

Fallon returns to Ariboslia to save lives...but the creatures she wants to save want her dead.

Aloft - Book 3

Fallon and Morrigan face off for the ultimate battle ... in their minds.

Alight - Prequel

Three friends. Evil seeks to corrupt them. If they survive... what will it cost?

Pepin's Tale - Companion

Can one small peach make an eternal difference?

THE CURSED LANDS SERIES

The King's Curse - Will Colleen turn her back on everyone, including God... or risk her life for strangers.

The Witch's Curse - Will Colleen face her fears to kill the witch... or remain trapped in a living nightmare forever? (Coming August 29, 2023!)

The Queen's Curse - Book 3

COMING IN FALL/WINTER 2023!

ACKNOWLEDGMENTS

First and foremost, I must thank God for changing my heart...and my story. He sent so many of you my way to help shape Astray and make it a reality. Thank you, my loving husband, Rick: for your support, your feedback, and for putting up with me. You're my rock. My beautiful daughter, Emily (aka mini-me): you enjoyed *Astray* enough to read it twice—something you rarely do. Thank you for your honest feedback and for finding so many editing issues. Your grammar skills are impressive! You were a huge part of this. I love you both so much!

Thank you, Pastor Nathan. I was petrified to reveal this story to anyone outside my family. Your glowing response encouraged me to get out of my comfort zone and dare expose my work to others. Emily Hendrickson: thank you for convincing me to seek a critique group and pointing me toward ACFW. Thanks to all the members of ACFW who provided input: Gretchen Engalls, Kari Wells, Amy Cattapan, and many more. Thank you, Yvonne Anderson: you took me under your wing and critiqued my entire manuscript without receiving or expecting much of a return for your efforts.

My critique group, Fantasy for Christ: when I was lost and desperate for other fantasy Christian authors, you sympathized with my plight and joined me. Sarah Grimm, Karen DeBlieck, Terri Proksch (Terri Luckey), Precarious Yates (aka Sarah Smith), Azalea Dabill, Kathrese McKee, Katie Clark, Sarah Witenhafer, Loraine Kemp, Tami O'Neal, and Phyllis Wheeler: You each brought wonderful insight to the group and played an integral part in piecing this book together. I couldn't have done it without you. You're all amazing writers who've become more than crit partners—you've become travel companions and friends. I love you all!

Thanks to the following groups: ACFW, Lost Genre Guild, and Realm Makers.

My editors, Deirdre Lockhart with Brilliant Cut Editing and my sister, Rebecca McKinney: thank you so much for taking the time to help *Astray* shine—no small task. You did an impressive job. Thank you all for your hard work, your patience, and your assistance in making this dream a reality.

My dad and fellow author, John Pilkington: You were always there for me. I can't thank you enough for fighting for me and for influencing my life.

I must also thank my family and friends: it would take pages to list you all by name. You all encouraged me in one way or another, helping this project and my journey far more than you realize. I'm grateful for you all.

I'm amazed at how many people participated in this seemingly life-long project. God's sovereign hand oversaw it all. My heart is full of gratitude.

STILL HERE?

LOOKING FOR MORE FROM J F ROGERS?

Be among the first to know when J F Rogers releases a new book.
Join her clan today.

https://jfrogers.com/join/

Made in the USA
Monee, IL
25 August 2023

41627531R00184